HIDDEN IDENTITIES

OTHER BOOKS AND AUDIOBOOKS BY TRACI HUNTER ABRAMSON

UNDERCURRENTS SERIES

Undercurrents

Ripple Effect

The Deep End

SAINT SQUAD SERIES

Freefall

Lockdown

Crossfire

Backlash

Smoke Screen

Code Word

Lock and Key

Drop Zone

Spotlight

Tripwire

Redemption

Covert Ops

Disconnect

Reconnect

LUKE STEELE SERIES

Hometown Vendetta

Victim #8

ROYAL SERIES

Royal Target

Royal Secrets

Royal Brides

Royal Heir

Royal Duty

Royal Intrigue

GUARDIAN SERIES

Failsafe

Safe House

Sanctuary

On the Run

In Harm's Way

Not Dead Yet

Unseen

Hidden Identities

DREAM'S EDGE SERIES

*Dancing to Freedom**

An Unlikely Pair

*Broken Dreams**

Dreams of Gold

*The Best Mistake**

Worlds Collide

FALCON POINT SERIES

Heirs of Falcon Point

The Danger with Diamonds

From an Unknown Sender

When Fashion Turns Deadly

Treasures of Falcon Point
(Coming June 2026)

PEN AND DAGGER SERIES

Novel Threat

Staged Evidence
(Coming April 2026)

STAND-ALONES

Obsession

Proximity

*Twisted Fate**

*Entangled**

*Sinister Secrets**

Deep Cover

Mistaken Reality

Kept Secrets

Chances Are

Chance for Home

A Change of Fortune

The Fiction Kitchen Trio Cookbook

Jim and Katherine

*Shadows of Trust**

* Novella

HIDDEN IDENTITIES

A GUARDIAN NOVEL

TRACI HUNTER
ABRAMSON

Cover image *Asian Woman* © Blvdone, Adobe Stock. *Singapore May 19, 2019* © Artinun. Icons © Adobe stock

Cover design by Christina Marcano
Cover design copyright © 2026 by Covenant Communications, Inc.

Published by Covenant Communications, Inc.
Salt Lake City, Utah

Library of Congress Cataloging-in-Publication Data

Names: Abramson, Traci Hunter author | Abramson, Traci Hunter. Guardian series
Title: Hidden identities / Traci Hunter Abramson.
Description: Salt Lake City, Utah : Covenant Communications, [2026] |
Series: A guardian novel | Summary: "When a CIA mission in Thailand goes wrong, undercover agent Jia Wu escapes—but her cover is blown. Suspecting a traitor within the agency, she turns to Erik, a covert Guardian. Together they infiltrate Singapore's criminal underworld to rescue her partner. As trust and attraction grow, so does the danger—and the enemy may be far closer than they realize"—Provided by publisher.
Identifiers: LCCN 2025032607 (print) | LCCN 2025032608 (ebook) | ISBN 9781524429584 trade paperback | ISBN 9781524429584 ebook
Subjects: LCSH: United States. Central Intelligence Agency—Employees—Fiction | Spies—Singapore—Fiction | Man-woman relationships—Fiction | Singapore | LCGFT: Fiction | Spy fiction | Thrillers (Fiction) | Romance fiction
Classification: LCC PS3601.B76 H53 2026 (print) | LCC PS3601.B76 (ebook)
LC record available at https://lccn.loc.gov/2025032607
LC ebook record available at https://lccn.loc.gov/2025032608

Printed in the United States of America
First Printing: February 2026

34 33 32 31 30 29 28 27 26 10 9 8 7 6 5 4 3 2 1

for Matt and Jen Leigh

Thank you for bringing Singapore to life.

CHAPTER 1

Erik eyed his bed in his simple studio apartment in Taipei. He knew better than to sleep while it was dark out, but that didn't mean he wasn't tempted. As a member of the elite guardian program, he did most of his work at night. An intelligence operative in trouble, someone in the military caught on the wrong side of a border, or a piece of critical information that needed to be shared with the CIA or one of the other intelligence organizations—nearly every situation occurred outside of daylight hours.

He checked his watch. Four in the morning. Surely, if he hadn't received any requests by now, he was safe to take a nap.

He sat on his bed and pulled off his shoes. Out the windows that made up two walls of his apartment, lights twinkled in every direction.

He should draw the curtains, but he rather liked sensing the life pulsing outside. In these quiet moments, he could pretend that his life was his own, that he could go anywhere and do anything. He could pretend that he wasn't dead.

Okay, so maybe he wasn't really dead, but his death certificate had declared him as such seven years ago, only two hours after he had testified against an organized crime boss in San Francisco.

The prosecutor had been so sure that Erik would be safe after he told the truth on the stand, but Erik had barely made it out of the courthouse when a drive-by shooting had killed two people and wounded three others. He was one of the three wounded who had survived.

He flopped onto his bed. There was no point in dwelling on the past now. His fellow guardians might have helped him fake his death, but he was still alive, and he had a purpose.

He closed his eyes, his body relaxing into that blissful state that came right before succumbing to sleep.

His cell phone ring startled him back into consciousness. He rubbed his eyes and checked his watch. 4:06.

He snatched up his phone and answered. "Yeah?"

His boss's voice carried over the line. "We may have a situation."

Erik sat up. "What kind of situation?"

"I'm not sure yet," Ace said. "But Vladimir Baranov is in Thailand again."

"Where this time? Phuket or Jomtien Beach?"

"Jomtien. Looks like he's using Chinese New Year as an excuse for another meeting."

A meeting with his Chinese counterpart. Monitoring the two players had become a commonplace mission that should have been handed off to the CIA months ago when the players had first been identified. But unfortunately, the CIA's chief of station in Bangkok had been sent stateside after a medical emergency, and his replacement was not only afraid to make a decision, but he was also stingy with his resources. The lack of leadership had left Erik fielding far more than his share of missions in Thailand.

He did a quick calculation in his head. If he left now, he could make the seven o'clock flight to Bangkok. "I'll get over there and set up surveillance."

"Thanks, Erik. And I'll let you know if anything new hits the database."

Erik ended the call and pocketed his phone. Then he grabbed his go-bag as he stifled a yawn. He'd sleep on the plane.

* * *

Jia had reviewed the intel from her source a half dozen times before making the trip from the CIA station in Kuala Lumpur to Bangkok. This wasn't the sort of information she could send through normal channels. If she was right, her source had handed her the information needed to stop another worldwide pandemic. Only this time, there was no doubt the virus was manmade.

She could have presented the intel on her own, but Shaun Fleming had joined her on this trip. He'd been by her side, sifting through the initial intel too. He'd also run the computer model that had confirmed her source's information. And the data clearly suggested the threat was greater than anything they'd ever dealt with before, particularly in the realm of biological warfare.

Now here they were, following Bangkok's acting chief of station into a conference room where three others already waited. The woman in the corner wasn't someone Jia had met before, but she was well acquainted with one of the men. Qian Zhang had crossed her path a dozen times before, and nearly every one of those meetings had resulted in his asking her out and her refusing. She had no interest in dating someone who, instead of treating her like an equal, viewed her as a traveling secretary who should be happy to fetch him a cup of coffee.

A touch of longing surfaced at the thought of her personal life. For so long, she had put her job first, but she couldn't deny that she missed the companionship of having a boyfriend or even a best friend. Sadly, she rarely had the time, energy, or trust to invest in a relationship outside her career.

Qian stood and cocked an eyebrow. "Looks like it's my lucky day."

Jia ignored him, focusing instead on the introduction of the other two in the room. After she and Shaun had met them, the acting station chief motioned for everyone to take their seats before claiming his spot at the head of the table.

"So what was so important that we had to rearrange our schedules to meet with you?" Acting Chief Faust asked.

"We have intel on a biological weapon," Jia said. "Or rather, a biological threat. A new virus has been developed, and the lab where it's being produced is here in Thailand."

Faust leaned back in his chair. "Where did you get your intel?"

"A worker in Singapore," Jia said. "She's been feeding intel to her sister in Malaysia, who gives it to us."

"So this is secondhand information?"

Jia fought back a sigh. As if she would travel this far without cause. "Technically, yes, but we've verified the source. And we've already identified her employer as someone who has both the financial resources and the education needed to create this virus."

Chief Faust rested his forearms on the edge of the table and fidgeted with his wedding ring. "Tell us what you've got."

Jia gave a subtle nod to Shaun, who proceeded to hook his laptop to the screen mounted to the wall.

Shaun remained standing and started his presentation. "Douglas Brandt is an American citizen living in Singapore. Our background information on him indicates he was adopted at the age of four into a family that ultimately developed some significant health issues. The grandfather died due to complications from type 1 diabetes when Douglas was twelve, and the grandmother moved in with Douglas's family shortly after."

"What does all this have to do with the threat?" Qian asked.

"That's a good question. If you'll give me a minute, I'll show you," Shaun said with far more patience than Jia would have managed. "The grandmother had both rheumatoid arthritis and kidney disease. Then the mother was diagnosed with MS when Douglas was sixteen."

Jia sensed the others' continued impatience and said, "From everything we've uncovered in his background, it appeared Douglas's life was consistently unraveled by people who were suffering from chronic illness."

"And this matters because . . . ?" Qian asked.

"Because this virus has been genetically engineered to target those who have autoimmune diseases and other significant health issues," Jia said. "We think he's deliberately targeting people who he feels are suffering unnecessarily." She gestured to Shaun. "Show them the numbers."

Shaun clicked his mouse pad to advance the image on the screen. "According to our source, these are the mortality rates for those exposed to the virus."

The chief of station's eyes widened, and he stood as though needing to view the screen from a different spot to make sure he was reading the information correctly. He turned back to face Jia. "And you think Brandt has a lab here in Thailand?"

"Yes," Jia said.

"We identified the location just last night," Shaun added.

And Jia and Shaun had been working nonstop ever since. "I already came up with the possible entry points and a basic mission plan," Jia said. "Once I know how many people we have going in, I can finalize the details."

"Going in?" Faust shook his head. "I'm going to need approval from headquarters for that. With the time difference, we can probably get authorization sometime next week."

Jia shook her head. "We can't wait that long. According to my source, we think the release of the virus is already in the final planning stages."

"I can do a few drive-bys tomorrow," Qian offered.

Again, Jia shook her head. "This lab is in a remote area, and a vehicle driving by is guaranteed to be noticed."

Faust stiffened and straightened his shoulders. "What do you suggest?"

"A direct infiltration. We go in, check out the lab, and get out," Jia said. "If we can get our hands on some of the virus, great, but even if we can't, we should be able to create a copy of their computer files."

"I don't like it." Faust fidgeted with his ring again. Definitely a sign of nerves. "It's too risky."

Jia gestured to Shaun to move to the next photo. "Here are the aerial shots from earlier this week." She stood and pointed at the tiny specks on the screen where the guards were positioned. "We can see the guard placement, and the area is surrounded by jungle. We come in on motorcycles from the road north of there and park far enough away to make sure we don't get noticed. Then we'll override the alarms and make a backup. No one will ever know we were there."

Faust hesitated a brief moment before he spoke. "You'd better make sure no one ever knows you were there."

"Does that mean you'll approve the mission?"

"Unofficially, yes. But if anyone asks, you went in on your own."

Lovely. This wouldn't be the first time Jia'd had to operate off the book. "Fine. Shaun can run my tech support, but I need two more operatives to help me on the infiltration."

"No, you misunderstand. I'm authorizing *you* to go in, and I'll provide your transportation, but that's all. I don't have enough staff to risk my people," Faust said. "I can't take the chance that this will tie back to the embassy here."

Jia's frustration bubbled over along with a hint of panic. "But it's a four-man op."

"Not anymore. You make it a two-man op, or you don't go."

Jia glanced up at Shaun, who spent his days working at a computer, who had a pregnant wife at home. And his eyes reflected eagerness rather than fear.

Did she dare take him with her? Under the circumstances, she had little choice. They certainly couldn't turn their backs on a threat that could affect millions.

* * *

Four years with the agency, over a year of which he'd spent in Malaysia, and finally, Shaun was getting the chance to work in the field. He'd been so excited when he'd scored the Kuala Lumpur position, but as a junior officer, and a computer specialist at that, no one ever let him do anything interesting—or fun.

"I don't like this." Jia shook her head as she sat down in the office the Bangkok acting chief of station had assigned to them. "You've never done fieldwork, and I need someone on the inside to disable the alarms."

"Which I've been trained to do."

"Shaun, I can't take you inside." She gestured toward the window overlooking the street. "Your wife would kill me if something happened to you."

"Nothing is going to happen to me." Without sitting, he leaned over and pulled up the floor plan of the lab on his laptop. "I recreated the likely layout of the lab, and I should be able to override any alarms."

"And security cameras?"

"Simple. I record a short segment of the empty hall and feed it back on a loop to the control room." Shaun gripped the back of the chair in front of him. "I can do this. You know I can."

Jia shook her head, but this time, it was in resignation. "I still don't like this." She gestured again, motioning toward the chief of station's office. "Faust has people he could send to back me up."

"He does, but since he isn't going to, how do you want to do this?"

She let out a heavy sigh and dropped into the chair beside Shaun. "Pull up the overhead images with the timestamps and see if you can figure out the guard rotation schedule."

"What are you going to do?" he asked.

"I'll talk to transportation. We need a couple of motorcycles that won't be traced back to the US government."

He nodded. "When are we going in?"

She dialed her phone. "Tonight."

CHAPTER 2

Erik sat on his balcony, his earbuds in place as he listened to the latest dialogue between the Russian intelligence operative and his Chinese source. The two made wide circles around each other throughout the conversation.

Erik recognized the dance all too well—two intelligence operatives eager to gain intel without sharing more than absolutely necessary.

Planting the listening devices had been easy enough. The two men might think they were good at varying their routines, but they both had their common vices. Or rather, they both had their common needs. Between Baranov's regular poolside massages and Duan's daily tai chi on the beach, slipping into their rooms this morning had taken little effort. And then Erik also had his backup plan of planting listening devices on the water bottles they always ordered upon their arrival. He supposed that was one positive about the tap water being unsafe to drink.

Today's conversation had touched on shipping lanes in the South China Sea, their suspicions about a possible plant by the American government in the Kremlin, and a Taiwanese dissident who was becoming problematic for China.

When the conversation finally ended, Erik ensured his laptop was recording everything coming off the listening devices and removed his earbuds.

Preferring to leave for dinner before the men he was surveilling did, Erik quickly grabbed the keys to his motorcycle and headed for the stairs, careful to avoid the surveillance cameras in the hall until he was outside.

He headed for a hotel a kilometer down the beach, one with an international chef who had proved his restaurant capable of creating gluten-free meals without poisoning Erik through hidden ingredients or cross-contamination.

Erik had suffered from constant headaches, fatigue, and abdominal pain for months without knowing what was wrong with him. Thankfully, the newest guardian, Lacey, was not only an expert in infectious diseases, but she had started her medical career specializing in autoimmune diseases. She had tested Erik and identified his problem, then had given him the simple—although often challenging—solution of avoiding gluten.

Erik reached the hotel restaurant and opted for a table where he could see the entrance and still remain mostly out of sight. He accepted the menu from the waitress, even though he already knew what he wanted. Best to look like a typical tourist, not a man who came to this part of Thailand at least once or twice a month.

He pulled out his cell phone and checked his messages. No operatives in danger, no mention of any upcoming missions. Maybe tonight he'd finally get a good night's sleep.

* * *

Jia breathed in the scent of industrial cleaners and a trace of curry, no doubt from someone's dinner hours ago. An empty hallway lay before her, security cameras located at regular intervals. She prayed Shaun had succeeded in bypassing them as well as the motion detectors that protected this secured area of the hidden lab.

She shouldn't even be here. Neither should Shaun, but Faust had been too afraid to step up and take the initiative. So here they were, two CIA operatives based out of Malaysia working in Thailand. And despite both of them speaking multiple languages, neither of them spoke Thai. She could also hardly forget that they didn't have diplomatic immunity in this country.

Jia couldn't think about that now. She took a tentative step forward followed by another. No blaring alarms. No sudden rush of footsteps coming toward her. She released the breath she hadn't realized she'd been holding. Shaun had held up his side of the mission; now it was up to her to achieve their objective, even without support from the local CIA station.

She still couldn't believe she'd been forced to accept Shaun's help. The man was a genius when it came to tech, but his having no experience in fieldwork meant it was up to her to make sure he got out of here safely despite the security system and the presence of a half dozen guards patrolling the grounds.

She drew in a deep breath. This wasn't the first time she'd taken such a risk, but today's objective hung heavily over her. If she was right—and she usually was—this lab wasn't being used to cure diseases. It was the birthplace of a new one.

Her pace slow and steady, she continued down the hall to the door leading to the main lab. A red light shone from the electronic lock. If her source was correct, and so far, they had been, this was where she would find the answers to her questions—and the confirmation of her fears.

Jia checked her watch. Two twenty-nine in the morning. Her watch rolled to two thirty, and the light on the lock switched to green. So far so good.

She entered the lab and zeroed in on the computer in the corner of the room. She slid her laptop out of her backpack and set it on the sleek countertop. Time to get to work.

* * *

Shaun checked his watch for the fifth time in as many minutes. Jia should have been done by now. He resisted the urge to duck out of the utility closet where he'd accessed the security feed and overridden it with an image of the empty hallway.

Footsteps approached, the squeak of rubber soles sounding against the linoleum floor in a steady rhythm.

Shaun's heartbeat quickened. The guard only had two places to go from this part of the building: outside or down the south hallway toward the lab. If the guard remained inside, one of his coworkers was sure to spot the inaccuracy that one of their men was in the hall despite the appearance of an empty space on their security screens.

Quickly, Shaun disconnected the fake feed for the hall, keeping the recorded images transmitting from the lab. Then he pulled his cell phone from his pocket and texted Jia. *Guard passing. Stay in place.*

Sure enough, the squeaking footsteps continued down the hall, the doors in the immediate area remaining closed.

Shaun glanced at his watch again. Ten more minutes before the full guard sweep would begin, which included all the rooms. Or so their intel suggested, the same intel the Bangkok station had been too cautious to act on.

But Faust's inaction had brought Shaun here and given him his first chance to prove he could operate in the field. Or maybe it was proving to him why he usually worked behind a desk. He was pretty sure his heart wasn't designed to beat quite this fast.

He wiped his sweaty palms on his black pants. Only another few minutes. Then he could reengage the fake security feed so he and Jia could get out of here.

* * *

Finally. Jia's shoulders relaxed slightly when her automated system finally broke through the security protocols on the lab computer. That had taken far longer than she'd hoped. She hit the button to begin a complete backup of the hard drive. The moment it completed, she plugged an external drive into her laptop and began a second backup. No way was she going to risk having only one copy.

Her watch buzzed with an incoming message. *Status?*

She pulled out her phone and texted back. *Almost done. ETA: 2 minutes.*

You're out of time.

Jia checked her watch. According to their surveillance, she still had six minutes until the next guard sweep. That gave her four minutes to spare.

Still, she had to remember that fieldwork was new to Shaun, and giving him a bigger window to clear the grounds would benefit them both.

She willed the second backup to copy faster.

Seconds ticked off in her head, and she estimated how much more time she needed.

Concerned that her rookie partner would need an extra minute or two, she texted him. *Clear the building. I'll be right behind you.*

A thumbs-up appeared on her screen a second later.

She had to give it to the guy. So far, he had executed his part of the mission perfectly. Now if they could remain unheard and unseen for a few more minutes, they'd be able to prove that their source had been correct and that Brandt and his associates needed to be stopped.

The backup finished, and Jia tucked the hard drive into the hidden pocket inside the back of her shirt, the same spot where she kept her passport holder, credit cards, and cash. Once her most valuable possessions were secured, she loaded her laptop into her backpack and hurried to the door.

Quietly, she opened it. After a quick check of the hall, she hurried past the security cameras and made it to the exterior door.

She messaged Shaun. *At the exit.*

Two seconds passed before his reply vibrated on her wrist. *All clear.*

With her gloved hand, Jia pushed open the door. Instantly, lights flashed overhead, and alarms blared.

Jia muttered her frustration under her breath. This was not how invisible worked.

She rushed outside despite the security lights illuminating the open courtyard. Palm trees lined the fence on the far side. If she could get that far without being seen, she had a chance of escaping this compound.

The door behind her burst open, and a shout followed.

Jia glanced back long enough to spot the guard now in pursuit, a gun in his hand.

He lifted his weapon. She ducked and darted to the left. A gunshot echoed, the bullet whizzing past her.

Her heart raced. The trees were still ten meters away. She dove to the ground.

Another shot fired, and the dirt beside her spat into the air.

Quickly, she pulled her own weapon from the holster at her waist and rolled over. She fired off two shots, both connecting with her target.

The guard clutched his chest and dropped to the ground.

Her stomach roiled at the thought that her target was a living human being. But he was involved with trying to murder millions of innocent people.

More shouts and pounding feet sounded.

Jia pushed back up and sprinted the last ten meters to the tree line. Multiple gunshots fired as she ducked behind a thick palm. Pieces of dried fronds flew into the air, and she closed her eyes to protect them.

A man yelled in Thai, which she didn't understand. Then he repeated himself in English. "Come out, or we kill your partner."

Jia forced her eyes open. Had the guards really found Shaun, or were they hoping they had guessed correctly that she wasn't working alone?

She slipped her backpack off and set it beside her. Then she ducked down and peered around the base of the tree trunk.

There in the center of the courtyard, two guards held Shaun. A fresh cut marked his cheek, and his eye was already swelling, likely from a fight with the guards when he'd been apprehended.

"Let him go," Jia called out in English. Not that she expected them to comply, but she had to make the demand.

"Give us what you stole from us," the guard standing behind Shaun shouted back. His body was protected behind his hostage, and the way he tilted his chin up suggested he held some authority even when he didn't have a gun to another man's head.

Shaun tried to jerk free, but that only earned him an arm around his throat to cut off his air supply.

"Let him go!" Jia shouted again.

"Hand over your bag, and I'll think about it."

Her bag contained her laptop and the information she'd downloaded, which was why she'd made an extra backup. But the backup wouldn't do her any good if she couldn't get out of here. She had to take out the guards, and she needed to break Shaun free of his captors.

With her weapon in one hand, she maintained her position behind the tree and held out the backpack.

"Don't do it!" Shaun croaked.

When no shots fired at the appearance of her hand holding the backpack, Jia stepped slowly out from behind the tree, her gun hand still hidden from sight.

"Throw it over," the English-speaking guard demanded.

Jia swung the backpack behind her before lobbing it into the air. It thudded onto the ground, and Jia could almost hear the laptop breaking inside the padded case.

The guard said something to his partner in Thai. The partner nodded and cautiously moved forward to retrieve the bag. He opened it and held up the laptop, the casing cracked and the hardware exposed.

"Now let him go," Jia said.

"I don't think so." The guard holding Shaun jutted his chin up slightly again.

The man with the laptop lifted his weapon and swung it toward Jia. She was faster. She fired a shot, downing the guard with the laptop. In the same moment, Shaun shoved his elbow into his captor's stomach.

With no clear shot at the head guard, Jia fired at the computer to ensure it was indeed broken beyond repair. She wasn't going to chance these guards uncovering her method for bypassing their security protocols.

She took aim at the scuffle going on across the courtyard, but Shaun managed to separate himself for only a split second before he was once again in the other man's grasp.

Jia fired wide, hoping to startle the man into diving for cover. It didn't work. He simply kept his grip around Shaun's neck.

Two more guards came into view, both of them firing in Jia's direction. She took cover once more, the bullets impacting the ground beside her and the tree. She sprinted to the next tree behind her, putting more distance between her and the guards.

Shaun shouted, "Go!"

Go and leave him behind? Jia couldn't do that. She peered around the edge of the tree once more with the intent of picking off the guards one by one.

In that same moment, one of the newcomers plunged a syringe into Shaun's thigh.

Through the darkness, Shaun's gaze met hers. "Go." The word died on the wind as he collapsed.

Jia's heart squeezed in her chest. As much as she hated facing the facts, she had no choice. She had to escape. Now.

CHAPTER 3

It was like an itch he couldn't scratch. Erik sensed a problem was brewing, but he had no idea if he'd missed a key piece of intel during his surveillance of Duan and Baranov or if there was something else causing this sense of unease.

He did a quick check on the audio from the two men he was currently monitoring, both of them now alone in their rooms for the night. With nothing left to do on that front, he pulled up the latest updates on the guardians' database, the one place where they could access all the different reports from US intelligence agencies at the same time. He started with the CIA reports out of Bangkok. After skimming through the activity there, what little there was, he moved on to the daily reports from Seoul, Taipei, and New Delhi.

When he reached the one for Kuala Lumpur, he paused when he read the travel orders for two CIA operatives, one of whom was Jia Wu. He'd met the woman only once, but she had made an impression. Chinese by heritage and American by birth, she spoke fluent Mandarin, Cantonese, and English, and she had expanded her language skills to Korean, Malay, and Indonesian since starting her CIA career six years ago.

The woman fascinated him, both because of her tenacity in her work and the way she could fit so well into whatever environment she happened to be inhabiting. If he hadn't known better back then, he would have sworn she was simply a beautiful Chinese woman who had decided to spend her leisure time hiking the border between North and South Korea. Which was exactly where he'd found her the first time they'd met. He still couldn't believe she'd taken on such a dangerous mission alone. Her extraction from North Korea had cost him four stitches on his forearm and had left Jia with a sprained ankle. Not bad considering she had been behind enemy lines and had succeeded in recovering stolen intelligence files from a North Korean spy.

That had been nearly two years ago, but he couldn't deny that he tended to notice when her name popped up on various communications.

Trying to take his mind off Jia, he continued looking through intelligence and military action in the area. He was analyzing the position of a US destroyer in the South China Sea when an anomaly finally caught up to him. He opened the activity logs for Bangkok again, this time homing in on the motorcycles that had been procured for the transportation of two unknown operatives. Since Bangkok's acting chief of station didn't authorize much of anything, Erik couldn't help but wonder what had prompted the purchase and who the motorcycles were for.

* * *

Jia fired off a warning shot at the guard currently chasing her through the trees. She had a decision to make: Should she remain on foot and try to disappear into the darkness in the hope that the guards would give up their search, or should she head for her borrowed motorcycle and hope she could flee without getting shot the moment she started the engine? Or should she circle back and try to find Shaun?

A gunshot fired, the displacement of air far too close for comfort. She took cover and evaluated her options again.

Though it pained her to admit it, rescuing Shaun on her own wasn't an option, especially when her only transport was a motorcycle, and Shaun was unconscious. As much as she hated the current situation, Shaun was at the mercy of Brandt's men, and the longer it took her to alert the CIA, the longer it would be before her colleagues could help her liberate him.

With Shaun's safety in mind, she sprinted forward, increasing her speed as she wove through the jungle.

Another gunshot sounded. Jia darted between two trees and headed to her left. Another fifty meters and she'd reach the motorcycles. But her pursuers were still too close.

She turned away from her intended destination into a thick cluster of trees, then took cover beside a downed coconut tree, the rotted husks of the fruit scattered around it.

Hoping for a bit of misdirection, she scooped up one of the coconuts and hurled it in the opposite direction of where she needed to go. She repeated the process twice more, each time sending the coconuts farther away from where she currently stood.

Barely breathing, she stilled and listened.

Footsteps sounded as someone ran toward where she'd thrown the coconuts. A spark of hope ignited inside her. A prayer circled through her mind, and she started toward her motorcycle again, this time moving more slowly to mask her footsteps until she reached her intended destination.

Her heart pounded, and she glanced over her shoulder to make sure she didn't have anyone pursuing her.

No one in sight.

Though tempted to send a message to her coworkers at the CIA, she refrained. The light of her phone could call attention to her if anyone were too close. And with the way tonight had gone so far, she didn't dare risk it.

Instead, she put the bike in neutral and pushed it to the road, leaving Shaun's ride hidden in the trees. She rolled the motorcycle a good twenty meters before she mounted it, slid the key into place, and started the engine.

A shout echoed over the sound of the motor, but she didn't wait to see how close the guards were to her. She put the bike in gear and sped off down the road.

She swerved to avoid becoming an easy target as someone shot at her. When she approached a bend in the road, the motorcycle skidded, and she barely remained upright.

More gunfire sparked through the air. Her heart jumped into her throat, and she could barely breathe. She'd lost her backup; she was outnumbered and outgunned.

But she couldn't give up now. She increased speed and made the turn to take her out of sight.

Once again, she debated her options. Someone would be coming for her. Of that, she had little doubt. Flee or hide?

This time, she opted for the latter.

She reached a roadside fruit stand and turned into the narrow drive beside it. She continued a few meters before she killed the lights and the engine. Rolling her bike behind a tree, she peeked out from behind a cluster of palms and willed her heart to settle, then she pulled her cell phone from her pocket as she waited for the inevitable.

As expected, less than two minutes passed before two vehicles raced past her.

She froze, barely daring to breathe.

As soon as the taillights of the second car disappeared from view, Jia dialed the Bangkok field office's emergency number.

No answer.

Her grip tightened on her phone. This should never happen.

She hung up and tried again. Again, no answer.

The closest safe house was behind her, but she didn't dare risk going to one so close to the lab. No, she'd spend a little more time on the road to make sure she was well hidden. But first, she needed to get a plan in motion to get Shaun back. She opened her secure messaging system and sent a text to the Bangkok chief of station. *S captured. On way to R27G.*

The words on the screen emphasized the failures of tonight, by her and Shaun and by the agency leadership in the region for not recognizing the intel for what it was—a viable threat that needed immediate action.

A renewed resolve swelled inside her. She was going to find a way to get Shaun back and get this intel into the right hands. But to do that, she needed to be invisible.

She pulled a tool from the back of her phone case and removed her phone's physical SIM card. After breaking it in two, she tossed her phone and the SIM card into the bushes. She then retrieved a burner phone and a protein bar from the storage compartment on the back of her bike. As soon as the cars chasing her returned to the compound, she'd leave her hiding place, trade out her bike for another, and make her way to the safe house, where she could regroup.

CHAPTER 4

Her weapon in hand, Jia circled the safe house twice before she unlocked the front door. She slipped inside, her chest tight with guilt. This was all her fault. Her source had tipped her off to the lab's existence. Jia had done the research on Brandt and interpreted the data to find the lab. And she'd personally written the mission plan that had resulted in Shaun's getting captured.

The magnitude of tonight's events crashed over her, and a hollowness expanded inside her until her emotions threatened to swallow her whole. She'd left a fellow operative behind—something she'd never thought she was capable of doing.

He was alive, she reminded herself. They both were, and with help, she could get him back.

She pulled out her new cell phone and again dialed the after-hours number for the Bangkok office. No answer. She huffed out an annoyed breath. Of all the times for the on-call officer to be away from the phone, this was not it.

She pressed a hand to her back, where the external hard drive remained hidden beneath her shirt. She needed to get this information to the agency, and she needed backup.

First things first. She gripped her pistol and kept it aimed in front of her as she passed through the streamlined kitchen and living area. The rickety table and two stools barely made for an adequate place to eat, and the rattan chairs in the living room were in desperate need of new cushions.

She moved into the hall, searching the bathroom and each of the two bedrooms. Like the rest of the small house, the furnishings were merely usable. The platform beds would provide a place to sleep, but the bedside tables were bare.

Satisfied that her location was secure, she accessed the security system and engaged the motion detectors outside. She then took stock of the supplies.

Basic clothing of varying sizes filled the closet, and three backpacks hung from hooks on the closet door.

She pulled open the trunk situated at the foot of the bed and pushed aside the stack of linens to reveal a safe. She unlocked it and did a quick inventory: cash, a prepaid credit card, a Glock 19M, three magazines of ammo, two blank passports, and two cell phones. But no laptop.

Jia let out a frustrated sigh. Communication with her office would have been so much easier if a secure computer had been included in the basic equipment here, especially since the duty officer in Bangkok hadn't answered her calls.

Hoping one of the cell phones would help her connect with the CIA one way or another, she plugged both in and set them aside to charge. Then she grabbed one of the backpacks from the closet and loaded it with a change of clothes, some cash, the credit card, and the gun and ammunition.

After closing the safe, she sat on the bed and picked up the charging phone nearest her. It opened without a passcode, and she tapped on the app for the security system. After connecting it to ensure it was synced, she dialed the Bangkok after-hours number. When there was no answer yet again, she leaned forward, resting her elbows on her knees. Maybe she could rest for a few minutes before she tried again.

That thought had barely formed when an alert rang on her new phone. Her heart raced, and she held up the phone. A motion detector had tripped, but no movement appeared on her screen.

Unsure of whether it was man or wildlife waiting for her outside, she unplugged the second phone and stuffed it and the charger into her backpack. After she slipped her arms through the straps, she checked the screen on the first phone again. The shadow of a man passed in front of where she'd parked her motorcycle. A second followed, both hands gripping a pistol as though ready to shoot.

Her pulse quickened. Brandt's men had found her. But how?

She'd consider that question later. First, she needed to slip past them and get out of here. She moved to the back window and waited for the two figures to close in on the front door.

Praying that they didn't have someone watching the back of the house, she opened the window and climbed out.

She dropped into the shadows beside the house and listened. The front door creaked open, and she quietly crept through the trees toward the stream that bordered the property. When she reached it, she dropped the cell phone she'd used to call the Bangkok station into the water to make sure no one could use it to track her.

With no way to get to her motorcycle without being seen, she continued along the edge of the stream. Once she was a full kilometer away from the safe house, she stopped and pulled the second cell phone from her bag.

She pulled up the contact list, but only one number popped up: Ghost.

Like many in the CIA, she'd heard the whispered rumors about the guardians, but she hadn't believed them until one had appeared out of nowhere when all hope had been lost.

She needed a dose of hope now. She drew a quick breath and hit the Talk button.

A man answered. "Who is this?"

That wasn't a question Jia was prepared to answer. "Is this Ghost?"

"Yes."

A wave of relief rushed through her. Finally, someone who could provide backup. "I need your help."

"Who is this?" he asked again.

Though she didn't particularly care to share that detail, she had little choice. "This is Jia. We met a while ago in Korea." She didn't specify which Korean country. "I have intel I need to get to the right people, but I don't have a way to transmit it."

"Do you have transportation?" he asked, clearly already focused on the logistics of what would happen next.

"I'm working on it, but there's more. My partner didn't make it out."

"Where is he?"

Jia gave Ghost the location of the lab.

"I'll make sure his status is reported. In the meantime, I'm going to text you a location. Find some transportation so you can bring that intel to me. Once it's secure and you're safe, we'll evaluate the situation."

The situation was that Shaun was in an enemy compound, and there was no way to tell how long he would remain alive. She opened her mouth to protest, to insist she join whatever rescue effort would come next, but the hard drive pressing against her back reminded her of how much more was at stake. Shaun was one man. If someone didn't stop Douglas Brandt and his group, millions could die.

A text message came through, and she looked at the screen. "When do you want to meet?"

"That's your call. You tell me."

Fatigue weakened her limbs, but she knew she wouldn't be able to sleep until she was sure the intel was in the right hands. "I'll leave now."

"I'll be waiting."

CHAPTER 5

"They found her."

The words spoken in English pushed through Shaun's semiconsciousness. The chill of a cool surface pressed against him, and he vaguely wondered why he wasn't in his bed.

More words jumbled together, but Shaun couldn't decipher their meaning.

He stirred and struggled to open his eyes. Bright light glared from overhead, and he tried to lift his arm to block it out. The effort only resulted in his wrists chafing against metal. Handcuffs?

Fragments of memory pushed through the fog in his brain. The intel reports on a deadly virus, the flight from Malaysia to Thailand, the meeting with the Bangkok chief of station, the guard grabbing him from behind.

The last piece replayed on a quick repeat—the alarms blaring, Jia facing down the guards, the pinch of the needle stabbing into his thigh before he lost consciousness.

He tried to push himself up from where he lay on the floor, but again, his bound hands prevented it. He squinted as his surroundings took shape. The light overhead wasn't from a single fixture but rather a bank of fluorescent lights. Judging from the metal counter beside him, the spotless linoleum floor, and the glass-fronted refrigerator filled with test tubes, he was in the same lab Jia had broken into tonight. Or last night? He had no idea how long he'd been out.

Two men stood beside the door. It took only a moment to identify Douglas Brandt. The other, with his blond hair, blue eyes, and thick accent, suggested he was from somewhere in Europe.

"Her computer doesn't have anything usable on it," the European said.

"You're sure she couldn't have made a second download?" Brandt asked.

The European shook his head. "I checked the system. One download was made, and I was able to retrieve enough from her hard drive to determine the time of the data transfer matched the one taken from the lab computer."

Which meant Shaun had been captured for nothing. If Jia didn't have proof, there was no guarantee the agency would understand the potential risks.

Brandt gestured toward the door. "Make sure she doesn't live to see tomorrow."

The European nodded. "My men have their orders."

"Good."

Shaun gulped. He'd been captured, but Jia was about to die. And he was certain to meet the same fate. He managed to push up on an elbow.

"He's awake." Brandt gestured absently toward him. "Take care of him."

Shaun's pulse quickened. Brandt was going to kill Jia, but Shaun was going to be the first to die. He tried in earnest to stand. But before he could manage it, one of the guards produced a syringe and grabbed his arm. The man plunged the needle into Shaun's flesh. Then the light faded at the edges of his vision, and within seconds, everything went dark.

* * *

Erik peeked around the edge of a large passenger van and looked into the dark parking lot of his hotel in Jomtien Beach, the same one where he'd been monitoring Vladimir Baranov and his Chinese informant. A couple passed by, speaking in Mandarin. Beyond them, a half dozen more people waited to cross the street to the 7-Eleven on the corner, Australians by the sound of them.

The group turned toward the line of vendors that lay beyond the convenience store. Rows of booths, where hawkers sold everything from street food to souvenirs for tourists and locals alike.

Erik took another look around, the lights from the evening street fair spilling onto the road that ran between them. More tourists, a foursome of Russians, walked by with kabobs in their hands. A Thai family followed behind them. The people Erik could see didn't worry him nearly as much as those who might be hiding in the shadows.

Ever thorough, he left his hiding place. He did a quick search of the perimeter of the parking lot and then walked up and down the rows of cars, vans, and motorcycles. Once he was satisfied that he was alone, he sent a single-word text: *Clear.*

The reply was nearly instant. *ETA 4 minutes.*

Just enough time to take another security precaution. Erik returned to his motorcycle and opened the storage compartment in the back. He retrieved a screwdriver and a license plate he'd lifted off an abandoned bike in Bangkok. Then quickly, he changed out his plates to make sure anyone who might have tracked him here wouldn't recognize his ride. Not that anyone likely would. After all, except for a few select people in the US government, the world didn't know he existed.

A little pang filled his heart as he thought of the grandparents who had raised him after his parents had died in a car accident. How he wished he could still have them in his life, but pretending to die had been his way of protecting them as well as himself.

A horn beeped, pulling him from his thoughts. There was no time to lose focus on his regrets of the past, especially when the person he was meeting tonight was Jia. He couldn't deny the odd sense of anticipation he'd felt when he'd learned she would be the operative he was helping tonight. Surely that was simply because of how much he respected her work. The woman was a force of nature, one who continually exceeded expectations.

The steady hum of traffic continued on the main road that separated the hotel from the beach, a couple of vehicles turning onto the narrow street that passed by the parking lot. Seconds ticked off as he waited for an engine to grow louder, for a car or motorcycle to turn into the parking lot. None did.

Instead, a woman emerged from the strip of street vendors. Petite in build, with black hair falling past her shoulders, she looked exactly like a local. But as she approached, her deliberate footsteps and obvious awareness of her surroundings made Erik suspect his contact had arrived on foot rather than in a vehicle.

She drew closer, and Erik stepped out of the shadows. It was her all right—Jia Wu, the American intelligence operative who was even more beautiful than he remembered.

She reached his side and glanced over her shoulder before asking, "Were you followed?"

Erik shook his head. "That's usually my line." Though, with how long she'd taken to reach him, he was sure she'd taken a meandering route to avoid discovery.

Another group of fair-skinned foreigners passed by on the side of the street.

"Come on." Erik gestured to the hotel's back door. "We can talk inside."

"I can't afford for anyone to track me."

"Don't worry." Erik retrieved a handheld device one of his fellow guardians had developed. The invention would allow him to not only bypass the locking mechanisms of their hotel rooms but also override the registration system to show that their rooms were occupied. The payment would ultimately come through the guardian financial system long after they left the hotel to make sure no one could trace them.

Erik swiped the key card against the keypad and glanced back at Jia. "No one will ever know we're here."

* * *

Jia stood in the empty hall and checked both directions while Ghost fiddled with what appeared to be a hotel key card attached to a cell phone. She suspected it was little more than a code breaker, but right now, she was more worried about staying out of sight.

The light on the keypad turned green, and Ghost opened the door. He gestured her inside and followed. As soon as he closed the door behind them, he flipped the extra bolt at the top and asked, "What's the situation?"

Leave it to the man to get straight to the point. She usually appreciated the direct approach, but right now, with her head spinning and her body fighting fatigue and hunger, she needed a minute to put her unprecedented situation into words.

Jia crossed the hotel room, passing the queen-size bed and reaching the table in the corner. Behind it, two french doors led to the balcony. She sat and faced the man she'd met only once before and who wouldn't even tell her his real name. But he was here, and he was her best chance.

Her gaze lifted to his, her eyes locking on his blue ones. Something was different about him since they'd last parted ways in Seoul. She'd sensed his respect when they'd first met, but that was likely due to the fight they'd waged together to gain their freedom a couple of years ago. Now, however, his expression held a softer emotion. Concern, maybe?

She must be imagining things. He probably barely remembered her. She swallowed and forced out the words. "I need your help."

"That's usually why people call me," Ghost said dryly, but she didn't miss the little twitch of a smile. He peeked out the curtains that hid them from the outside world before slipping his backpack off his shoulders. He lowered it to the floor and sat across from her.

Jia waited for him to turn his attention to her again before she said, "I think someone in Singapore is trying to develop a new biological weapon." She drew a deep breath and exhaled slowly. "If I'm right, it has the potential to kill as many as or more people than COVID-19."

"Where are you getting your intel?"

Jia's stomach clenched. Shaun had sacrificed himself to make sure she could share the data she'd collected. She had to see it through, even if she didn't have access to her typical agency resources. Slowly, she reached into the hidden pocket in her shirt and produced the hard drive containing the intel she'd downloaded. Her hand trembled as she passed it to him. "This is everything I have."

Ghost took it from her, and he studied her face. He frowned. "When was the last time you ate?"

When had she eaten last? "This morning, I think."

Ghost unzipped his bag and dug out a protein bar. He passed it to her with one of the two water bottles from his bag's side pocket. "Here. This will get some calories in you."

"Thanks." She unscrewed the top of the water bottle and took a sip. The warm liquid trickled down her dry throat, a reminder of how far she'd come today.

While she unwrapped the protein bar, Ghost plugged the hard drive into a small scanner of some sort. Then he slid his laptop free and set it on the table.

After he appeared satisfied that the external hard drive didn't contain any computer viruses, he opened his laptop and plugged it in.

"It's the first file." Jia took a bite of the bar and slid closer.

The spreadsheet popped up on the screen, the analysis laid out in black-and-white of how many people would likely die once the virus was unleashed.

Ghost's jaw dropped. He scrolled through the lengthy report before lifting his gaze to meet hers. "The fatality rates are off the charts for people with any kind of health problems."

"I know." Her grip tightened on her water bottle. "We've only identified one person involved, but we know there are others."

"Who's 'we'?"

Jia swallowed hard. The mere thought of Shaun going through an interrogation or worse turned her stomach. "Me and Shaun." She blinked against the tears that threatened. "I tried to free him, but once they drugged him and Shaun lost consciousness, it was three against one."

"You did the right thing in getting this intel here. And I already passed on Shaun's location to the military." Ghost furrowed his eyebrows. "But why are you bringing this intel to me? Why didn't you take it to the agency?"

"I tried. I called several times, but my calls went unanswered. And I only had time to call once from the safe house in Ang Thong before some unfriendlies showed up. I barely had time to grab the essentials." She set her water bottle on the table beside her, her mind racing. The possibilities of how she'd been found swirled in her head, and she verbalized them now. "As soon as I messaged my SITREP my intended destination, I shed everything electronic except the external hard drive, but I'd already scanned it to make sure it didn't have a tracking device on it."

Clearly picking up on her concerns, Ghost asked, "Could Shaun have given up the location of the safe house?"

She shook her head. "Like I said, he was sedated. My guess is he probably wouldn't have regained consciousness until an hour or two after those guys showed up at the safe house." Had it really only been this morning when she'd left Shaun behind? "And I didn't go to the nearest safe house. I passed three first. How could they have known where I was going?"

Ghost's eyes narrowed. "You're afraid someone on the inside leaked your location."

"The thought crossed my mind."

"It more than crossed your mind if you reached out to me." Ghost stood and peeked out the curtains again before he turned back to face her. "I want you to tell me every detail of how you found out about this weapon and the people behind it."

"Okay, but first, I need to get an update on Shaun, and we need to make sure this intel gets to the right people," Jia insisted. "If someone at the CIA is working with this group, there's no way of telling if they'll also block the information to keep it from getting to the president."

"Tell me everything. I'll make sure the right people receive what they need to know." Ghost settled back into the chair beside her. "And we'll find your friend."

CHAPTER 6

An operative in peril. A second CIA officer holding information that warranted immediate action. Erik was accustomed to the first situation, but not the second. Sharing the danger and planning a way to combat it had to take priority. But he needed to understand the big picture in order to do that.

"This man, Douglas Brandt—" Erik began. "Any idea why he's trying to release a deadly virus?"

"I have a guess, but that's all it is." Jia rubbed at her eyes, then she explained Brandt's background and family history. "It looks like instead of helping cure these diseases, he's trying to eradicate them through extreme measures."

"That's scary." Or perhaps *terrifying* was a better word, especially since Erik had one of those autoimmune diseases. He pulled up the database he and the other eight guardians used to share secure information and selected the file from the external hard drive Jia had given him. Leaving the new intel to upload, he pushed back from the table, where Jia still sat. He slipped his phone out of his pocket and called Vanessa Johnson, the guardians' liaison with the president. No answer.

Jia stifled a yawn. "Who are you calling?"

"Someone who can get this intel to the right people."

If Vanessa wasn't answering, she was likely somewhere in the White House where cell phones weren't allowed. Erik dialed again, this time choosing Kade's number. It was early in the morning on the East Coast, but of all the guardians, Kade had the most direct access to the White House.

The phone rang twice before Kade's grumpy voice came over the line. "What?"

"Don't tell me I woke you." Erik checked his watch. "It's already seven in the morning there."

"I had to secure a witness for a gun-running case out of Camp Lejeune last night." Kade's yawn carried over the phone. "Why are you waking me up?"

"I'm uploading a bunch of files into the database now. I need you to get it to V so she can verify the intel," Erik said, referring to Vanessa. He couldn't exactly use the names of his colleagues in front of Jia.

"Can it wait until after I get some sleep?"

"I don't think so. We also have a CIA operative who was taken captive early this morning in the Northeast region of Thailand."

"Way to bury the lede." Kade's voice sharpened. "Who and where?"

Erik relayed the details Jia had given him. "I've already sent the intel forward, but the military will need updated satellite imagery to see what we're dealing with before they can send a special forces team in after this guy."

"You're getting pretty demanding all of a sudden."

"I learned from the best."

Kade had come into the guardian program several years before Erik, but they'd spent a good deal of time training together.

"You should know by now that flattery doesn't work on me," Kade said.

"Nothing works on you." Except spelling out a problem. Kade might grumble, but he was loyal, and he always followed through. Sympathizing with his colleague over his lack of sleep, Erik added, "You can always have your wife do it." Kade's wife was former CIA and now worked with the guardians. "She's just as capable as you are."

"Probably more so, but I don't want her driving all the way to DC with the baby. Not by herself anyway."

Another guardian with a baby. Ace's little one was already a year old, and Kade's wife, Renee, had given birth four months ago. Erik could hardly imagine living his life in the shadows while also having a family.

He pushed aside that thought. "I'll leave it for you to decide who's getting the intel into V's hands, but it needs to happen today."

"Fine. I'll keep you updated."

"Thanks." Erik stifled a yawn of his own. "Who else is available right now? I need someone to keep an eye on things here while my client and I get some sleep."

"Try Troy. It's daytime in Helsinki, and it looks like everything's quiet in his part of the world."

"I'll send him a message once I get my cameras set up." Erik ended the call and focused on Jia again.

She blinked rapidly, as though trying to keep her eyes open. "Your friend will get the word out?"

"He will. And he'll let us know what's being done to get your partner back." Erik could only imagine how all-consuming her concern must be for her coworker. He checked to make sure the upload to the database had completed before disconnecting the cord. "For now, get some sleep. I'll have a friend watch the security feed here at the hotel to make sure we don't have any unexpected visitors."

She wiped at the dust on her cheek. "I need a shower first."

"Do you need me to go pick up some clothes for you?"

"I have what I need for tonight."

Erik nodded. He handed the external hard drive back to Jia. "You hold on to this. I have a backup on my laptop now."

She took it from him, and her fingers brushed his.

The simple human contact warmed him, a sad reminder that he rarely had the luxury of personal connections, much less with a beautiful woman.

He moved to the door. "Call me if you need anything. I'll be in the room directly across from you: 504."

"Thank you."

He gripped the doorknob. "We'll talk in the morning." Erik slipped into the hall and closed the door between them. Once he made a quick sweep of the hotel to make sure Jia was safe, he'd check the audio on his Russian and Chinese friends and then get some sleep. He suspected tomorrow would be a busy day.

CHAPTER 7

Light streamed through the thin curtains that covered the balcony door, and Jia rubbed at the grit in her eyes. Her shower last night had washed away the worst of the dust and grime she'd picked up on her long drive to this beach community located a hundred kilometers outside of Bangkok, but her whole body still ached from riding so many hours on a motorcycle.

Her stomach grumbled. The only food she'd eaten yesterday was grilled pork and rice, which she vaguely remembered picking up from a street vendor, and the protein bar Ghost had given her last night. But at least she'd eaten something. She had no idea if Shaun had been granted that same privilege.

The guilt gnawed at her, and she pushed out of bed. She needed to know if he was still being held at the lab or somewhere else. Once they determined that, they could make a plan to free him from his captors. Of course, first she needed to add more allies to her collective "they." She doubted she and Ghost alone could take on the task, but he'd mentioned a special forces unit. Whether or not he had the connections and resources to pull that off, she had no idea. Now that she'd had enough sleep to sort of function, she intended to find out.

She dressed for the day and debated whether to call Ghost or knock on his door. She opted for the simplest option and unplugged her phone from the charger.

A knock sounded before she could dial. She peered through the peephole to confirm it was Ghost before opening the door.

With his backpack hanging off his left shoulder, he lifted two paper plates into her view. One held a piece of pork on a stick and a blob of sticky rice, just like her breakfast the previous day. On the other plate, a Thai omelet topped a bed of rice.

"I thought you might want real food." He entered her room and crossed to the table while she closed the door behind him. "You can pick which one you want. I'll eat the other one."

"I'll take the omelet." She followed him to the table. "Any word on Shaun?"

"Not as much as I'd hoped." Ghost waited until she sat before he claimed the seat across from her. He slid the omelet closer to her and passed her a set of silverware wrapped in a napkin. "Satellite imagery showed a lot of movement at the lab you infiltrated. Whoever was there packed up and moved shop."

"And Shaun?"

"The Saint Squad already went in and cleared the building. No one is there."

They were too late. Her heart sank, the enormity of finding Shaun weighing on her. She repeated Ghost's words again and tried to make sense of them. "Who's the Saint Squad?"

"They're a squad of navy SEALs." He stood and turned to the minifridge behind him. After he retrieved two water bottles from inside, he returned to the table and passed her one.

She took it and twisted off the cap. "What about the wounded? I shot two men."

"They found blood but no bodies. Either the men survived, or they took their dead with them."

Jia hated the thought of killing anyone, but she couldn't imagine the first guard she shot had survived his wounds. "We need to assume they took their dead with them to keep us from identifying them."

"I had a feeling you might say that." He took a sip of water. "What else do you know about Douglas Brandt? You said an informant tipped you off?"

"Yes. Her sister works as a helper in Singapore. She overheard him speaking to someone on the phone about how much better the world would be once they were done," Jia said.

"And how did you find out about the virus and the lab?"

"My informant's sister sent her a photo of some documents she found. They included some mortality rates, although the ones I showed you last night were even higher than the first ones I saw." Scary. She cut into her omelet. "It took me the better part of three weeks to track Brandt's movements and locate the lab."

"Obviously, you found the right place, or no one would have been shooting last night." Ghost seemed to ponder for a moment. "Any chance you can have your contact get in touch with her sister again? Maybe we can arrange to meet with her. With the right evidence, we can stop this before it goes any further."

"I don't think that will be possible."

He lifted his eyebrows. "Why's that?"

"My contact hasn't heard from her sister since she received the message about the virus."

"That's not good."

Jia let out a sigh. "No, it isn't."

* * *

Shaun jolted awake, his body no longer on the floor but in the seat of a private plane. His right hand was cuffed to the base of the armrest, but his left hand remained free. He sensed someone behind him, but his focus immediately turned to three men sitting in the chairs surrounding a worktable.

Brandt sat across from one of the guards from the lab. The third man faced away from Shaun, but judging from the man's blond hair, he suspected the European from the lab rounded out the group.

"The rollout has to be simultaneous, or we run the risk of someone developing a vaccine or effective treatment options," the European said.

"With our current plans, the spread will hit nearly every continent within a few weeks." Brandt tapped his finger on the tablet that lay on the table. "Beyond our current distribution plans, I think we need to consider additional exposure events in the largest cities in North America and Europe."

"I suggest we also include Mumbai and a couple spots in Africa," the European said.

"I agree," Brandt said. "With the length of the contagious period, it shouldn't take long before we create a truly worldwide pandemic."

"What will the numbers look like under this scenario?" the European asked.

"Based on our initial estimates, we'll see approximately three million deaths in the US during the first year, between five and six million in Europe, and around eight million in India. I don't have good numbers on Africa yet."

Shaun barely kept his jaw from dropping. He'd seen the data, but their estimates hadn't been nearly that high. Sixteen million deaths and these men were treating the details as though they were discussing a simple business transaction.

Frustration hummed through the European's voice. "Those numbers aren't quite as high as I'd like in Europe, but we're getting closer to where we need to be."

A steward entered the passenger space of the private jet, a tray in his hand. Rice and curry scented the cabin, and Shaun's appetite stirred. He didn't know how long he'd been kept sedated, but he was starving. And thirsty.

The flight attendant set plates down in front of each of the three men.

Brandt picked up his fork and gestured toward the nearest cabin window. "With the woman still on the loose, we can't afford to wait. If she knew enough to break into the lab, she may know enough to warn the World Health Organization of what we have planned."

The European nodded. "At this point, it's too late for any of these countries to do anything to stop us. The woman is an inconvenience, but she doesn't know enough to get in our way."

"I hope you're right." Brandt glanced in Shaun's direction, and he lifted his eyebrows. "It appears our guest is finally awake." He turned his attention to the attendant. "Get our friend something to eat and drink."

The man bowed his head. "Yes, sir." He disappeared into the galley at the front of the plane.

Shaun swallowed to fight the dryness in his mouth, three questions surfacing in his mind: What was this group's timeline, where were they taking him, and why was Brandt keeping him alive?

CHAPTER 8

Erik sat at the table across from Jia and used his laptop to read the latest updates. No sign of Shaun, a dead end with Jia's asset, and a suspicious breach of security two nights ago with the Bangkok field office. This wasn't good.

After he and Jia finished breakfast, he'd used his laptop to check the guardian database for any updates while Jia did her own digging into the backgrounds of her coworkers, using his spare laptop. Lacey, their newest guardian, who specialized in infectious diseases, had completed her initial analysis of the virus, her conclusions supporting what Jia had told Erik last night. If the data Jia had recovered was accurate, the virus would be deadly for millions.

And then there was the whole scenario of someone showing up at the safe house two nights ago. It hadn't sat well with him then, and reading Kade's report only furthered Erik's concerns.

He looked at Jia. "One of my colleagues pulled the video feed from the safe house's security cameras yesterday."

"And?" Jia's eyes narrowed. "Please don't tell me I ran from someone who was coming to help me."

"You didn't." He expanded the image of one of the two men who had been there and pushed his laptop toward her. "Niran has suspected ties with the Ling crime family. Same with Klahan."

Jia sighed. "Sounds like enforcers to me."

"I agree." But with how fast they showed up, it only made sense that someone had tracked her, likely through her phone. Yet even with this new insight, it still didn't make sense that the CIA hadn't given her the backup she'd needed. "After you escaped the compound, when was the first time you tried contacting the agency?"

"I tried calling the Bangkok office soon after I lost the people following me. No one answered, so I sent a text message to report Shaun was compromised."

"Did you also tell them where you were going?"

"Yes, but I used the coded identifier for the safe house. There wasn't anything that indicated the town, much less the address." She tucked a lock of her straight black hair behind her ear, the ends brushing her shoulders. "Then I tried calling the Bangkok office again as soon as I arrived at the safe house, but again, no one answered."

"An after-hours call should never go unanswered."

"I know." She furrowed her brow. "Maybe the phone lines were down."

Erik tapped his fingers on the table. "That's not likely without some outside interference."

"Maybe the guys following me blocked my call without me realizing it."

"If they did, they would have had to be right behind you the whole time." Erik shook his head. None of this was making any sense. "Why let you get all the way to the safe house if they already knew where you were?"

"You're right. It makes far more sense that someone knew where I was going, and these guys were trying to catch up."

Which brought them right back to the possibility that someone inside the CIA could have set her up to fail.

"We need to make a plan." Jia pursed her lips and tapped a finger against them. "Until intel can track down where Shaun is, that op is on hold. For now, we need to figure out how, when, and where Brandt plans to release the virus."

"I can put some of my colleagues on that. One of them specializes in medicine."

"Great. After you pass that project off, our next move is to fly to Singapore to look for my contact's sister and Douglas Brandt. That might be the only way to track down where the people at the lab relocated to."

Our next move? Erik shook his head. "The intel is already in the hands of the Thai authorities and the White House. One of my colleagues is sharing it with the World Health Organization. And I'm sure we can hand off the details about your informant's sister to the CIA's Singapore station."

"You might be sure, but I'm not. If someone on the inside is undermining my communication with the agency, there's no way to guarantee that whoever it is couldn't send someone else after me to keep all this quiet."

She had a point, but he wasn't sure he liked where this was leading.

"Your job is to keep people like me safe, right?" she asked.

"Yes. I did that. Twice." Which was already an anomaly. Rarely did he assist an operative more than once.

Jia held up both hands. "And if you stick close to me, we can make sure there won't be a third time."

"What are you proposing?"

"I have the phone number for my informant's sister." She lifted her eyebrows. "I say we trace it and track her down in Singapore. If we find her, we should be able to find Brandt."

"What if Brandt finds you first?"

"I doubt he knows who I am, but if he does, I'll have you there to watch my back."

Or some other operative from the CIA would fill that role. Either way worked for him. He was used to being on his own, and rather liked it that way. He couldn't deny, though, that he wouldn't mind extending his time with Jia.

"I'll put in your suggestion to my superiors. I doubt they'll want me to run your support, but I can take you as far as Singapore."

A hint of panic flashed on her face. The fact that she showed any emotion in her expression surprised him and revealed she wasn't happy about losing him as her backup.

She clenched her jaw and studied him for a moment before she nodded. "It's a start."

* * *

Jia adjusted her sunglasses and leaned back in her chair on Ghost's balcony. Unlike her room, which had a view of the resort's swimming pool, his looked out over the street and the beach that lay just beyond it. A steady stream of cars passed by, and dozens of beachgoers lounged on chairs in the sand or waded knee-deep into the water. And here she was, free to sit and enjoy the faint breeze and the scent of meat grilling while Shaun was who knew where.

Her stomach knotted. She drew a deep breath and tried to push images of Shaun out of her mind. She couldn't help him if she couldn't find him, and she had to trust that Ghost's friends were taking that task seriously.

Ghost stepped outside, two water bottles in hand, and scanned the scene before them. He passed her a water and took the seat beside her.

"Why are you always handing me water bottles? Do I look thirsty?"

"No, but in this heat and humidity, it doesn't take much to get dehydrated."

Her last eighteen months living in Malaysia had taught her that lesson well. A bead of sweat trickled down her back. She took a long drink of the cold liquid and looked out at the view, where palm trees lined the edge of the beach. She gestured toward the wide stretch of sand below. "How come you got the beach view?"

"Because I needed to monitor the street," Ghost said. "And you needed sleep last night more than I did."

She'd assumed he'd turned surveillance over to someone on his support team. Not that she had much of an understanding of what his support team consisted of. "Did you get any sleep?"

"Enough." He turned his chair so he was facing her while also being able to see the street. "I just got off the phone with my tech guy. He was able to trace the origin of the call between your informant and her sister."

Jia lifted her eyebrows. "That was fast." Requests for such details at the CIA typically took at least a day or two. "Where is she?"

"The call came from a condominium complex in Orchard."

Jia hadn't spent a lot of time in Singapore, but she was well aware of Orchard Road and the high-end retail shops located there. Which made sense. Her source's sister was a helper—a maid of sorts—and in that area of town, she was most certainly one who resided with her employer. "I don't suppose your guy was able to narrow it down to a specific apartment?"

"No, but he did check other calls to and from that number. It could be that the informant lives in tower two." Ghost took a sip of his water. "There are eighteen units in that section, but it looks like they all share the same elevator."

"So theoretically, if we can watch everyone coming and going in that tower, we'll be able to find her."

Doubt flashed in his expression. "We'll be able to narrow our suspect field anyway. There is one catch."

"What's that?"

"These condos are gated."

"Great." Jia blew out a frustrated breath. "Normally, I'd say we could try to get in undercover with a job as a helper or with maintenance, but I don't know if we have that kind of time."

"I agree. I already looked for job openings for anyone in the complex looking for domestic help, but I didn't find any," Ghost said. "And trying to use the deliveryman cover means we would have extremely limited access."

"So what do we do?" Jia asked. "We can't just ignore this lead."

"With the short amount of time we have, I think the only way we'll be able to move about freely is to actually buy or rent a unit in the complex. Unfortunately, there's only one vacant unit in that tower, but it's for sale, not rent."

"We don't have time to buy."

"I know. My friend is looking into options to see if we can put down a contract, which will allow you to take possession early under a rent-back agreement."

"You mean *us*. The owner will let *us* do a rent-back agreement." She couldn't take on Douglas Brandt alone, not without agency resources, and right now, she didn't trust herself to use them. Ghost was the only one she could trust right now, with Shaun captured and someone else in the agency potentially sabotaging her.

"We'll see." Ghost stood. "Any chance you're up for going through the list of agency personnel in the region? If you can narrow down who knew about your mission here in Thailand, we'll have a better chance of finding out if there really is a leak."

"Yeah." She finished off her water and pushed to her feet. "Let's get started."

CHAPTER 9

Eight employees at the CIA had knowledge of both the safe-house location and Jia and Shaun's mission here in Thailand. Erik tried to ignore Jia's incessant pacing as she crossed from the balcony to his hotel room door and back again. He didn't know how she could transition so quickly from her relaxed state out on the balcony to someone in constant motion, but she'd clearly taken it upon herself the past two days to make sure they didn't have any unwanted visitors.

She peered through the glass of the balcony door before wearing a path on the tile floor back to where she could peer through the peephole.

Concentrating on his task at hand, Erik loaded the list of possible leaks into the guardian database. He then entered a support request into the message board. Hopefully, someone had time on their hands and could do the background checks for him as well as go through the latest audio on the men he'd originally come to Thailand to monitor.

Jia must have sensed he'd accomplished his task because she stopped in the center of the room and asked, "How much longer are we going to wait here?"

"Until we get new intel on Shaun's location or we sort out your accommodations in Singapore."

She closed her eyes as though blocking out a bad memory. After several seconds, she shook her head, and her gaze met his. "I don't even want to think about what Shaun must be going through right now."

"How much intel does he have that could compromise you?"

"My name, the alias I was using here in Thailand, the identities of our personnel in the Kuala Lumpur station, our contacts in Bangkok."

Erik took a moment to reassess the situation. He had assumed Jia was assigned to the Bangkok station. "You're assigned to Malaysia?"

She nodded. "My informant is Malay. When the trail led us to Thailand, we coordinated with the acting chief of station here, but he's stingy with resources. He wouldn't give us any extra manpower without approval from headquarters, and we didn't have time to wait."

Which would explain why Jia and Shaun had gone in without sufficient backup. It also shed light on why four of the eight employees on their list of suspects were out of the Kuala Lumpur office.

Erik leaned back in his chair. "Tell me what you know about Andrea Morrow, Tyrone Porter, Chesah Abalos, and Dylan Floyd."

Jia checked out the balcony door again. "Andrea has been station chief for almost two years. She's fluent in Malay and Mandarin and passable in a half dozen other languages."

"Family? Hobbies? Signs of unexpected wealth?" Erik asked.

"Married, two kids—both attending universities in the US. Her husband is some big-shot consultant in the oil industry, so they've always had money."

"And how does she spend her free time?"

"She doesn't have a lot of that, but she's a fan of the theater, and she and her husband travel a lot, mostly to different parts of Malaysia."

Erik added those details to his notes in the database.

Jia sat across from him. "I know her personal life might make it sound like she could be getting money from some outside source, but of the eight names on our list, she would be at the bottom for me."

Jia's loyalty to her boss was admirable, but was it misplaced? "Explain to me why."

Jia lifted her hand and held up one finger. "For one thing, she's a patriot. She spent six years in the army before she joined the agency."

Another finger lifted. "Second, she has no weaknesses to exploit, no skeletons in her closet."

Erik tilted his head to the side. "That you know of."

Jia narrowed her eyes and stared for a moment before she gestured absently with her hand that still had two fingers up. "Okay, fine. That I know of."

"What else?"

She lifted her third finger. "I already shared my suspicions with Andrea about the possibility of a biological weapon targeting people with health issues."

"Does she have health issues?"

"No, but most of her family does. Her mom and daughter both have heart issues, and her husband is diabetic," Jia said. "If any of them were exposed to the virus, it's unlikely they'd survive."

Just as Erik's celiac put him at risk. "Okay, what about Tyrone Porter?"

"Our finance officer. He only transferred in a few weeks ago. It's doubtful someone could have recruited him that quickly."

"January isn't a typical time for a transfer."

"I know. His predecessor retired at the end of December," Jia said. "Tyrone wasn't even named as the replacement until the week before Thanksgiving."

Which made him an unlikely target for Brandt's organization.

"Dylan Floyd?"

"This is his second overseas assignment. He was in India for two years before a stint at headquarters. He's been working in the Kuala Lumpur office for about a year now."

"And Chesah?"

"She's smart, ambitious." Jia shrugged. "Her dad is Filipino, so her coloring gives her an edge over some of the other people in our office." She tapped a finger on the table. "The two of us don't work together often."

"Any particular reason why not?"

"We're both women of Asian descent with similar language skills. No point in doubling up when we share similar abilities." She shrugged. "Plus, Chesah wasn't in my circle of need to know on this case. I doubt she even knew Shaun and I came to Thailand."

Jia's descriptions of all four of her colleagues in Malaysia suggested the leak had come from somewhere else.

"How long have you been assigned to Kuala Lumpur?" Erik asked. The last time they'd crossed paths, she'd been working out of Seoul.

"About a year and a half."

He updated his notes again. "Any chance you've worked with the other four people on our list?"

"Only in passing." Her gaze met his. "If there was a leak, it could be any of them."

So four prime suspects in the potential-leak category and four secondary suspects.

Erik's phone rang, and he pulled it from his pocket. The letter K filled the screen. Kade.

"What have you got?" Erik answered.

"A headache from staying up so late."

Erik glanced out the window, where the sun hung high in the sky. If it was midday here, it was most decidedly the middle of the night on the US's East Coast. "I hope you called for something else besides a chance to complain."

"Yeah. The real estate broker just called. You just bought yourself a condo."

"We bought it? How'd you manage that so fast?" Erik asked.

"The owner wasn't willing to rent, but he was open to a quick sale. Because of the size of our deposit, he's letting us take possession early."

"I'll take it." Erik sat back down at the table. "How soon can Jia move in?"

"Tomorrow, but it isn't just Jia who will be living there. Ace wants you there too."

Erik glanced at Jia, who was still standing in the middle of the room. Spend more time with her? He hadn't worked with a partner since he finished his training when first joining the guardians. That had been years ago. "Why does Ace want me to go too? Jia's capable of handling this on her own."

"Under normal circumstances, but Ace doesn't want her cut off from intel resources, not while she doesn't trust the people in her own agency."

He supposed that made sense. Doing an intel job without access to intel was a way to get killed. "How long am I supposed to partner with her?"

"For as long as it takes."

Torn between wanting to support Jia and his regular duties, Erik laid out the challenges before him. "We can't leave this region without support for that long."

"I know. Troy's heading down to Frankfurt so he'll be more centrally located in Europe, and Cas is going to work out of Istanbul so she'll be closer."

"Istanbul is still a full day's flight from here." And Erik averaged a boots-on-the-ground type of operation at least once a week.

"She has to tie up something there, but once she does, she'll head over to Mumbai for a few weeks. Seems like she's willing to do some shopping while she plays backup to you."

Which meant this was really happening.

* * *

Jia sat beside Ghost in the back of the hired car, their driver a kind man in his forties who didn't speak more than a handful of words in English or Mandarin.

For the entire hour-and-fifty-five-minute drive, Jia had checked over her shoulder at regular intervals, but their location had thus far remained hidden from Brandt and his cohorts. Despite that fact, Ghost had given her a new phone before leaving the hotel, this one a smartphone that had Ghost's phone number programmed into it as well as her flight information and boarding passes.

Dawn broke over the Bangkok airport as they approached, Jia's tension rising. If she were to try to acquire a target, this was where she would start.

Ghost tapped their driver on the shoulder and said something in broken Thai. The Grab driver nodded and pulled to the curb.

As soon as the car came to a stop, Jia put her hand on Ghost's arm. "Are you sure about this? Maybe we should drive down to Phuket and fly out of there."

"If they're watching one airport, they'll be watching both." Ghost opened his door. "Trust me. I have a plan."

She kept her hand on his arm to hold him in place. "Want to share?"

"Just follow my lead."

Follow his lead, when they'd already had to dump their weapons to fly today. Not the most comfortable situation.

She released him. They were here. She prayed Ghost's plan would keep them both alive.

Ghost grabbed his backpack and climbed out of the car. She drew a deep breath and stepped beside him. Her quick scan of the area didn't reveal anything unusual. People climbing in and out of cars, vehicles jockeying for a spot beside the curb.

They said goodbye to their driver and headed for the nearest entrance. They were nearly to the door when she caught a glimpse of movement and sensed something familiar.

A glance to her left revealed the nightmare she'd hoped to avoid—the guard who'd held Shaun at gunpoint.

Jia grabbed Ghost's arm and pulled him forward through the automatic sliding-glass doors.

Ghost must have sensed her urgency because he sped up and turned toward the escalators. "What's wrong?"

"It's one of Brandt's guards." Jia rushed to the escalator and stepped on before she glanced behind her. As she feared, the man was already inside, and he was heading toward them. "Green shirt, tan shorts."

Ghost gestured for her to continue up the escalator in front of him. He glanced over his shoulder, no doubt to identify their pursuer.

Jia pushed her way past a woman and her carry-on bag and then climbed several more steps before she had to stop behind a family of four who were blocking their path.

Jia's heart pounded as the escalator slowly ascended. She turned to check the guard's position, but Ghost's face filled her view.

"Keep looking forward," he whispered. "When we get to the top, turn left and head for security."

"He'll catch us there." Worst case, the man would pull a gun and try to kill them. The alternate situation of involving the Thai authorities might very well land her in jail for breaking and entering.

Urgency swept through her as they neared the top.

"Just do it," Ghost whispered.

Trust him. That was what he was really saying.

The family of four stepped off the escalator, and Jia pushed forward, sidestepping their group.

She rushed toward security as though late for her flight.

Within seconds, Ghost was beside her.

A quick peek over her shoulder revealed the guard was nearly to the top of the escalator, his path impeded by a middle-aged couple and their large suitcases.

Jia blocked out the mix of Thai, Mandarin, and English humming around her. She ignored the scents of curry and spring rolls and the underlying stench of humanity. Instead, she quickened her pace and focused on the two options before her—the exit to her left and the security line to her right. The exit was closer.

She started to turn toward it, but Ghost grabbed her arm and tugged her toward their original destination.

"Faster." He released her arm and broke into a jog.

Torn between instinct and trust, Jia surprised herself and chose trust. She matched his pace and then increased her speed until she was sprinting past passengers and luggage.

They turned a corner, and she checked the guard's position. He was closing in on them, but she'd already made her choice. The only escape was through the security checkpoint, where a line of people would very soon cut off their forward progress.

The guard would catch them any second. It appeared she'd trusted Ghost one too many times.

CHAPTER 10

Shaun didn't trust these men, and they clearly didn't trust him. He'd fought to stay awake throughout the flight, but more than once, the effects of the drugs they'd given him overtook his consciousness. Because of that, he had no idea how far they'd flown or where they were going.

The plane started its descent, and Shaun could only hope that someone at the airport would be waiting to free him. He gripped the arm of his seat, the handcuffs forcing him to remain in place.

Within minutes, they touched down, and the three men in the passenger cabin stood and left him behind. For a moment, Shaun thought they'd forgotten about his presence. Then two guards climbed aboard. One lifted his AK-74 and aimed it at Shaun. The other one approached with a pair of handcuff keys.

As soon as Shaun's hand was free, the man with the keys grabbed him by the arm and pulled him out of the plane and down the airstair. Shaun squinted against the bright light, trying to identify his location. Thick palms surrounded both sides of the single runway, and a van waited at the base of the stairs. A second vehicle, this one an SUV, pulled away, likely with Brandt and his associates inside.

In the distance, a single low-rise building occupied the space near the end of the runway—the only runway. This wasn't an airport. It was simply a place for Brandt and his friends to land a plane. But where they were or what would happen to Shaun now, he had no idea.

* * *

Erik slowed when they reached the security checkpoint. They had forty seconds to spare, maybe less, before their pursuer would reach them. Praying the man wouldn't pull a weapon so close to armed security personnel, Erik veered toward the Fast Track lane.

"I don't have Fast Track," Jia managed between breaths.

"You do now." Erik had tended to that detail yesterday. He reached the line and took his place, urging Jia to move to the spot in front of him.

A couple followed them into the Fast Track line right before the man pursuing them reached it.

"When you pass through, don't wait for me. Head for concourse F."

Jia nodded and retrieved her passport from her backpack. Her turn came, and Erik remained in his spot, deliberately using his body to shield her from view as best he could.

He glanced back when the couple behind him protested and their pursuer pushed past them.

Jia passed through the checkpoint, and Erik stepped forward before the guard could try to jump in front of him as well. He'd barely handed over his passport when the guard rushed up to the security agent beside Erik.

He'd hoped the man wouldn't have a right to go beyond the security checkpoint, but with the methodical way the passport control agent was checking the man's documentation, Erik suspected he'd bought a ticket in anticipation of a situation such as this.

Erik willed the agent processing his ID to work faster.

The agent finally finished, and Erik passed through the checkpoint. The guard followed only seconds later.

Erik turned away from the international terminal and followed the signs leading to terminal B. If he was lucky, the man would follow him.

He glanced over his shoulder in time to spot the man emerging from the security checkpoint. But he didn't follow Erik. He turned toward the international gates.

Erik reversed direction and roles. Now the pursuer rather than simply the protector, he fell in behind a woman pushing a stroller and holding a young child's hand.

After several meters, he sidestepped the woman, the stroller, and the child.

Erik picked up his pace, weaving through the various passengers. He had only two options: hope Jia would remain out of sight until they boarded their flight or eliminate the threat against her.

Though he preferred the invisible option, the stakes were too high for him to risk Jia's being found.

Keeping his pace quick and steady, Erik closed the distance between them until no barriers remained.

When the sign came into view for the men's toilets, he further quickened his step until he was walking beside the guard, only two meters between them. The moment they reached the opening for the men's restroom, Erik charged the guard, wrapping his arms around his waist and using his forward momentum to force him through the open doorway.

Erik rammed the guard into the bathroom wall. A man stood at the sink and yelped in surprise.

Ignoring him, Erik pressed his arm against the guard's windpipe. The guard retaliated by thrusting his fist into Erik's ribs.

Erik's hold loosened, but he managed to deliver a hard jab to the guard's gut.

The guard punched Erik again, this time in the stomach.

Erik's breath whooshed out. The guard broke free. Rather than try to face off again against Erik, he tried to sidestep him.

But Erik blocked the exit, his fists raised.

The guard swung at him, this time aiming for Erik's face. Erik ducked. Lowering his shoulder, he charged the guard again.

They rammed into the wall a second time, and the guard's head bashed hard against it.

The man at the sinks scuttled past them.

No doubt, airport security would show up any minute.

Before the guard could regain his balance, Erik grabbed his arm, turned the man's body, and hooked his arm around the guard's throat. Erik tightened his hold, the guard struggling against him. An elbow jabbed backward into Erik's ribs, the pain bringing tears to his eyes. Erik held firm.

The struggles continued for several seconds until, finally, the man's body went limp.

Breathing heavily, Erik dragged the now-unconscious guard across the floor and into a bathroom stall.

He then unzipped his bag and changed his shirt, exchanging tan for blue.

He slipped his backpack back into place and hurried to the exit. Taking care not to limp, he walked out as though he'd simply come out after using the facilities. Staying close to the wall to avoid the overhead cameras' view, he made his way toward the F gates. Two security guards raced past him, and Erik turned his head to keep his face from being seen. He slowed his steps and glanced over his shoulder as the two uniformed men continued toward the men's toilets.

Erik resumed his forward progress, increasing his pace. Time to collect Jia and make their way to their real gate on the E concourse.

* * *

Jia tucked herself behind a vending machine that distributed earbuds, phone charging cords, and several other items travelers might need while at the airport. The entrance into the F concourse was only fifteen meters away, but the man following her had yet to come into sight.

She hated waiting, but more, she hated relying on someone else to protect her.

Nearly twenty minutes had passed since Ghost had sent her ahead—twenty minutes of wondering and worrying.

Passengers continued to walk by or, in some cases, run. Thai, Chinese, European, Malay, Indonesian, Australian, American. The list of languages and accents continued. At the moment, she cared more about Ghost's status than evaluating the people passing her.

She checked the time on her phone. What could be taking him so long? Unless he planned to create a diversion to keep the other man from finding her so she could continue to Singapore on her own. That thought shouldn't have created a sense of unease, but it did. Shaun was in Brandt's custody, assuming he was even still alive. She didn't know if she could handle the guilt if another person fell victim to Brandt and his band of hired killers.

Passengers continued past her in a steady stream. Another two minutes passed, and Jia peeked around the corner of the vending machine. Still nothing.

Dread formed a knot in the pit of her stomach. She lifted her cell phone and found the contact that simply read *Ghost*. Unable to stand not knowing his situation, she hit the Talk button.

The ringing of the phone carried from both her cell and somewhere nearby.

"Where are you?" Ghost answered. Again, the sound came from both the phone and her natural hearing. He walked past her before she could respond.

"I'm right behind you."

Ghost stopped and turned, lowering his phone to his side. He stepped up to the vending machine as though contemplating a purchase.

"Head for gate E-9," he said, his voice low. "I'll be right behind you."

"What happened to the guy following us?"

"I took care of him." Ghost remained where he was. "I moved us onto an earlier flight. It should be boarding any minute. Text me when you get on the plane."

"I will." Jia kept her phone in her hand and abandoned her hiding place. She passed Ghost, a little surprised that except for the color of his shirt, he looked exactly as he had when she'd seen him last. Had he confronted the man, or had he somehow managed to get him detained by the authorities?

Whichever it was, she doubted he would share much beyond the details he'd already offered.

Her phone dinged with an incoming text as she left the F concourse and headed toward the E gates. As Ghost suspected, their flight was already boarding. She went to pull up her boarding pass, unsure if it had been updated from their previously planned flight. It wasn't, but a text from Ghost included the new one.

She retrieved her passport from her bag and fell into line with the other passengers waiting to board. She made it all the way to the front of the line before she took the time to look at her seat number: 2B. Ghost had upgraded her to first class.

CHAPTER 11

Erik struggled to walk normally as he followed Jia to their plane. His ribs throbbed with each step, but he was pretty sure they were bruised rather than broken. He'd had more experience with both than he cared to admit.

Jia passed into the Jetway, another twenty passengers still in line behind her.

Erik used his phone to update his flight information on the guardian message board along with the details about the man he'd left hidden in the men's toilets. Less than thirty seconds passed before his phone rang. Kade.

"Making a mess over there, I see."

Erik checked the line again as the next boarding group was called. "It wasn't by choice."

"Renee is pulling the security feed from the airport to see if we can ID this guy. She'll override any images that might implicate you," Kade said. "In the meantime, I set up a drop at a local hotel where you can pick up your new IDs, weapons, and other basics."

"Thanks." Erik considered for a brief moment. "Any chance you can help me with a quick trip over to Batam?"

"You want to go through border control twice in one day?"

"Three times, actually." Erik glanced around to make sure no one was in earshot. A couple passed by before he continued. "I want a roundtrip on the ferry with two hours in Batam."

"Why?"

"Because we'll have already filled out our entry card to go into Singapore. If we manipulate the system to let us use the same one twice, I can make it look like we went into Indonesia and stayed there."

"Not a bad idea." Kade's approval hummed through the line.

Ideas, Erik could manage. The electronics, he needed help with. "You can manipulate the system for me, right?" Erik asked.

"No problem," Kade said. "I'll also put a hold on the pickup at the hotel and book the ferry tickets."

"Wait until we're en route. I don't want to risk someone tracking us there."

"You got it," Kade said. "I'll buy the tickets right before I go to bed." With the thirteen-hour time difference, that meant Kade would have another late night.

"I appreciate it."

"Yeah, well, you can always send me some of those fruit-flavored walnuts to thank me."

Erik smiled. Kade almost always had something he wanted for a bribe. As often as not, it was food. "I'll see what I can do."

Erik ended the call and approached the line leading to his flight. He handed his passport to the gate agent, the name on the document the same one he had used to cross international borders since his official death date. The increase in the use of biometric scanners dictated he consistently use the same one.

He reached the plane, and the flight attendant checked his boarding pass. "Welcome, Mr. Hays." She gestured to the seat in the second row beside Jia. "Your seat is right here."

"Thank you." Erik winced as he sat down.

He caught Jia's questioning glance and took care to shift carefully so he could face Jia more fully. As though he'd never seen her before, he extended his right hand. "I'm Steve Hays. Nice to meet you."

Jia put her hand into his. "Nice to meet you too."

* * *

Ghost had a name. Or an alias. She wasn't sure which. Personally, she hoped it was an alias. He didn't look like a Steve.

After they landed in Singapore, Jia followed him off the plane and through the airport to the passport-control kiosks. Signs on the pillars provided a QR code and a reminder to nonresidents to fill out their entry card online.

Jia pulled up the camera on her new phone to do just that.

Ghost put his hand on her arm. "I already filled one out for you."

Which meant he had access to all her personal information, including her passport number. That was a bit unnerving.

He gestured for her to go first, and she pressed the ID page of her passport against the kiosk scanner.

The first set of fiberglass doors opened, and she stepped into the center of the kiosk, where her photo was taken and biometric scans would confirm her identity.

After a few moments, the second fiberglass barrier swung open, and she passed through to the other side.

Though signs in English and Mandarin dictated she not wait in the open area past passport control, she couldn't resist glancing over her shoulder to make sure Ghost made it through as well.

She spotted him in the scan section of the kiosk next to the one she had just exited.

Not wanting to draw attention to herself, she continued walking, albeit slowly. She reached the open space that led to the airport exits, and Ghost appeared beside her. Maybe he really was Steve Hays.

With no luggage to collect, they made their way toward the exit.

They cleared customs without incident, and Ghost turned away from the signs for ground transportation.

Jia stepped closer to him. "Where are we going?"

"To the Jewel. It runs at ten."

Jia had witnessed the Jewel Changi before, with its impressive indoor waterfall located in between two of the airport terminals, but stopping there now, when they had a job to do, wasn't high on her priority list.

Questions burned on her tongue, but her training dictated that she avoid questions as much as possible while in a public setting. And Ghost had gotten her this far.

He followed the signs to the Jewel Changi, opting to follow the ramp up to the observation deck rather than to the ground level, where they could get closer to the Jewel. Then again, if they walked down there, anyone from above would have an easy view of them—not something either of them wanted right now.

When they reached the observation deck, the enormous column of water was already falling from the high ceiling. Jia took a quick scan of the others clustered nearby, their cameras out, all aimed at the man-made phenomenon before them.

Ghost tapped her shoulder and led her away from the doorway. As soon as they reached an open area of the railing, he nodded toward the lower level. "See anyone you know?"

Or rather, someone she didn't want to see. Jia took a step forward and did another scan. "No one."

"In that case, let's go out this way." Ghost guided her to the elevator leading to the lower level.

The waterfall was still running when they reached the ground floor, everyone's attention on the impressive sight. Ghost and Jia skirted along the edge of the circular area surrounding the Jewel until they reached a side door.

Within moments, Ghost stepped outside, the heat and humidity fighting its way into the air-conditioned airport. He gestured her forward and led the way to a waiting Kia SUV.

They both slipped into the back seat. The moment the door closed, Ghost tapped his hand on the driver's seat. "Let's go."

The driver nodded, put the car in gear, and pulled away from the curb.

Jia turned to look out the rearview window. No familiar faces, but if Brandt had the right resources, it was only a matter of time before he learned she was in Singapore.

* * *

Shaun stood in the ornate entry hall of the grand home situated a good kilometer beyond the private runway. While the building he'd seen from the plane had been rudimentary at best, likely nothing more than a place to store fuel and equipment, the structure before him could pass for a palace.

At the moment, he hardly felt worthy of such surroundings. After leaving the plane, he'd been left to sit beside the tarmac for what must have been hours while various boxes had been unloaded, the plane refueled and serviced, and more boxes loaded into the cargo hold. The walk from the private runway through the heat and humidity had pushed him to his physical limits, another sign that he should stay out of fieldwork in the future.

Perspiration beaded on his brow and dripped down the center of his back, and Shaun tried to focus again on his current surroundings. Two guards were visible through the windows that flanked the heavy wooden front doors, and two more stood beside the marble statues on either side of him. A gold chandelier hung overhead.

With each passing minute, the knots in Shaun's stomach tightened a little more.

Another guard appeared from deeper inside the house and spoke in a hushed tone to the guard to Shaun's left. Then suddenly, the guard grabbed his arm and pulled him down a hall to the side of the entryway.

They walked past several rooms before he said something to another guard, who appeared to be barely into his twenties. At the older guard's command, the younger one pulled out a set of keys and unlocked the door beside him.

The older guard pushed Shaun forward, and Shaun stumbled into a simple room, barely managing to avoid falling onto a woman to his left. The younger guard closed the door, and the lock clicked into place.

Shaun rushed to the door and tried to turn the knob, but it didn't move. Then he slapped his hand against the door, pressing his head to the wood for a brief moment. He was a prisoner, but he didn't know where, and he didn't know if anyone had any way to find him.

Slowly, he turned to face the only other occupant in the room. It took only a moment to recognize her from her photo. Nur, the sister of their informant, the woman who had started him and Jia on this journey that had led him into captivity.

"Nur?"

The woman's eyes widened, and she backed away from him.

"I'm not going to hurt you." Shaun said the words, but based on the fear still in her expression, he suspected she didn't understand them, or her fear had prevented her from translating them into her primary language.

He tried again in Malay. Her fear seemed to subside, and she stared at him for a long moment.

Indistinct voices rumbled into the room, and Shaun turned as he tried to identify the source of the sound. He spotted a vent in the ceiling and moved closer to it.

The voices grew louder, and slowly, he was able to make out the words.

"The latest report just came in," a man said, his accent identifying him as Brandt's European friend. "It looks like the timing is going to be tighter than we expected."

The sound of movement followed, like something sliding across a table.

"What's the holdup?" another man asked, likely Brandt. "You said the testing was finished weeks ago."

"It was, but we're still trying to get sufficient supplies to create enough of the vaccine to take care of all our employees," the European said.

"How much longer?"

"We've already secured the vaccines in Tokyo and Rome, but we need at least another week before we'll be ready to release the virus."

"This is cutting it way too close," Brandt said. "We already have everything in place for the twenty-seventh."

February 27. That couldn't be more than nine or ten days from now.

The European hesitated a moment before he answered. "I'll make sure we're ready before the first event."

"See that you do."

CHAPTER 12

Taking care to not aggravate his bruised ribs, Erik shifted his backpack onto his shoulder and waited for Jia to join him on the sidewalk beside the mall. He'd taken a couple of painkillers on the plane, which had thankfully taken the edge off.

Jia narrowed her eyes. "Are we shopping?"

"Yes, but not here." They walked by a number of shops and took the escalator up to the next level.

When they passed under the sign leading to the ferries, Jia put her hand on Erik's to stop him. "Where are we going?"

"Batam." He leaned close and whispered in her ear. "Just for a couple of hours so it looks like we left Singapore right after we arrived."

Jia lifted her eyebrows and shot him a skeptical look. "I hadn't planned on being in three countries in one day."

"It's just a precaution," Erik said quietly. "And the ferry will take us right to one of the main shopping areas on the island. We could both stand to enhance our wardrobe before we arrive at the condo." The condo that cost nearly three million dollars and would be his residence for the near future. He cast another look at Jia. He wasn't used to having a roommate, much less being in proximity to anyone for more than a day or two.

"Do you really think our taking a quick trip to Indonesia is going to fool anyone?" Jia asked.

"I don't know, but we need to create some doubt if we want to stay here with any degree of safety."

Some of her own uncertainty faded from her face, and she nodded.

Erik looked around for a spot to sit, but he needn't have bothered. Almost as soon as they arrived, the boarding process began.

They passed through passport control to leave Singapore and boarded the ferry. An hour later, they went through passport control yet again, only this time, the control agents stamped their passports to indicate the date they entered Indonesia.

As soon as they were clear, Erik led Jia out of the loading area into where a handful of shops and fast-food booths were located.

"We're shopping here?" Jia asked.

"No. This way." Erik headed for the escalator, and they made their way to the skybridge that connected the ferry terminal to the shopping mall next door.

As soon as they entered, Jia nodded her approval. "This is more like it."

"Do you want to eat something before we shop?"

"If we only have two hours, we should shop first." Jia headed for one of the larger department stores. "We can always get something to eat for the ferry ride back."

Erik's stomach grumbled in protest, but her suggestion made sense. Plus, there would be less likelihood of him eating something he shouldn't if he stopped by a market and bought whole ingredients instead of eating at a restaurant.

He stopped beside the shoe section, where rows and rows of shelves were laden with displays on top and shoeboxes stacked below. "Get what you need, and meet me back here."

She narrowed her eyes. "You want me to use my credit card here so it will be easy for Brandt to track me?"

"Yeah." Erik appreciated that she had followed his logic so easily. "There's a nearby hotel we can check you into before we book a flight to Bali."

"A flight I won't be on?"

"Exactly."

"If we need to check into a hotel, we'd better shop fast." Jia took a step toward the women's department. "I'll meet you back here in forty-five minutes."

Erik didn't know how much she could accomplish in that amount of time, but he nodded. "I'll see you then."

* * *

Jia leaned back in her seat on the ferry and nibbled on a black-bean pastry she'd picked up at one of the bakeries in the mall. As far as desserts went, it wasn't bad. Bite-sized and not too sweet. She debated if she wanted to eat another one, but the announcement of their impending arrival made that decision for her.

Ghost stood and winced as he collected his backpack and the duffel bag that held his new purchases.

"Are you okay?"

"Yeah. Just a bit sore."

"From your time in the airport?" Jia asked.

He shrugged and fished a bottle of Tylenol out of his backpack. He then popped two pills into his mouth, chasing them with a swallow of water.

"I'm sorry you got hurt."

"I'll be fine once I rest a bit."

Jia hoped so. She compared her luggage to his. Her shopping spree had been much more extensive: clothes, shoes, makeup, a hair dryer, toiletries, a new purse, and two towels. If nothing else, she'd be able to take a shower at the condo without needing to go to the store again.

She reached for the handles of her two new suitcases.

"Want me to take one of those?" Ghost stretched out his hand.

"But you're hurting."

"I can carry one of your bags."

That would let her keep a hand free in case they ran into any unexpected obstacles, which was likely why he was offering even though he was clearly in pain. She handed the lighter of her two suitcases to him. "Thanks."

They made their way to the exit and hauled their luggage off the boat and onto the dock.

"Are we good to go to the condo now?" Jia asked.

"Almost." They cleared through passport control yet again and headed for the mall exit. Ghost turned toward the MRT station, Singapore's version of the subway.

"We're taking public transit?" Far fewer people would see them if they took a Grab instead.

"I need to make one more stop." He paused and looked down at the suitcase gripped in her hand. "If I take the luggage, can you go into the market and pick up the basics so we can eat in tonight? I'll text you a list."

"I can if you have some Singapore dollars. I don't want to use my credit card now that we're back in Singapore."

Ghost pulled out his wallet and held out several bills. "Text me when you're done. I'll call a Grab and meet you here."

She took the money, the everyday exchange driving home what they were about to do. "Are we really going to move in together?"

"Yeah, we are." He looked almost apologetic. Turning his attention to the luggage, he shifted the duffel strap on his shoulder so he could relieve her of her second suitcase.

Even though Jia didn't look forward to sharing living quarters with a man she barely knew, she was the reason they were in this situation—well, Brandt's activities had landed them here. Yet Ghost had fallen in line with her plan with minimal complaint. A seed of appreciation sprouted inside her.

Ghost turned back to her. "Oh, and do me a favor: Don't buy any durian. I can't stand the smell of it."

"Deal." She didn't care for the strong-smelling fruit either. She doubted the market would sell it anyway. It was much more likely to be found in roadside fruit stands around the city.

She turned toward the grocery store as Ghost headed in the other direction laden with all their luggage.

She walked into the market, grabbed a basket, and went to work.

* * *

Shaun awoke disoriented, his vision blurred. He remembered flying on a plane and then being brought into a locked room. And there had been a woman. At least, he was pretty sure there had been a woman.

His wife wouldn't be happy if he were conjuring one up in his subconscious. His wife. Concern for her was enough to push through the fog in his brain likely caused by the drugs still in his system.

He cracked an eye open and took in the room. Yes, this was the place he remembered before losing consciousness shortly after eavesdropping on Brandt's conversation. The scent of sticky rice and durian carried on the air, and he sensed he wasn't alone.

He turned his head, his focus once more on the woman sitting on the sofa across the room. She turned her attention from the window to Shaun, fear once again reflected there.

Even though she hadn't understood him previously, he spoke slowly in Malay. "Where are we?"

She stared at him, and he tried to formulate the same question in Thai.

Before he could pull out the right words from his limited vocabulary, she spoke in English. "I don't know where we are."

"You speak English." That would make communicating so much easier. With his legs still unsteady, Shaun scooted closer to her rather than trying to stand. He faced the woman who worked for Brandt, the woman who had been feeding information to the CIA through her sister. "How did you end up here?"

"Mr. Brandt said I couldn't be trusted," she said in a thick Malaysian accent. "He put a needle in my arm, and I woke up here."

"Did you wake up at all on your way here?" Shaun asked.

She shook her head.

If Jia's source was correct, Nur had disappeared shortly after sharing the intel about the lab. That had to have been three or four days ago.

Shaun turned his attention to the door. "Are there guards in the hall?"

"I don't know." She clasped her hands together and rested her elbows on her knees. Rocking forward, she whispered, "They come in and bring me food morning and night."

"What about letting you use the bathroom?"

"It's in there." She pointed at an adjoining door.

Shaun struggled to his feet and kept his hand on the sofa until he steadied himself. Slowly, he crossed to the bathroom, which consisted of a toilet, a sink, and a shower stall with two towels stacked on the counter. No towel racks or hooks in the walls. Nothing he could easily fashion into a weapon.

He returned to the room that had likely been a bedroom at one time. "What else can you tell me about Brandt and the people working with him?"

"I only know what I saw." A flicker of something flashed in her eyes.

"You know more than that."

Her gaze darted to the door, and she lowered her voice. "Whatever they're planning, it's happening soon."

CHAPTER 13

Erik loaded his and Jia's luggage into the trunk of the hired car. The number of suitcases had nearly doubled since his stop at the hotel. He wasn't sure what all Kade had provided for him, but he suspected laptops and clean phones along with the weapons and new IDs Kade had mentioned.

He climbed into the back of the vehicle and settled two backpacks into the center seat, the one he had brought with him from Thailand and the one he'd just received.

The driver slid behind the wheel. "Are you ready?"

"Not quite. Let me make sure I have everything." Erik opened the new backpack and located the new US passports. He opened the first, Jia's photo staring back at him. Except her name was now listed as Jingyi Mallory. He turned to the first page of his new passport: Richard Mallory. Same last name. Apparently, Kade wasn't kidding about making them look like a couple.

He slid the passports back into the outside pocket and texted Jia. *Are you almost done?*

Heading to the checkout line now.

Be there in a minute.

Turning his attention back to his driver, he said, "We need to swing by VivoCity to pick up my wife on the way home." His wife. The mere use of the word brought the level of craziness to new heights.

The driver put the car in gear, clearly unaware of Erik's churning thoughts.

Erik guided the driver to the correct entrance. They'd barely pulled up when Jia walked outside, her hands full of groceries.

"I'll be right back." Erik climbed out of the car and strode toward her. As soon as he reached her side, he relieved her of several of the bags.

"Thanks," she said.

"You're welcome." He lowered his voice and added, "The driver thinks we're married."

Her eyebrows lifted, but she followed him to the car without comment.

They loaded the groceries into the trunk, keeping the few bags that wouldn't fit up with them as they climbed into the back seat.

"Okay, we're all set," Erik said.

Fifteen minutes later, their driver turned onto the private street that led to their condominium complex. The driver stopped at the guard booth, and the guard approached.

"May I help you?"

Erik pulled out the two new passports and handed them to the guard. "We're the Mallorys. We're moving in today."

"Oh, yes. In tower two." The guard checked their IDs and handed them back. "Welcome."

"Thanks."

"That's your elevator over there." The guard pointed between two of the buildings. "Your real estate agent should have given you the access codes to get into your apartment. If you have any trouble, let us know."

"Thanks."

The guard let the driver pass.

Jia leaned close. "Do you have the codes?"

"I hope so." Erik opened the new backpack again, this time locating the legal paperwork that included the sale documents for the condo. Attached to the front was an access code for the elevator and the instructions on how to get into their apartment.

With the Grab driver's help, Erik and Jia transferred all their belongings to the private lobby for their tower's elevator. As soon as their driver left them alone, Erik punched the security code for the elevator into the keypad.

The doors opened, and Jia hauled one of the suitcases, her backpack, and most of the groceries into the elevator car. Then she pressed the seven on the control panel before hitting the Door Open button. "I'll man the doors if you get everything else in here."

Erik rolled her other suitcase into the elevator before transferring the rest of their bags inside. As soon as he entered, Jia let go of the button, and the doors slid closed.

Neither of them spoke as the elevator rose to the seventh floor. The doors opened to reveal a private foyer.

The previous owners had left behind a shoe rack and a single umbrella hanging from one of the hooks affixed to the wall.

Erik set both of the rolling suitcases on the tile floor and used his foot to push them closer to the apartment door. Jia grabbed groceries, and Erik helped with the rest of the bags.

"Ready to see our new home?" Erik asked, the words surreal even as he said them. "The door should be unlocked. My contact said the keys would be on the kitchen counter."

"Let's take a look." Jia stepped past him and opened the door.

She made it only two steps before she stopped and stared. "Oh wow."

Erik followed her inside and took in the walls of windows on three sides of the living room, the open curtains inviting the view of Singapore's skyline inside. It was like his apartment in Taipei, only better.

* * *

Jia transferred the last of her new clothing into the cubbies in the closet of her new bedroom. She'd have to remember to buy hangers on her next trip to the store. Then again, if she and Ghost found Brandt quickly, maybe she wouldn't be here long enough to need them.

She stifled a yawn and did her best to ignore the shakiness in her limbs. She needed food and a good night's sleep. Maybe once she managed those two necessities, she'd be able to think clearly and find a way to locate their suspect.

Though tempted to leave her new suitcases where they lay open in the middle of the floor, she removed the last remaining items and took her toiletries into the adjoining bathroom.

Ghost had been kind enough to give her the master bedroom, which thankfully had a bed and two side tables. The other rooms were far less accommodating.

Two of the other three bedrooms were completely void of furniture, and the other had been outfitted as an office, with two desks, matching chairs, and floor-to-ceiling bookshelves.

She shoved her suitcases into the open space in her closet—more to make sure she wouldn't trip over them than for tidiness's sake—and walked down the hall to the kitchen, where Ghost was putting away groceries.

The sizzle of meat filled the air and stirred her appetite. When she caught sight of the frying pan on the stove beside another pot with rice cooking in it, she asked, "Did the previous owners actually leave us pots and pans?"

"No. I bought kitchen essentials in Batam." Ghost picked up a wooden spatula and stirred the meat.

"Well, whatever you're making smells good."

"I'm just cooking up what you bought. I hope beef and broccoli is okay with you. It was the easiest thing to make with what was in there."

"Sounds great." That was exactly what she'd planned when she'd purchased the thinly sliced steak and fresh broccoli. Of course, most of what she'd bought had come from the extensive list Ghost had texted her. She'd never known anyone to be quite so picky, right down to brand names and tamari instead of soy sauce.

Jia rested a hand on the counter. "Need any help?"

"Want to help me put the rest of this away?" He gestured to the few remaining grocery bags and the open suitcases that contained boxes of dishes and silverware.

All she really wanted was to sit down and rest, but she nodded. "No problem."

She opened the box of dishware. "Any chance you bought dish soap?"

"It's already under the sink in the wet kitchen." Ghost gestured to the doorway leading into the small additional kitchen, where the dishwasher and main sink were located along with a bank of storage cabinets. Beyond it lay the washer and dryer, an overhead wooden drying rack, and the back door.

Two additional doors opened off the narrow space, one leading to a small bathroom, which included a toilet, sink, and tiny shower. The other space looked like a storage closet, rows of shelves lining the top half and a cot set up against the back wall. A single folding chair hung on a hook opposite the door. No doubt, this was where the previous owner's helper lived. She shook her head against that thought. She couldn't imagine having live-in help and confining them to this little space.

Then again, it wasn't her place to judge someone else's choices, not unless those choices impacted others' lives without their consent.

Jia gestured toward the back door. "Have you already checked out what's back there?"

"Yeah. It leads to the service elevator, the stairs, and the other apartment on this side of the building."

"Maybe we'll get lucky, and Brandt will be in the other unit on our floor." Jia set the dishes on the counter.

"I already checked. The other apartment on our floor is owner occupied, but not by Brandt."

"How sure are you?"

"Very. I had a contact from the embassy do a quick meet-and-greet to verify the occupants."

"You involved someone from the embassy?" Jia whirled to face him. "Why would you do that? We already talked about the danger of a mole."

"Don't worry. It wasn't the American embassy I contacted. It was a contact at the Australian embassy. He thinks he was doing a location check for a potential Russian asset."

"How did you pull that off?"

Ghost shrugged but didn't answer. Protecting his sources and his methods. She couldn't fault him for that.

She set about washing the dishes and silverware. "I don't suppose you have any dish towels, do you?"

"No. Maybe we can use the dishwasher as a drying rack for now."

"Good idea." She completed her task and returned to the kitchen as Ghost slid the pot of rice off the burner.

"This will be ready in about five minutes." He gave the beef and broccoli a stir before he reached into the outside pocket of his backpack. "Here. This is for you." He passed her a new US passport. "We're now Richard and Jingyi Mallory."

Jia narrowed her eyes. "I didn't realize we were going to have to pretend to be married."

"I didn't either." He reached into his backpack again, this time producing two ring boxes. He opened one and passed her the other.

She took it and flipped open the top. A stunning wedding set sparkled beneath the overhead lights. The diamond had to be over a carat, the matching band lined with smaller stones. "Wow. This is beautiful. It actually looks real."

"It is real." Ghost held up his open ring box, revealing the simple platinum band. "So don't lose it."

"Why would you invest in real rings if we're only pretending to be married?"

"Because one of our neighbors is a jeweler. We don't want to risk him spotting a fake."

She looked down at the rings again. There had been a time when she'd hoped to someday wear a ring like this, to have a man she cared about enough to want to spend the rest of her life with.

She pulled the rings out of the box. Real or not, they were simply props.

Ghost held out his hand. "Here. Let me help you with that." Before she could protest, he took the rings from her and then held her hand.

An unexpected connection rippled through her, startling her enough that she froze in place.

"I hope these fit." Ghost slid the rings onto her left ring finger. They fit perfectly. He rubbed his thumb over the back of her hand, a delicious shiver rippling over her skin.

Startled by the unexpected connection, she pulled her hand away. "My turn." She took his ring box and pulled the wedding band from it.

Ghost held out his left hand, but her attention was drawn to the scar on his forearm. She caressed it with her fingertip. "Is this from Korea?"

"Yeah." Their eyes met again and held. "A souvenir from the first time we met."

Her skin heated beneath the intensity of his gaze. What was wrong with her? He was just here until they could take down Brandt. Then he would disappear out of her life again. It would be best to remember that. She slid the wedding band onto his finger and tried not to think about what it represented. Their rings bound them together.

She shook that thought away and focused on a more practical aspect of their current situation. "What am I supposed to call you? You don't look like a Steve, but you don't look like a Richard either."

"How about Rick?" Ghost asked.

Jia nodded. "Still not quite right, but we're getting closer."

CHAPTER 14

Erik stood at the kitchen counter and ate another bite of his dinner. The skyline lit up at night really was incredible.

Beside him, Jia gestured to the wall of windows. "This view is so beautiful. It's hard to imagine anyone wanting to close the curtains and block it out."

He couldn't agree more. Rarely did he close the curtains in his apartment in Taipei.

He took in their view, ensuring they could keep their curtains open without risking anyone in neighboring buildings watching them. Their windows looked out over the street, away from the other units in the complex, and the nearest high-rises were far enough away that the copper shielding should prevent anyone from seeing much more than shadows against the backdrop of light in their apartment.

Erik gestured to the corner where the curtains had been pulled back. "We should close them when we go to bed."

"First, you need a bed." Jia carried her dish to the small sink in the main kitchen. "You gave me the only one."

"I can crash on the cot in the helper's room." Erik ate his last bite of beef and broccoli.

"Now you're making me feel guilty." She jutted her chin toward the empty living room. "Even a couch would be more comfortable, and we don't even have that."

"We don't need a couch."

"No, but it's easy enough to order something for you to sleep on." She pulled out her phone and started scrolling through Amazon. She turned her phone toward him. "What about something like this? It can be delivered as soon as tomorrow."

Erik leaned closer. The futon couch was more suited for a living room than a bedroom, but it would be nice to have some furniture in their living space.

"Text me the link, and I'll order it." Along with a mattress and a platform bed. He could always use the furniture to set up a safe house in Singapore once this mission was over.

"We should get a couple of stools, too, so we'll have a place to eat at the counter."

"See if you can find some that will be delivered after tomorrow."

"Why?" She looked up from her phone.

"Because the more deliveries we have, the more likely we'll be to run into the other residents without anyone becoming suspicious."

"True." She turned her attention back to her phone.

"I left my laptop in the office. Want to work in there for a bit? I need to check the latest intel reports."

"So you're going to work while I shop?"

"Shopping is work." Erik set his dish in the sink and headed into the office. He retrieved his laptop from his backpack and set it on the desk closest to the door.

"Maybe another one of our purchases should be a new laptop for me so you don't have to be the middleman."

"No need." Erik opened one of his new suitcases, revealing a neatly organized arsenal of electronics and weaponry. Two laptops, four Glocks with holsters, ammunition, two Tasers, three handheld containers of pepper spray, a half dozen syringes, a flash grenade, a stack of spare cell phones, and a host of chargers.

"Impressive."

"Take what you need." He settled at the desk and pulled up the guardian message board.

While Jia retrieved a laptop and the matching cord, Erik scrolled through the latest messages.

Jia set the new computer on the desk beside his. "Anything from your friends?"

"This may be something." He turned his laptop toward her as he opened a file from Kade's wife, Renee. "It's a list of CIA employees who have access to the location of the safe houses in this region."

"There have to be hundreds of them."

"Yes, but my friends will help us narrow it down, and we can focus on the eight suspects we already identified," Erik said. "Everyone won't have access to every safe house. And we only have to connect one person to Brandt and his people."

"It would help significantly if we knew who Brandt's people were."

"I agree." Erik opened the next communication on the message board, this one from Lacey. "Looks like my colleague made some progress with the virus."

"What kind of progress?"

"According to her, we're dealing with an airborne virus." Not what Erik had been hoping for.

Concern lit her eyes. "I was afraid of that."

"Me too, but that does narrow down the likely forms of distribution." Erik lifted a hand. "Air vents, fans, or some sort of vaporizer."

She sighed. "We still have too many options."

"I know, but my friends will keep looking into any clues that will help us narrow it down." Although based on the summary Lacey included, it didn't sound like there was much more she could do beyond helping search for possible targets.

Not wanting to dwell on the negative, he worked through the list of resources Kade had provided for the rest of the guardians until he located the backdoor access to the surveillance feed for the Bangkok airport. "Are you up for finding a screenshot of the guy who followed you today? If we send it to my friends, they should be able to run facial recognition for us while we sleep."

"I will if you can get me access."

"I'm forwarding you a link." Erik emailed the link to the generic email address already set up on her new laptop.

A chime announced the arrival of the message on her computer.

Jia tapped on her mouse pad. "That was fast."

"In our line of work, time is usually of the essence."

Her expression clouded. "Yes, it is."

It didn't take a genius to figure out where her thoughts had gone. "You're worried about Shaun."

"How can I not be?"

"We'll find him."

Jia gripped the arms of her desk chair and let out a sigh. "You said that before."

"And I still mean it." Unable to resist, he reached for her hand. "Trust me."

She drew her eyebrows together, and an odd expression flickered over her face. "I do trust you."

The simple words filled him with an unexpected warmth. "Good."

She looked down at their joined hands, and a blush rose to her cheeks. "We should get to work."

"Right." He released her and begrudgingly turned his attention back to his laptop.

They worked in silence for several minutes. An incoming message popped up on his screen. When he opened it, three images appeared of the man he'd confronted in the men's toilets. "I'll upload these to the message board. By the time we wake up, we should have some answers."

"Oh no you don't." Jia shook her head. "First, you're going to order that futon. You need something more comfortable to sleep on."

"Would you mind doing it?" Erik asked. "I need to do a security check of the grounds."

"Sure, but do you already have a secure account created?"

"Yeah." Erik stood and turned her laptop to face him. He logged in to one of the fictitious corporate Amazon accounts he'd created for just such an occasion. "There's a credit card already on file."

"Thanks." She turned the laptop toward her again. "You really trust me to spend your money?"

"I trust you won't buy more than what we really need."

She nodded. "I'll do my best."

CHAPTER 15

Erik rolled over on the cot and bumped his shoulder into the wall of the narrow walk-in pantry. Pain shot through his ribs from the bruises that had formed after his run-in at the airport. Time for some pain meds.

He sensed the presence of someone nearby and jerked upright, his head connecting with the shelf directly above the cot, and he moaned in pain.

Rapid footsteps followed, and Jia appeared in the pantry doorway. "Are you okay?"

Erik rubbed his head and slid off the cot, careful to avoid hitting his head a second time. He didn't speak, instead focusing on the woman in front of him, clad in a stylish one-piece swimsuit with a cotton sarong wrapped around her waist. She really was gorgeous. "Where are you going?"

"To the swimming pool. I want to check out the area." She cocked an eyebrow as though the answer should be obvious.

He supposed it would have been if he weren't still half asleep. And then the instinct to protect kicked in. "Maybe I should come with you."

Jia folded her arms, a you've-got-to-be-kidding-me expression flashing across her face.

Erik caught the unspoken message that she could take care of herself, but that didn't lessen his concern about her being outside without him. "Give me a minute to change."

"We'll have a better chance of finding Brandt if we go out at different times during the day." Jia stepped back to give him room to exit the pantry. "It'll be too noticeable if we're constantly going out together."

Erik moved into the laundry area. "I don't like the idea of you going downstairs unarmed and without backup."

"I won't be unarmed." She continued into the main kitchen and gestured to a canvas bag with a beach towel sticking out of it. "My gun's already hidden at the bottom of my bag."

That made him feel a little better. And she did have a point. They needed to look like two people exploring their environment, not two government operatives on a stakeout. "How long do you plan to be down there?"

"An hour or two." She gestured to their window. "It's only seven right now. Maybe you can watch the people coming and going from the complex to start establishing patterns."

Erik wasn't used to someone telling him what to do, nor was he sure he liked the sensation. Okay, maybe Kade could get a little bossy at times, but he lived on the other side of the world, so he was easy to ignore. Jia, however, was a presence—a distracting one at that.

But the simple fact remained: Her suggestion was a good one, and it didn't make sense to fight against it. "Are you expecting Brandt to be someone who comes and goes every day or someone who rarely leaves?"

"From the intel I have so far, he doesn't follow a set schedule."

"I'll watch this morning," Erik agreed. "But after you get back, I want to set up some surveillance around the complex."

"Can you do that without being noticed?" Jia asked.

Now it was Erik who cocked his eyebrows. "I'm a ghost, remember?"

She nodded slowly. "How could I forget?"

* * *

Light streamed into the room through the window, and Shaun struggled to remember where he was. The running water in the nearby bathroom must be from his wife showering for the day. But why was his head pounding and his body aching? The whole ordeal in Thailand must have been a bad dream. Or was it?

He cracked one eye open and took in the room. Not a dream. And the person showering wasn't his wife; it was the woman who was also being held captive.

The water shut off, and Shaun sat up.

A shadow crossed in front of the barred window, a man visible as he walked by. No doubt a guard who was patrolling the inner courtyard.

The urge to escape, to gain his freedom pressed in on Shaun. He rose to his feet and checked the door. Locked. Of course it was.

He circled the room, taking in every detail. The air vents that were too small for a person to fit through, the closet that had been stripped of hangers and hanging bars. As he'd previously discovered, the simple furnishings were void of anything he could brandish as a weapon.

Either someone had recently remodeled this room and hadn't finished decorating it, or they had used this room as a prison cell before.

The bathroom door opened, and Nur emerged, her hair damp, her cotton pants and tunic-style shirt identical to the clothing she'd worn yesterday, except that the color was now faded-blue instead of tan.

"Did you bring extra clothes with you when Brandt brought you here?" Shaun asked.

"No. They gave me a change of clothes the day after they locked me up." She nodded toward the bathroom. "I have to wash my other set every day so I have something clean to wear."

An inconvenience, but it also demonstrated Brandt's desire to keep her alive and well for the foreseeable future. But why hold captives? Unless, perhaps, they'd be used for some sort of hostage exchange. Or human testing.

That thought chilled Shaun's blood.

The doorknob rattled. Nur stepped back. Shaun clenched his hands.

The door opened, and two men appeared in the doorway. One held a rifle, the barrel raised and aimed at Shaun. The other man entered holding a basket. He removed two wooden bowls and set them on the coffee table. The scent of fried eggs and rice carried to Shaun, but he kept his gaze on the man with the gun.

The other man removed something else from his basket before backing away.

As soon as the door closed, Shaun looked down at the coffee table. Sure enough, two bowls with white rice and a fried egg on top had been served as their breakfast. A stack of clothing lay beside the food.

It appeared as though they expected Shaun to be their guest for a while longer.

CHAPTER 16

Jia strolled along the architectural pool, the fifty-meter length interrupted on one side by islands, complete with palm trees to provide shade. Built-in seating areas also lined the shaded side of the pool. A light breeze rippled over the water, creating a sense of serenity Jia rarely experienced.

This early in the morning, the temperature fell into the comfortable range, but the thick humidity already had Jia debating whether she should take advantage of the water to cool off.

A short flight of steps on the far side of the pool led to what appeared to be a large hot tub and picnic area. Looking at the beautiful scene, she could understand why the units in this complex went for so much money.

A woman approached wearing workout clothes, and Jia guessed she'd just come from the gym. At least, she assumed the complex had a gym.

"Good morning," Jia said. Following her curiosity, she asked, "Do you know where the gym is?"

The woman nodded. "Just through there, to the left." She furrowed her brow. "I haven't seen you here before. Did you just move in?"

"I did." She reminded herself of her cover story. "My husband and I. We just got here yesterday."

"Oh, well, welcome." The woman's accent suggested English wasn't her first language, and Jia guessed she was from somewhere in eastern Europe. Ukraine maybe?

"Thanks. How long have you lived here?" Jia asked.

"Four years." She glanced at her watch. "I should get going. I have an appointment this morning."

"Nice meeting you." Jia held out her hand. "And I'm Jingyi."

"Irina." The woman shook Jia's hand. "Enjoy your swim."

"Thanks." Jia watched the woman leave, noting that she passed the elevator for tower two and continued toward the last set of elevators.

It would have been too easy if Jia had been able to befriend someone who might live in her tower to help her eliminate an apartment. She settled her bag next to one of the chaise lounges, adjusting the contents so her Glock was out of sight but easy to reach. She dipped a toe into the water, surprised that it was significantly cooler than the air temperature.

With the building still shading a large portion of the pool deck, she settled into her chair and pulled a paperback novel from her bag.

For the next hour, she alternated between pretending to read, checking her cell phone, and discreetly taking photos of the residents who passed by.

A trickle of sweat ran down her spine, and she abandoned the idea that she could remain dry throughout her early-morning surveillance. She checked to make sure she was alone before she set her bag on the deck so it would still be in easy reach. Then she slipped into the cool water.

Her feet had barely hit the bottom of the pool when a woman emerged from an elevator with a puppy. The poodle sniffed at the deck, pulling at its leash. Judging from the woman's features, she appeared to be from the Philippines, and her dress suggested she was a helper rather than a property owner here.

Another woman appeared, this one with two children beside her. The kids made a beeline for the puppy, leaning down to pet it. The two women chatted briefly, their words distinct enough for Jia to pick up that they were speaking Tagalog. After a moment, the woman with the children ushered them away, and the woman with the puppy headed in the other direction.

Jia climbed out of the pool, hoping the woman with the puppy would speak to her as she passed, but the woman simply lowered her eyes and continued toward a path on the other side of the pool.

Jia used her towel to dry off and then reclaimed her seat. So far, she'd yet to speak with anyone besides Irina, and Jia hadn't seen any sign of Brandt or her informant. She hoped Ghost was having better luck.

* * *

Erik lasted only an hour before he gave up on trying to watch the cars coming and going. Even with his binoculars, he wasn't in the right position to see the license plates until the cars pulled through the gate and turned onto the main road. And by then, they were turning away from him, making it difficult to see the full plate numbers. Plus, sitting still in this position wasn't helping his ribs any.

With a better option in mind, he abandoned his post and retrieved his backpack. According to the paperwork in his closing documents, this unit came with a parking space in the garage below. And if he were lucky, Ace or Kade had already arranged for a car to be parked there.

Erik checked his watch before he headed downstairs. Almost nine o'clock. Surely by now, the people heading to office jobs would have already left. He took the elevator to the garage level and stepped off, surprised to find half the parking spots full. After he took note of the security cameras already present in the garage, he passed a Lexus SUV and a Ferrari, lifting his gaze in search of a spot to plant surveillance cameras that wouldn't be noticed. He circled through the main part of the lot, passing another Ferrari, a Lamborghini, and an assortment of motorcycles. Based on the number of vehicles that had already left this morning, he suspected the garage would be nearly full by tonight.

He reached the space designated for his unit and found a Toyota Corolla there. Not exactly an impressive vehicle among the sports cars in the garage, but the fact that they had a vehicle in Singapore at all would help them fit into this ritzy area of the city. Once he located the key, it would also give him and Jia an escape route should they need it.

He pressed a surveillance camera to the side of the pillar beside the Toyota and continued to where several motorcycles were parked along the wall behind it, a dozen or so bicycles mixed in.

Circling through the garage again, he planted more cameras beside the ramp leading out of the garage and beside the elevator for tower two.

He was placing another one on the wall near the Lamborghini when an elevator chimed. A woman emerged from a path leading behind the elevator for his tower, a bucket in one hand and a sponge in the other.

She spotted Erik and nodded in greeting. Then she approached a Lexus sedan, set down the bucket, and promptly dipped the sponge into what appeared to be soapy water.

Not comfortable placing any more cameras while the woman washed the car—most likely her employer's—Erik followed the path she'd come from. He spotted another elevator, but this one was wider than the one leading from his tower's lobby. Curious, he hit the Up button.

It took him a minute to figure out how to put in his code on the keypad, which was different from the other elevator's. Once he had that sorted, he waited for the elevator to finally reach the garage level so he could get on.

When the doors opened, a deliveryman stepped out and moved past him with barely a glance in Erik's direction.

After Erik confirmed that the man didn't match Brandt's description, he entered the elevator car. Would it be so much to ask that Brandt magically appear in front of him so he and Jia could determine where he lived?

Then again, finding Brandt was only the first step in the process of learning what he had planned. They also needed to know who else was involved, and they needed to determine the targets. Neither could they forget the other issue at hand—the possibility that someone in the CIA really was leaking intel to the man who planned to kill millions.

* * *

Jia had barely stepped out of the shower when she heard the knock on the door. "You have to be kidding me." She muttered the words to herself and quickly dressed.

If Rick hadn't wandered off, he could have answered the door, but no, he'd been nowhere to be found when she'd returned from the pool.

Zipping up her shorts, she hurried to the front door and opened it. No one was there.

The knock repeated, followed by Rick's voice. "Jingyi!"

The back door.

Jia reversed course and passed through the kitchens. She opened the door and glowered at him. "Why are you pounding on the door instead of coming in the other way?"

He stared at her a moment as though he'd never seen a woman with wet hair before. No matter the case, if they did their job right, he wouldn't see her at all after this week. That thought brought with it a pang of regret.

"I came up the back elevators and didn't have my key." He stepped inside and closed the door behind him. "Sorry. Did I catch you in the shower?"

Jia didn't bother to answer the question. "Where did you go?"

"I went downstairs to set up some surveillance cameras."

"You know, we could have just tapped into the complex's security system."

"Maybe, but those cameras are easy to spot, and anyone who lives here would avoid them if they're doing anything they're not supposed to."

"With as many surveillance cameras as they have in this city, I don't know how anyone can get away with anything."

"But you think Brandt did."

"Yes." A new realization formed. "Maybe we can dig through the old security footage to see if we can find my source."

"Assuming she's still alive."

Her stomach twisted uncomfortably. "Alive or not, we should be able to determine whether she's here or if she's been taken somewhere else."

"True." Ghost . . . Rick—she needed to think of him as Rick—continued past her and entered the office.

By the time Jia caught up with him, he was already seated at his desk, his laptop open.

He glanced over his shoulder. "I'll put in a request for someone on my support staff to review the footage." He tapped on his keyboard before looking at her again. "What day did you last hear from her?"

"I met with her sister last Monday, but she spoke with her sister the day before."

"That's over a week ago." He shook his head but didn't comment further.

Jia interpreted his expression, her hopes fading. "You think she's dead."

"I don't know, but right now, our focus isn't on finding the people who are missing. It's on finding out when and where Brandt plans to release this virus."

"That might be our priority," Jia said, trying to let her intellect dominate instead of her emotions, "but that doesn't mean I'm going to forget about finding Shaun."

Rick stopped typing, and he lifted his gaze to hers. "Of that I have no doubt."

* * *

For the past two days, Shaun had debated what to do next. With he and Nur sharing this room, which was little more than a furnished cage, he had tried to use his time to ferret out every bit of information possible about what she'd learned during her time working for Brandt, but so far, she'd been able to share only that Brandt had a partner, based on a meeting she'd overheard in which there had been two voices besides her employer. Based on her descriptions, one was the European Shaun had seen on the plane. Likely, the third was some sort of bodyguard.

What Shaun really wanted to know was why these men had brought him here and what their motivation was for holding him and Nur captive. Logically, they would have either let them go or killed them. Not that he wanted them to seriously entertain the second option.

With nightfall complete, he crossed to the single window in the room. He closed his eyes, wishing he were home, wishing he were in his own bed with his wife beside him. What she must be going through right now. Or maybe she didn't know he'd been taken captive. It was entirely possible she believed he was still on an assignment where he couldn't safely call home.

He certainly didn't want to admit that he'd been so anxious for the chance to go on a mission that he'd gone in underprepared and understaffed.

He should have known better when even Jia had questioned the wisdom of inserting on their own.

It was all the Bangkok acting chief of station's fault. Had he given them the necessary resources, one of the operatives out of Bangkok would have been the person backing Jia up, and Shaun would have remained firmly in a support role, where he belonged.

Instead, here he was with nothing more than a vague memory of his previous training on the farm and no clue how to use it.

At least there was a chance Jia had made it out. He hoped she had. If she hadn't, Brandt would continue with his plan, and no one would know what the man was up to until it was too late.

CHAPTER 17

All morning, Erik ran through license plate numbers to determine which of the vehicles belonged to Douglas Brandt. He had his answer now—none of them.

At least the throbbing in his ribs had finally eased to tolerable, and he could focus on his work without the constant pain. He turned his office chair to face Jia. "When was the last time Brandt was spotted in Singapore?"

"Last Sunday."

"So around the same time your source heard from her sister."

"Yes. Why?" Jia furrowed her brow. "Don't tell me you think he isn't here."

"I could, but I'd be lying." He waved at his laptop. "None of the vehicles parked in the garage belong to him."

"Maybe he left before you started watching the garage."

"It's possible, but the timing fits for him to have left after his plans were compromised." Which would mean Erik had just spent millions of the government's dollars for nothing.

"I really hope you're wrong."

"Me too."

A buzzer sounded, and Jia stood. "That's probably the furniture delivery."

Erik pushed back from his desk. "Do you want me to deal with it?"

"I've got it." She disappeared into the living room. Within minutes, Jia's voice and two men's sounded from the living room. By the time he reached the open space, the men had carried a full-sized couch inside, and Jia was directing them where to set it.

He smiled when they turned it to face the windows. He had a bed. Sort of. The actual bed for his room wouldn't be delivered for two more days.

Jia walked the delivery men out and returned a moment later. "You know what we need?" she asked.

"To cancel the order for my bed since Brandt isn't here anyway?" Erik asked.

"No. I was thinking we should get a dog."

"Excuse me?"

"There are a couple of people I've seen walking their dogs both yesterday and today, and every time, all the kids come up to talk to them."

"So?"

"So, if the kids talk to us, so will the adults caring for them."

"Maybe you missed my earlier comment: Brandt isn't here."

"Or his car isn't here, assuming he even has a car."

Erik narrowed his eyes. He suspected most people who lived in this complex owned a vehicle, but he supposed it was possible Brandt didn't have one. Focusing on the more pressing challenge, he said, "We don't need a dog."

"Don't you like dogs?"

"Of course I like dogs. But having one is sure to get me noticed. That's the opposite of what my job entails."

"Not on this assignment." She passed by him and disappeared into the office. Before he could follow, she reappeared with a laptop in her hand.

"What are you doing?" he asked.

"Googling what it takes to buy a dog in Singapore."

"How about we look at what it takes to find Brandt instead?"

She let out a heavy sigh. "Fine." She dropped onto the couch and shifted her body so she could face Erik. "But you're not canceling the delivery of your bed. If we find out Brandt really isn't here, we can always send it back."

That seemed fair enough.

Jia readjusted her position on the couch, leaning back into the cushions as she balanced the laptop on her legs. Erik looked out at the view and wished he'd thought to claim that particular spot for himself to work.

Resigned, he left Jia alone and returned to the office. He sat at his desk and put in a request for Kade to hack into both the security cameras for the garage and the passport control for Singapore. One way or another, he needed to know if Brandt was in the country.

A knock sounded on the doorjamb, and Erik looked up. Jia stood in the doorway with her eyebrows lifted. "You don't really want to work in here, do you? The view is so pretty from the living room."

"I didn't want to intrude on your space."

Jia simply shook her head. "It's our space." She gestured down the hall. "Come on. We should work for a while together, and then after dinner, we can watch a movie or something."

Watch a movie with someone by his side? That was something he hadn't experienced in years. He stood and picked up his laptop. "I'd like that."

* * *

Brandt and his guard were talking again. Shaun leaned closer, straining to make out the words.

"They don't appear to be a problem," the guard said.

"How sure are you?"

"Their background check came back consistent with what they told our man."

"Backgrounds can be forged, and the timing is a little too convenient," Brandt said. "I want someone on the inside, and I want ears on this new couple."

Shaun furrowed his brow. Who was Brandt spying on? And why?

On the couch behind him, Nur shifted her position, the movement masking the next words.

"Shh," Shaun whispered, holding his finger to his lips.

She widened her eyes as though she were a small child who had just been caught with her hand in the cookie jar.

Shaun pressed his ear to the vent again.

"Make it happen soon," Brandt said. "I want to be there when the big event goes down."

"What about the prisoners?" the guard asked.

"Keep them here."

Shaun swallowed hard. They were being left here—alive, he hoped—but for what purpose?

A new voice came through the vent, this time the man with the European accent. "I have the new doses calculated. Everything is ready except testing the vaccine on someone who weighs less than fifty kilos. Once we have that tested, we can monetize the vaccine."

"Nur can't weigh much more than forty-five kilos."

"Then I have your permission?" the European asked.

"Do what you need to do," Brandt said.

Shaun scrambled back from the vent and turned to Nur. He needed to protect her, but what could he do? If he banished her to the bathroom, the guards would simply break down the door. And if Shaun took protective measures, Brandt might realize that he could hear their conversations.

"What's wrong?" Nur asked.

He opened his mouth to warn her, but the words died on his tongue when the door opened and three guards entered with the European.

One guard moved toward Nur, and Shaun stepped between them. "Leave her alone."

A second guard grabbed him by the arm, allowing the first to reach Nur.

She cried out, clearly unaware of what these men intended.

The European produced a syringe filled with an unknown serum. He really was going to use Nur as a human test subject.

Shaun strained forward, nearly breaking free of the guard restraining him.

"Hold him back," the European ordered.

A second guard came to assist the first, grabbing Shaun's other arm. Even as Shaun tried to resist, the European plunged the needle into Nur's arm.

* * *

Jia tucked her feet up underneath her as she and Rick watched the first episode of a new Korean drama series. Since they didn't have a TV, they'd pulled a folding chair from the storage closet and set her laptop on it.

Rick had propped his foot on the bottom crossbar of the chair, and he was more relaxed than she'd ever seen him. She liked this side of him, a side she was quite certain he revealed to very few others.

Out of the corner of her eye, she took in his facial features. He really was one attractive man, from the stubble on his face to his toned physique. How he managed to remain in the shadows was beyond her because right now, his mere presence was becoming an increasing distraction.

He sat up and clicked to exit the show. When he turned to face her, he narrowed his eyes. "Why are you looking at me like that?"

Her cheeks heated, and she was grateful the lights were low to hide her blush. "I was just thinking it's nice to see you relax for a change."

He continued to stare at her as though he weren't sure how to respond.

When he didn't speak, she stood. "Do you want some dessert? I have some ice cream in the freezer."

"Sure, I'll have some of the vanilla." He picked up his laptop from where he'd set it on the cushion between them. By the time she returned with two bowls of ice cream, he already had surveillance feed up on his screen, the comings and goings of their new neighbors documented on video.

"How far back did you go?" Jia asked.

"The day before your source last spoke to her sister." Rick zoomed in on several parking spaces.

"Do you know which parking spaces belong to people in this tower?" Jia asked.

"No, but when I looked at the garage tonight, I made a note of the ones that haven't had anyone in them all day." He set his laptop aside again and took the bowl of ice cream she offered.

She sat beside him and curled up her legs again. Curious about the man beside her, she asked, "Can you tell me how you became a guardian?"

"It was the classic example of being in the wrong place at the wrong time."

"Seems to me that every time I've needed help, you've been in the right place at the right time."

"That's the job. Or it is now."

"How long have you been doing this?" Jia asked.

"Sorry, that's classified."

Jia couldn't remember the last time someone had pulled the classified card on her. Her security clearances were high enough that it was rarely necessary for someone to hide intel from her. "Is the CIA looking for me yet?"

"No. I put in a report that you had to go to the hospital to be treated for injuries sustained during your escape."

"I escaped the lab compound three days ago, and my passport will show us coming into Singapore and then traveling to Indonesia," Jia said.

"I know. The report claims your injuries were aggravated during your travel."

Jia scooped ice cream up with her spoon. "I doubt anyone is buying that story, especially since I haven't reported in."

"Whether they believe it or not, you're in the system as being on sick leave. And no one besides the guardians knows where you are."

"Until we find out who is leaking intel, that's a good thing."

CHAPTER 18

Sitting by the wall and listening through vents really was taking spying to a new level. Or maybe not. Shaun supposed this technique had been used all the time before advances in electronic surveillance had made old-fashioned spy craft far less common.

This morning's conversations had been primarily between the European and one of the guards, the topic focused on last night's soccer game. At least, Shaun assumed they were talking about soccer, even though they called it fútbol.

Brandt's words came through the vent. "I have those projections for you."

Excitement laced the European's voice. "Will the virus do what we hope?"

"Whether it will eliminate the weak is your department, but the population control measures are within the range you'd hoped."

"What are the numbers?" the European asked.

"We're looking at a 15 to 20 percent reduction in population over the next three years, with the heaviest reductions coming in the Americas, Africa, and Asia."

Shaun shook his head, unable to fathom that he'd heard correctly. A 15 to 20 percent reduction in population? That would mean that out of every five people he knew, one would die.

"What about Europe?" the European asked.

"It will run around 8 percent."

Eight in a hundred. Almost one in ten. Shaun tried to wrap his brain around the devastation of so much death, of a pandemic that would touch even more lives than COVID did.

Footsteps echoed, followed by a woman's voice. "The vaccine is ready to administer. Who wants to go first?"

"I will," Brandt said. "And then you can take care of Kenneth."

"Sit here, please," the woman said. A minute passed before she spoke again. "And now you."

"Let's get this over with," the European—presumably Kenneth—said.

Silence followed.

Then Brandt said, "Thank you, Cynthia. That will be all for now."

"Yes, sir." The woman's footsteps retreated until Shaun could no longer hear them. A door clicked shut.

"You said you have the death-toll numbers. What about the financials for the vaccine?" Kenneth asked.

"We'll wait until the virus has adequately spread, but once it does, we expect we'll both be multibillionaires overnight."

"What about our little CIA informant?"

Shaun straightened. An informant within the agency? If they really had someone on the inside, Jia's escape route could have been compromised. His stomach curled. His first and only partner in the field could be dead.

After a brief pause, Brandt spoke, his words breaking into Shaun's thoughts. "Let the Chinese have her back. If we leak that she was the one responsible for spreading the virus, we'll have a fall guy, and we won't have to share any profits."

"She'll point her finger at us being involved if we don't pay her off."

"No, she won't. She'll be too dead," Brandt said. "Her Chinese handler isn't known for his patience, and both of his parents are likely to die from the virus. That will make him even more unwilling to listen. Besides, she knew the dangers when she agreed to spy on the Americans for the Chinese. We're just lucky she was greedy enough to work for us too."

"Just make sure this doesn't come back on us. We stand to fix the world's population problems, improve health, and get very rich in the process," Kenneth said. "Don't let one woman get in the way."

"Trust me. I won't."

CHAPTER 19

For nearly a week, Erik had spent his time walking through the different areas of their complex, planting surveillance cameras as he'd gone. He'd also finally located the keys to his new car. A drive around the neighborhood had revealed what he'd already known—this complex was in the ritziest part of Singapore, and the nearby shopping district catered to the wealthy.

He'd even stopped by Marks and Spencer to pick up a few items to round out his limited wardrobe because while he personally was fine to recycle the same few outfits, if they stayed here long enough, someone might notice. And he had no idea how long he and Jia were going to be here.

If all went well, Kade and his wife, Renee, would finish running through all the license plates of the other residents before too much longer. Hopefully, Erik would also gain access to the passport records here. But for now, he had another issue to deal with. His bedroom furniture.

His bed had arrived yesterday, but unbeknownst to him, the next delivery had included two bedside tables, which Jia and the man who had brought them in were now placing. Why it mattered where they went was beyond Erik.

Table, bed, table. Nice and simple. But no, Jia had made the poor deliveryman move them twice already as well as shift the position of the bed.

Then again, Erik couldn't explain why he felt the need to stay and supervise. Jia could take care of herself, but something about the deliveryman had his senses heightened.

On the surface, the man seemed harmless enough, but with the way Jia was drawing out their conversation, it was as though she were conducting a soft interrogation.

"How long have you lived in Singapore?" she asked in English.

"All my life."

"Really?" Jia said, now switching to Mandarin. "Is all your family here?"

"Most of them," he said, answering in English. "What brought you to Singapore?"

"My husband's work." Jia pointed at the spot where she wanted one of the end tables.

"Really?" The deliveryman turned to face Erik. "What do you do?"

"I'm in the oil industry." The only truth to that statement was that he drove vehicles that relied on the oil industry. And while the man's question was natural enough, it felt like he was probing as much as Jia was.

Jia and the deliveryman continued their conversation while Erik did his own analysis, searching for whatever clue he might have missed. Mid-twenties, a typical age for this type of work, Chinese heritage, the most common cultural background in Singapore. His clothing was basic: cargo shorts and a T-shirt and a pair of sandals on his feet.

Sandals. That was what Jia must have noticed. No furniture deliveryman would wear shoes that left his toes exposed.

Entering into the conversation again, Erik asked, "How long have you been doing this kind of work?"

"A couple years." The man slipped his hands into the pockets of his shorts and stepped back before asking Jia, "Is everything where you want it?"

She nodded. "I think that will do. Thanks."

Jia followed the deliveryman to the back door before she turned to Erik. "Honey, would you mind walking him down?"

"I'd be happy to."

"Thanks." She pushed up onto her toes and brushed a kiss across Erik's cheek before whispering, "Car keys?"

A wave of goose bumps rippled over his skin, and it took him a second to translate her words.

"You don't have to walk me down," the deliveryman said.

But Jia wanted him to, probably to slow him down until she could get to their car.

"It's not a problem. And sometimes the freight elevator shuts down if you don't have a security code." Erik reached for the door and opened it with one hand. He slipped his other hand into his pocket and retrieved the car keys, discreetly passing them to Jia. He turned back to face her. "I'll see you in a minute."

Jia nodded and headed back into the main part of their apartment. If Erik's suspicions were correct, she would reach the garage long before the deliveryman left the parking lot.

* * *

Jia checked her weapon before she slipped it into the holster inside her waistband. She hadn't expected to need to be armed to accept a delivery, but the man who'd brought the two end tables into her current residence wasn't who he claimed to be. Even if she hadn't noticed the anomaly that the man was wearing sandals instead of closed-toe shoes, his watch was far more expensive than a man in that career would be able to afford, and his face was one she'd seen only last month when he'd been spotted in a restaurant with Brandt here in Singapore.

Yuzi might have cut his hair shorter and shaved his mustache and beard, but she recognized the eyes. And she didn't miss his probing questions or the way he could understand Mandarin but chose not to speak it.

With Rick's keys in hand, she hit the button for the express elevator. A few seconds later, it dinged and the doors slid open for her to enter. And for the first time since her arrival, it wasn't empty. A woman with blonde curly hair stood inside, her mini Australian shepherd sitting obediently beside her.

She really would love to have a dog.

"You must be the new neighbors," the woman said, her accent clearly Australian. "I'm Elanora."

"Good to meet you. I'm Jingyi." Jia pressed the button for the garage. "Have you lived here long?"

"Ten months. My husband works at the Australian embassy."

"How long are you here for?" Jia asked, even as she willed the elevator to go faster.

"Probably five years, but I don't mind. I love the city, and it's so easy to travel from here."

"I look forward to exploring more of the area."

"I'm sure you'll love it." They reached the lobby, and Elanora left with the dog trotting behind her. "Have a good day."

"You too." Jia gave a quick wave. Under normal circumstances, she would have gotten off at the ground level, too, and tried to gain more knowledge about her neighbor, but today, she had other priorities.

She hit the Close Doors button to force the elevator doors to close faster. As soon as she reached the garage level, she hurried to the car and hit the fob to unlock it.

After she slid behind the wheel, she quickly started it and pulled out of the tight parking space. She drove past the blue Ferrari and a handful of luxury vehicles.

When she emerged from the underground area, she spotted Yuzi's truck already pulling past the guard shack. She started to follow, but before she could make the turn, Rick strode toward her with purpose.

He opened the passenger door as though he'd expected her to pick him up and climbed in. "Who is he?"

"Yuzi Song." Jia cast him an approving glance before pulling forward and driving past the guard shack and onto the road. "His photo crossed my desk last month after he was spotted with Brandt."

"Any more intel on him?"

"Nothing beyond knowing that he was here a month ago eating dinner with Brandt." Jia switched lanes to mirror the delivery truck's movements. "Since he didn't speak Mandarin back to me, my guess is he's not really a local."

"You think he was afraid you'd notice his accent?"

"It's the only reason I can think of that he would keep speaking in English even though he clearly understood me."

The truck made a right turn, and Jia followed.

"Hang back a bit, or he's going to spot you."

She should follow Rick's advice, but the sense of urgency flooding through her kept pushing through her mind. "I don't want to lose him."

"You won't." Rick lifted his phone into her view. "I'm tracking him."

Relieved and impressed, she eased up on the gas. "How did you manage that?"

"I put a tracker under his back bumper."

She spared Rick a quick glance. "You carry a tracker around with you?"

He turned his head to look at her. "You don't?"

The surprise in his voice nearly made her laugh. "No." She turned her attention back to the road. "But maybe I should."

* * *

Shaun rolled his shoulders before leaning back against the wall. He'd taken to sitting here in case Brandt said something of value, but for the past day, the conversations had been few and far between. And Shaun had had to scramble up off the floor far more frequently, as the European came regularly to take blood samples from Nur.

She lay on the couch now, just as she had for the past three days since she'd been injected with the vaccine. Other than sleeping a lot, she seemed to be okay. He hoped she was.

Shaun's senses heightened now at the sound of voices, nothing more than mumbles at first. Then the words began to take shape.

"What level of access do we have so far?"

"We have our people hired at every venue in either food services, custodial, or maintenance."

"What happened to getting someone in on the security team?"

"No one made it past the initial interviews."

Shaun sensed Brandt's frustration through the following silence and the footsteps that pounded above him. Shaun did a silent high-five to whoever had done the background checks for the security team Brandt was trying to infiltrate.

"How do you propose we transport the virus?" Brandt asked finally. "We need someone who can bring it inside without being detected."

"I know, which is why we're planning to hide the extra vials of the virus inside the metal framework of the set at the concert here in Singapore," the European said. "Those will be impossible to see through if they go through any kind of X-ray machines."

"And the distribution?"

"It's just like you planned. It will be hidden in the stage equipment. The minute the virus is dispersed into the air, everyone will be exposed."

Shaun glanced at Nur. Assuming she continued to regain her strength, someone like her would be protected. But the people at whatever show they planned to infiltrate would be instantly vulnerable.

The voices faded again, and Shaun stood and paced the room. He had to find a way out of here. He had to warn someone that Brandt had a target. And he suspected it wouldn't be long before Brandt would be putting thousands of people in danger.

"What did you hear?" Nur whispered.

"They're planning to release the virus at some sort of show in Singapore," Shaun said, his voice low. "It sounds like they're going to do the same thing in other places too."

"It's not a show." She shifted to sit up. "It's a bunch of concerts. Singapore, Tokyo, Seoul, Berlin, Paris, Rome, London, and New York. Eight cities in three weeks."

"How long does it take for the virus to show up after exposure?"

"Seven to ten days." Tears filled her dark eyes. "By the time anyone realizes the connection of where it started, the damage will be done."

And millions could die. Shaun's heart squeezed painfully in his chest.

He walked to the window, searching for any weaknesses in the bars covering it. The bars didn't budge.

He caught a glimpse of movement and jumped out of sight. Staying to the side where he would remain unseen, he peeked through the glass.

A guard crossed the inner courtyard, followed by two men: Brandt and Kenneth. They disappeared from sight, leaving the courtyard quiet and still. Only ten minutes passed before engines started up nearby. Not car engines but an airplane's.

Shaun strained forward, looking upward as the sound increased. Within moments, the tail lights of a small jet came into view.

Brandt and Kenneth had left, but where they had gone, Shaun had no idea.

CHAPTER 20

The delivery truck had disappeared from sight, but Erik guided Jia on a parallel route using the tracker.

Jia stopped at a red light. "Any thoughts on how this guy knew to step in for our real delivery guy?"

"No." The same question had been rolling through Erik's thoughts for the past ten minutes. "But the fact that he wasn't armed bodes well in our favor."

"I appreciate that he didn't try to pull a gun on us."

"Me too. It also shows that he wasn't expecting to encounter a problem." Erik caught the little furrow on her brow. The light turned green, and he pointed at it to make sure she saw it.

"I guess it's possible that he came in to check us out simply because we're new residents, and Brandt wants to have a pulse on everyone in the building." She fell into the flow of traffic. "But if that's the case, what happened to the real delivery driver?"

"I don't know. Mostly likely, this guy paid the real driver to take an unscheduled day off." Erik hoped that was the case. "The more important question is whether he recognized you."

"I've never seen him in person before."

"But it's possible he's seen you or your photo, just like you saw his. I'm sure the lab had security cameras."

"It did, but we overrode them. Only the guards who captured Shaun would know what I look like."

"How many are still alive?"

A little flash of remorse flickered across her face. "Best guess, three."

"So it's possible this guy is one of Brandt's enforcers and was sent in to see if we pose a threat."

"That seems like overkill to me."

"Maybe, but if your suspicions are correct about what Brandt is planning to do, he could be taking extra precautions."

"If that's true, it's likely that Brandt knows someone was leaking intel."

"I'm sure he does. Otherwise your source wouldn't have disappeared."

Jia glanced at him. "You really do think Nur is dead, don't you?"

"I have no idea, and there's no point in worrying about that right now." Erik gestured in the direction of where the delivery truck was currently traveling one street over. "The bigger issue is if you've been identified as the person who broke into the lab."

Her grip tightened on the steering wheel. "If I have been, our aliases have already been compromised."

"Again, our delivery guy wasn't armed." Erik checked the little blue dot on his screen. "He's slowing down." After a quick check of the map, he gestured to the upcoming intersection. "Take the next left."

Jia signaled and took the turn.

The blue dot came to a stop beside what appeared to be a restaurant in Little India.

"Speed up. I think he just parked."

Jia did as Erik asked, but when she turned the corner beside one of the local Hindu temples, a crowd stepped out into the street to cross to the other side.

Erik made a quick decision. "Up the street to the right." He pulled open his door. "I'll meet you there."

Before Jia had the chance to object, he climbed out and hurried past the pedestrians blocking their car. Erik darted into one of the alleys that ran behind the temple and the businesses that lay beyond it. When he emerged from the alley, he spotted the delivery truck parked on the side of the narrow road.

Erik quickened his step, keeping to the sidewalk the best he could, both to take advantage of the shade and to stay clear of the various security cameras in the area.

When he reached the truck, the cab was empty.

Erik kept walking to avoid appearing as though he were overly concerned about the vehicle. He reached a sidewalk sale of various scarves and purses and picked up a wallet, not because he was interested in it but because he wanted to look like he had a reason to stop.

He turned as a man approached the delivery truck, keys in hand. But it wasn't their deliveryman. It was a man of Indian heritage who appeared to be in his early twenties. The man opened the door and climbed in at the same time Jia turned onto the street.

Erik set the wallet back on the display table and stepped to the side of the road.

Jia pulled up beside him, and Erik leaned forward as she rolled down her window.

"It's a different driver."

"Where did ours go?"

"I haven't seen him," Erik said. "I'll send you the tracking code so you can follow the other guy. I'll keep looking for our friend."

Her gaze lifted to meet Erik's. "Be careful."

His heart lurched at the simple command. "You too."

* * *

Jia parked the car in the garage under her apartment, her back tense from driving around town for the past two and a half hours. The man who was currently driving the truck had made three furniture deliveries, and it had only taken a brief glance at his clothing and shoes to determine this was likely his regular job.

Rick had messaged her over an hour ago to let her know that he'd been unable to find their deliveryman, and he'd offered to meet her back at their condo so she wouldn't have to go back to find him.

She stepped out of the car and stretched her arms over her head. She needed a long bath and a good meal. She was starving.

With food in mind, she headed for the elevator. When she stepped into the foyer, she immediately smelled meat cooking. She hoped it was coming from inside her apartment and not one of the neighbors' places.

She opened the door, and Rick looked up from where he stood in the kitchen. "Hey. I thought you might be hungry, so I made some pad thai."

"That smells so good." She dropped her purse on the couch. "How long until it's ready?"

"It's ready now." He turned off the stove and passed her a plate. "Help yourself."

She took the plate. "I love you so much right now. I'm starving."

He smiled. "I thought you might be. It's been a long day for both of us."

She walked into the kitchen and scooped some food onto her plate. Rick served himself as she circled the counter and sat on one of the stools.

He came around the counter, too, and set his plate beside hers, but he didn't sit down. She was surprised when he put his hand on her back and pointed at the underside of the counter.

"Did you want lemonade to drink?" he asked.

"That sounds great. Thanks." She leaned over to look under the counter and spotted the small listening device pressed to the underside of it. They'd been bugged.

Jia pointed at it and asked, "How many bottles of lemonade do we have left?"

"Three." He set her glass down and pointed at the serving bar. He then held up one finger on each hand and gestured down the hall, each hand motioning to the opposite sides. It didn't take much to determine that one of the remaining bugs was in Rick's bedroom and the other was in the bathroom from when their deliveryman had asked to use the toilet.

Thank goodness Rick had locked the office before the delivery had arrived, and the man never made it as far as the master bedroom.

Jia took a bite of her food. "This is so good."

"Glad you like it." He slid onto the stool beside her.

"So how was your day?" Jia asked, twirling more rice noodles onto her fork.

"I'll be glad to get the last of these furniture deliveries behind us. I really need to spend more time at the office."

Jia played along. "It's been nice to have you working more from home."

"Yeah, it has been, but I'm not sure I can accomplish everything I need to from here. Do we have any deliveries coming tomorrow?"

"Yes. The new end table." Jia considered their current dilemma. "But you weren't sure you liked that one. Do you want me to cancel it so we have more time to shop?"

"You don't need to do that," Rick said. "I was thinking though. Do you want to go explore the city a bit after dinner?"

The idea of going back out was not high on her list, but she suspected he had a reason to plant the idea, likely to get them back to their car so they could speak more freely. "What did you have in mind?"

He winked at her. "It's a surprise."

CHAPTER 21

Erik had hoped he and Jia could spend the night relaxing and watching a movie, but since discovering the listening devices in their apartment, he didn't have much choice but for them to find another spot where they could speak privately.

So once they finished the dishes, they left their apartment and headed out past the pool and out the back gate of their complex.

"Where are we going?" Jia asked as soon as the gate closed behind them.

"There are some gardens up by the embassies. I thought we could check them out."

"That sounds good." She leaned closer. "Not as good as sitting at home, watching a movie though."

"I know. I had the same thought."

A woman walked toward them, a dog trotting beside her. Her eyes lit with recognition, and a streak of panic shot through Erik. He wasn't supposed to have people recognize him. Or was he? Right now, he was supposed to be passing for someone who was living a normal life. He wasn't supposed to be a ghost.

"Hi, Jingyi." The woman lifted her free hand. "This must be your husband."

"Yes." Jia gestured to Erik. "Rick, this is Elanora."

"And this is Shelby," Elanora added, gesturing to her dog.

"Good to meet you." Erik shook Elanora's hand.

"Isn't Shelby adorable?" Jia asked.

Erik glanced down at Jia, not sure if she was being serious or playing her part. "Yes, but that doesn't mean we're getting a dog."

Elanora laughed. "You sound like my husband. Or how he sounded before we got Shelby."

Jia shot Erik a hopeful look.

Erik simply shook his head and took a step forward. "It was nice meeting you." He continued down the sidewalk.

Jia leaned down to pet the dog before she said a quick goodbye and caught up to him.

"You weren't kidding when you said you wanted a dog," Rick said.

"Not at all." She shrugged her shoulders. "That's the one thing I regret about my current occupation. No way to have one."

"Maybe you just need to find a neighbor who can take care of it when you aren't around."

"That would require me letting someone know when I'm coming and going."

"True, and since your coming and going tends to put you in some not-so-great situations, I can see why you wouldn't want to announce your travel plans."

"Exactly."

They crossed the street and continued past the US embassy.

"Elanora said her husband works for the Australian embassy."

"What does she do?"

"She didn't say, so I guess she isn't working."

Or she wasn't working in a job she wanted to announce to a complete stranger. "Did you catch her last name?"

"No." Jia leaned closer. "But maybe one of your friends can check property records."

They reached the botanic gardens and passed through the entrance into a lush area filled with a variety of plants.

Several other people walked along the path, and Erik searched for any place that would afford them some privacy. They needed a plan to protect their identities and their work while not tipping their hand that they were aware of the listening devices in their apartment.

The sound of running water carried to them, and it wasn't long before they reached a small waterfall.

Erik stopped beside it, waiting for a nearby couple to pass before he spoke. "We need a way to be able to work in our apartment without anyone knowing that we found the listening devices."

"So we need to sound like we're really an oil exec and his wife," Jia said.

"Yes, and unfortunately we won't be able to talk to any of my contacts while we're in our apartment."

Jia shook her head. "That's inconvenient."

"I know. I need somewhere secure to work."

"What about by the pool?"

"Sitting out in the open where anyone could see my computer screen or hear me talking?" Erik shook his head. "I don't think so."

"Just hear me out." Jia stepped closer and slipped her hand through the crook of his arm. "The area by the Jacuzzi has a wall behind it—no reflective surfaces. And with the waterfall flowing from the Jacuzzi into the lower pool, you would have some background noise to mask your conversations."

Conducting classified business outside in the constant heat and humidity—this could be an interesting experience.

"Do you have a swimsuit with you?" Jia asked.

"No, why?"

Another couple passed by, and Jia didn't answer until they moved past them. "Because if you're working outside, you'll want a way to cool off, and the pool is your best option."

Erik shook his head. "I can't leave my laptop unattended."

"No, but if I work down there with you, we can take turns getting into the water."

Working outside in plain sight, wearing swim trunks. "This is the strangest assignment I've ever had."

"Same." She put her hand in his as though they really were a couple. Erik suddenly wished they were. That thought shocked him. After all, he was used to living on his own. Maybe he was getting too comfortable with having Jia around.

"Come on," she continued. "Let's see the rest of the gardens."

"And then what?" Erik asked.

"Then we go back home and watch a movie." She flashed him a smile. "A really loud one."

CHAPTER 22

Jia waded into the pool as Rick sat in the covered picnic area beside the Jacuzzi. He'd been there for the better part of two hours, but he'd yet to take advantage of the pool to cool off.

Throughout the morning, Jia had met a half dozen other residents, most of them people who had chosen to take a morning swim before heading to work or to whatever activities they had planned for the day. And so far, she hadn't caught sight of Brandt or Nur, even though Jia had deliberately chosen to stay where she could clearly see the tower two elevator.

She climbed out of the pool, the water cascading off her as she made it onto the deck. After she wrapped a towel around her waist, she climbed the steps to the upper swimming pool.

Rick was focused on his laptop screen, and sweat beaded on his upper lip and brow.

"You should go for a swim," she said.

"I will in a minute."

"You're going to get overheated." When he didn't respond, she reached out and snatched his laptop from him.

"Hey!"

"Go cool off, and I'll give it back." She tilted the laptop so the screen was facing the ground and wouldn't be seen by anyone passing by.

"Fine." He stood up and took the laptop from her, closing it, then handing it back. "I'll be right back."

Rick stripped off his shirt and tossed it on a chaise lounge beside the Jacuzzi. She wasn't surprised by his muscular physique or even the quick flutter in her stomach when faced with an attractive man she had come to care for. What she hadn't expected were the scars on his back that looked very much like bullet wounds.

She lowered into one of the chairs in the picnic area and watched him jog down the stairs. And for a moment, she let herself pretend they were really a couple, that he was someone she would always be able to come home to.

Rick reached the side of the pool and stepped in without hesitation. He bent his knees as his feet hit the bottom of the pool, and he ducked below the water's surface.

He straightened and ran his hand through his hair to push it out of his face. Then he waded to the water's edge as though the water had no ability to slow his movements. With the way he climbed out with minimal effort, Jia suspected swimming pools had been a frequent part of his life at some point.

When he returned to where she waited, he snatched up his shirt and pulled it on without any regard to the fact that he was still wet.

"How long were you a swimmer?" Jia asked.

He furrowed his brow. "What makes you think I was a swimmer?"

"You move like one."

He picked up a towel from the bench beside where he'd been sitting, dried his hands, and reached for his laptop.

When he didn't acknowledge her observation one way or the other, she lowered her voice and asked, "Have you had any luck tracking down Brandt's movements?"

"Nothing yet. I did confirm that none of the cars downstairs are his, but we already suspected that."

"Yes, but I was hoping we were wrong."

"Me too." He let out a sigh. "My guess is that if Brandt isn't in Singapore, he probably left by boat. That's the only way I can see him slipping past passport control."

"That still wouldn't be easy."

"No, but if he knows the right people, he might be able to pull it off. Or he could claim that he's been sailing within Singapore's territorial waters."

"We've been here a week. I'd think someone would notice if he left for that long."

"Assuming anyone knows to look for him."

"I guess that's true." Jia stood. "I'm going upstairs to get something to drink. Do you want anything?"

"Some water would be great. Thanks."

"I'll be back in a minute."

Jia headed for the elevator and spotted a cluster of people in the glass-encased lobby. She was nearly there when she spotted Douglas Brandt himself.

Her breath caught, a combination of excitement and apprehension filling her. She quickened her step, reaching the door to the lobby as Brandt and several other people entered the elevator. Jia quickly punched in her security code to open the lobby door, but she accidentally hit one button twice and had to start over. By the time she gained entrance, the elevator doors had already closed.

She hit the code beside the elevator to call it back to the lobby and turned her gaze to the numbers illuminated above her.

The elevator passed her floor and continued upward. It stopped on the ninth floor before going up again, this time stopping on the eleventh floor. It stopped twice more, once on the fourteenth floor and again on the sixteenth floor.

Four possibilities. That was way better than when she'd started.

She nearly rushed back to give Rick the news, but then she remembered. She had a part to play. First, she needed to go get her "husband" a drink. Then the two of them could sit by the pool and discuss how they were going to narrow the possibilities even further.

* * *

"You saw him?" Erik had nearly given up hope on finding Brandt in Singapore. And Erik certainly hadn't expected to feel relieved that he'd be able to spend more time here. He really was getting used to having Jia around.

"Unfortunately, there were a bunch of people on the elevator with him, but I'm pretty sure he got off on the ninth, eleventh, fourteenth, or sixteenth floor."

"That helps." Erik pulled up the surveillance feed from the garage. It took only a moment to determine that no new vehicles had arrived in the past fifteen minutes. "He must have been dropped off out front."

"That would make sense. Otherwise, he would have taken the elevator from the garage level." Jia sat beside Erik and handed him his water. "Here. You need to drink something."

He took the glass, sipped some of the cool water, and set it aside. "Why isn't he driving his car? Records show that he owns one."

"I don't know."

Erik hadn't really expected her to have an answer, though he was afraid the car had disappeared because Brandt needed to hide evidence of a crime.

Erik kept that thought to himself. He didn't need to cause worry for Jia about the possible death of her asset, not until he was sure of the woman's fate.

"I already have a camera aimed at the lobby and garage elevators. When he shows up again, we should be able to narrow down which unit is his."

"And when we do?"

"I'll slip in and see if there's anything to find."

"Maybe I should do that instead of you."

Erik set his laptop aside. "You sneaking in somewhere without proper backup didn't work out so well in Thailand."

"I know, but I'll have you watching out for me this time."

"Or *you* could watch out for *me*." He leaned forward. "Ghosts are good at the whole invisible thing."

"Maybe so, but if someone sees a woman going into his apartment, they'll think I'm either a girlfriend or a helper," Jia said. "If someone spots you, there isn't a logical explanation besides you being an intruder."

She had a point. And he wasn't happy that she was right.

"We need to figure out his pattern before I let you go in there."

"Before you *let* me?"

"That's not what I meant." He put his hand on hers. "This is just me being an overprotective husband."

Humor flashed in her eyes, replacing her earlier annoyance. "You may be taking this whole married-couple thing too far."

"Maybe." Erik caught sight of a man as he emerged from the path leading to their elevators. It didn't take long to identify him: Dylan Floyd, one of the men Jia worked with at the agency.

Dylan took in the empty pool area as though looking for someone.

Adrenaline flowed through Erik when Jia's coworker took another step forward. Any second, he was going to look their way, and when he did, there was no way he'd be able to miss Jia.

Erik shot to his feet and did the only natural thing he could think of to hide Jia's face. He stepped in front of her, put his hand on her waist, and kissed her.

CHAPTER 23

Shock came first when Rick's lips met hers. Jia stood there in a stunned stupor as his lips moved against hers in a slow, dreamy kiss. She should push him away. She would have, but by the time her mind had caught up to what was happening, she no longer wanted to step away from the sensation of being in his arms or the way his kiss made her mind simply shut off.

Giving in to the magic created between them, she leaned closer and let her lips move with his.

He increased the pressure on her waist, guiding her as though in a dance, her feet moving in time with his. He tilted his head into the kiss, his fingers trailing up to her neck.

The gentle rhythm of the waterfall created an almost mystical sensation, and she could barely feel the pool deck beneath her bare feet.

The humidity thickened, the air backing up in her lungs until she could barely breathe. But with Rick's lips still on hers and the delicious shiver working through her, she decided breathing was overrated.

When Rick pulled away, he kept his hand on her back to hold her in place, his face close to hers. Then he drew her closer and whispered in her ear. "Don't turn around. Dylan Floyd is here."

Instantly, Jia stiffened, and she tried to decipher the tangle of sensations knotted inside her. The kiss had been a tool, nothing more. But it hadn't felt like nothing. And Dylan Floyd?

Not able to deal with her feelings at the moment, she focused on the reason Rick had stirred these unexpected emotions. "Are you sure it's him?"

"Yes. He looks like he's doing a surveillance sweep."

Jia mulled that over while fighting the urge to turn around to see for herself. "Maybe he's the one leaking the intel."

"Or he could be tracking Brandt."

She supposed that was possible. If she were still working inside the usual CIA channels, she would certainly be part of the surveillance to try to find Brandt, especially if the intel she'd gathered in Thailand had been shared. "Does the CIA know about the virus?"

"The intel has been passed along to US intelligence agencies, but I can't be certain who it's been distributed to."

"Logically, the nearby stations would have been informed of the potential threat, or at least that Brandt is a person of interest."

"When we get back to our apartment, I'll check on what intel has been disseminated."

"What's he doing now?" Jia asked.

"He's looking right at us." Rick paused. "And he's heading this way."

Not prepared to face her coworker, particularly one who might be in league with their prime suspect, she pushed up onto her toes. Then she leaned in and prepared for the onslaught of emotions she'd surely experience when she kissed Rick a second time.

* * *

Erik had barely managed to keep his eyes open when he'd kissed Jia the first time. Now, with her leaning into him and her lips caressing his once more, he fell into the kiss. His eyes closed, and his senses heightened.

He couldn't remember the last time he'd kissed a woman. Okay, that wasn't true. It had been seven years ago, three weeks before he'd testified. Sally Ann Palmer had been his girlfriend at the time. They'd broken up the next day.

Not once since he'd joined the guardians had he opened himself to the possibility of any kind of relationship, nor had he ever been in one place with a woman long enough to consider one.

But even his months dating Sally Ann had never brought out the reaction in him he was experiencing now.

Everything about Jia was vibrant and somehow brighter than any woman he'd ever encountered before. She'd established herself in the intelligence world as someone who was willing to take risks, someone who would fight for what she believed in. He admired that about her, even though he worried about how frequently she ended up on missions far more dangerous than he would like. But she'd demonstrated the ability to adapt in even the most unpredictable circumstances.

Personally, Erik tried to avoid the unpredictable, preferring to follow caution when possible. He'd abandoned his norm today, and his impulsiveness in kissing Jia was definitely impairing his judgment now.

She trailed her fingers over his back, pausing when she reached one of the scars from the drive-by shooting that had caused his fictional death.

And for all intents and purposes, he was dead. But in this moment, he felt more alive than ever before.

Fighting against the desire to lose himself in the sensation of holding Jia close, he reached deep inside him to let his protective instincts take over. Regretfully, he forced an eye open long enough to spot Dylan, who had apparently already completed his search of the area on their side of the pool and was now walking away from them.

Relief came first. Regret second. He accepted the first emotion and ignored the regret.

He should pull away, but he quickly discarded that thought. Surely he could enjoy his good fortune a moment longer. After all, he'd be crazy not to relish his time with this beautiful, intelligent, capable woman. He let his eyes flicker closed, lost once more in the overwhelming sensation of being held. His chest swelled, and his heartbeat quickened.

Far too soon, Jia pulled back, her dark eyes meeting his, her confusion reflected there. Could it be that she'd been as affected by the kiss as he had?

She swallowed and rubbed her lips together. "Is he still there?"

"He's heading down the path toward the back gate."

Jia stepped out of Erik's embrace. "Do you want me to back you up or disappear?"

He wanted her close, but logic dictated he keep her out of sight. "Can you take our stuff up to our apartment? I'll follow him."

"Be careful."

Unable to resist, he leaned in for one more quick kiss. "Always."

* * *

Jia had nearly managed to convince herself that the kisses she'd shared with Rick were nothing more than part of their cover story and a way to keep her hidden from Dylan. Then Rick had kissed her before leaving to follow their suspect. What had that been all about?

With Rick's laptop in hand and her towel slung around her neck, she took the elevator upstairs to their apartment. *Their apartment.* Just the sound of those two words took on new meaning since their kisses a few minutes ago.

She shook her head and exited the elevator. What was wrong with her? She didn't have any desire to get into a relationship, and certainly not with a man who had yet to tell her his real name. Or did she? She couldn't deny that thoughts of her future had been more on her mind in the last few days than ever before, and Rick had infiltrated those future plans whether she wanted to admit it or not.

She set his computer on the serving bar in the kitchen and opened it. When she couldn't bypass the main screen, she hurried into the office and grabbed her laptop. She logged in to the surveillance feed he'd set up and then found Rick and Dylan on the screen.

They were nearly to the gate that led out to the street, which required a code to exit.

Jia leaned closer. She sensed Rick slowing down as he approached Dylan, probably to see if Dylan had a code.

Rick reached into his shirt pocket, and a second later, an alert popped up on her screen to indicate a listening device had activated.

Reminding herself that their apartment was bugged, Jia grabbed the headphones sitting on the desk and connected them through Bluetooth so she could listen.

At first, there was nothing more than footsteps and the breeze rustling through the palm fronds and leaves of the nearby bushes.

When Dylan reached the gate but didn't immediately move to unlock it, Rick quickened his pace. "You must be visiting. Do you need me to unlock that for you?"

Dylan turned, his surprise instantly banked. "Oh, yeah." He stepped aside to give Rick access to the security panel. "Thanks."

"No problem." Rick stepped forward and shifted his body so Dylan couldn't see him key in the code. Then he pushed the gate open. "So, who are you visiting?"

"Actually, I was just checking out the area. I'm going to be working in the city for a month or two, and I needed to find a short-term rental."

Jia shook her head. Dylan should have known better than to fall back on that cover story around here. This complex didn't allow short-term rentals.

The two men passed through the gate and disappeared out of sight of the surveillance cameras.

"What do you do for a living?" Rick asked.

"I work for one of the oil companies."

"Really? Me too," Rick said as though delighted to have discovered a common connection. "Which company are you with?"

Jia anticipated what Dylan might say, surprised that he had been foolish enough to give this much information to a stranger.

Dylan clearly didn't expect the question because he hesitated slightly before he answered. "I work for Exxon."

"No way. You must be the guy Wyatt brought in to help while Nina is out on maternity leave."

For someone who typically worked in the shadows, Rick was playing his part far better than Dylan, who had been trained to handle such situations.

"You're in the main office, right?" Rick continued.

"Uh, yeah." Dylan hesitated. "You're with Exxon too?"

"I am. I just transferred here. I'm looking forward to getting to know everyone better."

"Yeah. Me too."

A faint thump sounded over the audio, but Jia couldn't identify the sound. Then Rick said, "Sorry. I need to watch where I'm going."

"No problem." Dylan paused. "Well, I'm headed this way, but I'm sure I'll see you around."

"Yeah. Have a good day."

The sound of footsteps and cars driving by replaced the voices. Jia hit the record button on her laptop in case Dylan met with anyone else of interest after leaving Rick. Then she removed her headphones and headed for her room. She needed a shower, and then she and Rick needed to have a talk, somewhere away from the listening ears of whoever had deemed them worth spying on.

CHAPTER 24

Erik continued walking toward the botanical gardens, not able to follow Dylan into the MRT with his swimsuit still wet and his transit pass in the apartment.

He took the time to walk part of the garden before he turned around and headed back to his current home.

So much had changed in the past hour, and he needed to talk to Jia, both about how they should proceed now that Brandt had shown up at their building and now that they'd seen Dylan Floyd in Singapore. How they were going to find a place to speak privately was going to be a struggle.

He used his code to enter the complex through the back gate and scanned the nearby area. What had Dylan been doing walking down here? Had he simply been checking out the area and searching for weaknesses in the security system?

Playing back the other man's movements, Erik suspected that was the case. And if that were true, it was highly likely that he was working with the Singapore CIA station in the hope that he could spy on Brandt without being IDed as a government operative.

He hoped the listening device he'd planted on Dylan's shirt would give them some clue as to his real allegiances, but as soon as he changed his clothes, they would lose the ability to hear what was happening in his world.

Erik quickened his step as he headed toward the elevator. When he hit the Up button, he glanced at the display. The elevator was heading up, stopping on the ninth floor before heading back down.

His heartbeat quickened. This elevator only went to one apartment on the ninth floor. Could it be that Brandt lived in that apartment and one of the people who had entered with him was heading to the lobby? It could even be Brandt himself.

Not wanting to miss an opportunity, he hit the Down button, too, in case the current elevator occupants were headed to the underground garage instead of the lobby.

The elevator stopped, and the door slid open. A man stood inside, his car keys in his hand. Not Brandt but someone Erik hadn't seen before.

Erik waited to make sure the man didn't plan to step out of the elevator before Erik entered and nodded a greeting. Not wanting to appear overly friendly, Erik didn't speak, instead letting the older man dictate if he was interested in conversation or silence. The man chose silence.

When they reached the lower level, Erik followed him into the garage and headed toward his own car. He cast a glance over his shoulder to determine where the other man was headed. The man clicked on his key fob, and the lights of a Lexus sedan flashed.

Erik noted the parking space so he could easily pull the license plate and registration on the vehicle before he approached the car parked two down from his.

He waited for the other driver to get into his car and pull out before he headed back to the elevator to go upstairs.

When he walked into the apartment, Jia sat on a stool beside the spot where one of the listening devices had been planted. She'd changed clothes, her eyes and cheeks enhanced with makeup, her lipstick making her lips even more tempting than when she'd been by the pool. Or maybe it was because he now knew what it felt like to kiss her, and that was making it hard to think about anything else.

She looked up, her gaze steady on his. "You've been working so long today. What do you think about the two of us going out for lunch?"

Going out to a restaurant wasn't his idea of a good time. Too many people around, too many people taking pictures of their food and anything else that might catch him in the background. And he couldn't afford to have his photo leaked online. Not now, not ever.

And then there was the food itself. He'd need to research possibilities for gluten-free options before he dared to eat out here. And he didn't particularly want to use his gluten sensor to test his food for gluten while in public. "I don't know."

She stood. "Come on. We can decide where to eat on our way to the MRT."

He caught the gleam in her eye, the one that suggested her words were more for the people listening to their conversation than for his benefit.

"I need to send a message and grab a quick shower, but after that, we can head out."

"Great." She nodded her approval. "I'll be waiting."

* * *

Jia led the way into the MRT station and followed the signs for the brown line.

When they stepped onto the escalators, Rick leaned down and whispered, "Where are we going?"

"Gardens by the Bay."

She glanced over her shoulder and caught the look of alarm on his face. If her suspicions were correct, the man she was currently calling her husband rarely went anywhere prone to high tourist traffic.

He leaned closer. "I'm not sure that's a good idea."

"Don't worry. I've been there before, and I know a spot where we can stay out of everyone's way." A spot where they could speak freely without worrying about listening devices or passersby.

They reached the subway platform, where a businessman waited in the otherwise empty space.

A minute later, the train came to a stop beside them, and the doors opened.

They entered the car nearest them, with just a handful of people seated inside.

"Do you want to sit down?" Rick asked.

She shook her head. "It's only a couple stops before we switch trains. I'll be fine." She'd checked their route while she'd waited for him. And now she was eager to be alone with him, where she could get his impressions of Dylan and whether Rick thought he was working with Brandt or spying on him.

One transfer and a half dozen stops later, they reached their destination.

Jia moved away from the gardens and toward the row of street vendors. "I say we grab some food first. Then we can go find a quiet spot to talk."

Rick nodded.

They walked the length of the food stands, grilled meat, rice, and fried noodles mixing in the air. Jia ordered a batch of spring rolls, while Rick opted for a simple bowl of white rice.

"Are you sure you don't want anything else?" Jia asked.

"I'm fine." He leaned closer. "I get sick if I eat gluten, and this is my safest option."

"Gotcha." She couldn't imagine how hard that must be to eat at restaurants. No wonder he'd hesitated when she'd asked about going out to eat.

Each of them holding their plates and water bottles, Jia looked around for a spot to sit. She should have thought to bring a blanket to sit on, but with or without that amenity, it appeared they were opting for a picnic lunch.

After getting her bearings, she turned down the path that led to a quiet spot alongside a bridge that wasn't well traveled.

She stopped at the edge of a wooden pathway. "We should be able to talk here." Jia motioned to the stream below them. "The water will mask our words, and no one will be able to get close to us without us seeing them coming."

Rick set the bowl he held on the railing of the bridge. He looked both ways before he spoke. "I ran the license plate of someone who was on the elevator when I was coming back up. The guy came off the ninth floor."

"And?" Jia took an egg roll off the plate closest to her.

"He works for a financial management firm here." Rick pulled out his phone and showed her a photo. "Any chance he was one of the people you saw get on the elevator?"

"Maybe, but I was so focused on Brandt that I didn't get a good look at the others."

"Either way, I have a friend tapping into his personnel file to check his address."

She blew on her spring roll and took a bite, savoring the crispy outer shell and the mix of carrots and cabbage in the middle. "This would be so much easier if we could check the property records for everyone in the building."

"We did, and I double-checked them again after my shower," Rick said. "It looks like the unit on the sixteenth floor is owner occupied by that woman we met, Elanora."

"Did her story check out about her husband working for the Australian embassy?"

"It did. My contact over there verified it and the fact that Elanora doesn't work."

"Which leaves us the units on the eleventh and fourteenth floors. Who are they owned by?"

"They both appear to be corporate owned, but we haven't been able to connect either company back to Brandt."

"Two units is manageable." Even though it would be so much simpler if Brandt's name were on one of the property records.

Rick scooped up another bite of rice. "We can stake out both if we need to."

"With the way this building is set up, maybe we should stake out the freight elevator to look for patterns of deliveries going to those floors," Jia said. "We can use the same ploy our delivery guy used on us."

Rick took a drink of his water. "Since Brandt just showed up, my guess is he had those bugs planted to make sure we weren't a threat before he came back home."

"Which means we've fooled him so far." Jia picked up another spring roll. "What was your take on Dylan?"

"His cover story wasn't very well thought out."

"I know. He should have been better prepared, but the fact that he wasn't makes me think he didn't anticipate speaking to anyone."

"A quick recon mission." Rick nodded slowly. "If that's all this was, he was likely brought in from the Kuala Lumpur office to make sure no one recognized him as agency."

"I had the same thought," Jia said. "If he was here visiting Brandt, he would have been more likely to say he was visiting someone and give a generic answer when asked who it was."

"Agreed. So that knocks him down on our list of suspects for the potential leaks."

"I just wish we could figure out where Shaun is."

"I know." Rick put his hand on hers. "But we'll find him. We just need more time."

"I hope he has time."

CHAPTER 25

SHAUN SCOURED THE BEDROOM AND bathroom for the thousandth time since his arrival. When yet again he didn't find anything that would help him escape his current prison, he leaned against the wall and slid down until he was sitting on the floor.

Nur, her strength now fully restored after receiving the vaccine, spoke quietly from her usual spot on the couch. "There's nothing we can do."

She'd said the same thing on numerous occasions, but today, with his knowledge that the virus would be unleashed in mere days, his emotions boiled over. "How can you be so calm?" Shaun leaned his head back against the wall. "Don't you understand how many people could die?"

She stood. "I'm here because I tried to help. If we don't cause any trouble, they might let us live."

"Might." Shaun pushed himself back to a stand, towering over her. "Do you truly understand what's at stake? Can you even visualize what it would look like for a million people to die? Or millions of people?"

She stared up at him, silent.

He tried to imagine that many people and couldn't. Sixty thousand people watching a football game. He could visualize that. But millions? Such a number truly was beyond his comprehension.

Nur blinked against the tears that had formed in her eyes. Maybe she was starting to understand. But it didn't matter. Even if they worked together, they were outmanned, and they had nothing to use as a weapon to overpower their guards, much less a way to save the millions of people in danger.

Nur lifted both hands and fiddled with the hair at the back of her head. Then she held one hand out, two bobby pins now resting in her palm. "Will these help?"

"Where did you get them?" And had she been hiding them this whole time?

"They were in my hair when they brought me here." She lifted her hands, both of them trembling. "They took all the pins out of my hair, but I tried to pull away. These two must have fallen out. I found them under the sofa."

"Why didn't you show me these earlier?"

"If you tried to escape while Mr. Brandt was still here, I was sure he would decide to kill both of us."

Her logic was sound, and Shaun couldn't deny that he would have tried.

A flicker of hope crossed her face. "Can you get us out of here?"

Shaun held up the bobby pins. "I think so, but we'll have to time it right." He looked around the room again. "And we'll need something I can use to disarm the guard after I unlock the door."

"I don't know what." Nur held up her hands again. "The only thing they ever give us is food, and even then, they make us use our fingers to eat."

"But the food comes in a bowl or on a plate." At this point, he was willing to use any available object as a means to escape.

"Tableware doesn't sound like it would be very effective as a weapon."

He let out a sigh. "Maybe not, but it may be all we'll have to work with."

"How soon do you want to try?" Nur asked.

"I don't know. As soon as we can be sure we have a real chance of getting past the guards."

"That may never happen."

* * *

Erik and Jia arrived back at their apartment fifteen minutes ahead of their next delivery. This time, Erik took possession at the back door, refusing to let the deliveryman enter their apartment. As soon as he slid the oversized box into the laundry room and closed the door, he took a step back so he could read the words on the side. "Jingyi?" he called out. "Did you order a TV?"

"Is it already here?" She joined him in the laundry room and put her hand on the edge of the box. "Oh good, we should set it up in the living room."

"Why did you get a TV?" Erik asked. "We can use our laptops if you want to watch something."

"I know, but those screens are so small." She winked at him, but Erik wasn't sure exactly what part he was supposed to play in whatever plan she was putting into place. "Can you help me set it up?"

"If you want." But he'd rather get back to work to see if any of the surveillance feed today had given more hints about which unit Brandt lived in.

Together Erik and Jia pushed the television into the living room.

"Where do you want it?" he asked.

"I think right here." She pointed at the only wall in the living room that didn't include windows. "There's supposed to be a mount included in the box."

"Let's see what we've got." He grabbed a pair of scissors from the kitchen and opened the box. Once he removed the television and the mounting kit, he determined which tools he would need.

"Oh no. You'll need a drill for that," Jia said.

He opened his mouth to let her know he had one in the toolkit in his room, but she held up her hand to stop him from speaking. "Maybe one of the neighbors has one you can borrow."

An ulterior motive. He should have known. "I'll see if someone upstairs might have one," Erik said. "Any idea which floors have people on them who might be home this time of day?"

"I'm not sure. Maybe go up a few floors and work your way down."

"Good idea." Erik tipped the box against the side of the counter. "I'll be back in a few minutes."

"Okay. While you do that, I'll start on dinner."

He started to go into his room to retrieve his pistol but thought better of it. Even if he stumbled onto Brandt, the man didn't know him, and showing up armed was not a good way to look innocent in the event he was searched or detained.

Instead, he headed for the back door. The service elevator took a full two minutes to arrive. Erik entered the empty car and took it to the fourteenth floor. When he stepped off, a man stood outside the apartment door of the unit to his left. Though his clothing consisted of shorts and a tan T-shirt, his posture screamed security, and Erik suspected the man had a weapon tucked at the small of his back.

Doing his best to appear nonthreatening, Erik took two steps toward the man before he asked, "Hey, is this your apartment?"

"What do you want?" the man asked.

"I just moved in downstairs, and I was hoping you might have a drill I could borrow to mount our TV."

"Why didn't you hire someone to install it for you?"

Erik held up both hands. "I have no idea why my wife does this to me." Now he shook his head. "Sometimes, I think she wants to see if I even know how to use power tools."

"I don't have a drill."

"Well, thanks anyway." Erik hit the Down button for the elevator. Though he suspected he'd already found Brandt's apartment and would have preferred to go straight to the eleventh floor to confirm his suspicions, he took the elevator down to the thirteenth floor. A Filipino woman answered the door and insisted that they didn't have a drill he could borrow.

Erik hoped for the same results on the twelfth floor, but the man who answered this time was all too happy to accommodate him. After a short visit and an exchange of phone numbers, Erik headed back downstairs, resigned to miss the eleventh-floor unit.

When he returned to his apartment, Jia was indeed in the kitchen making dinner. The bottle of tamari sauce sat on the counter along with the empty box from some rice noodles.

It wasn't often he could enjoy eating a meal that he didn't have to prepare, and he looked forward to that treat tonight. The sautéed mushrooms and meat grilling already had his mouth watering. He held up the drill. "I found one."

"Oh, good," Jia said. "Let me know when you need help with the TV."

"We can do it after dinner."

Jia offered him a little smile. "In that case, want to set the table?"

"We don't have a table yet."

"Okay, fine. You can set the counter," Jia said. "And after you finish setting up the TV, we can shop for a kitchen table."

Erik moved into the kitchen and retrieved two plates. At the rate Jia was going, this apartment was going to be fully furnished by the end of next week.

* * *

Jia returned the drill to their twelfth-floor neighbor, and she took the stairs both ways.

Based on Rick's description of the bodyguard on the fourteenth floor, the likelihood was that they'd already found Brandt's location. Now they needed to make sure by eliminating the other alternative.

No bodyguards or other signs of enhanced security on the eleventh floor. A bicycle chained to the railing near the back door.

Ever thorough, Jia approached the back door and knocked. A diminutive woman answered, with her long black hair pulled back in a ponytail. Jia guessed she was in her early twenties, likely working as a live-in helper for the family who lived here.

"I'm sorry to bother you," Jia began in English. "I just moved in downstairs, and I wondered if you have a cup of rice I can borrow? My husband forgot to buy some at the store."

"Yes." She nodded and held up a finger. She closed the door partway before she disappeared from sight. A moment later, she emerged with a plastic sandwich bag filled with rice. She held it out. "You take."

"Thank you so much." Jia took it from her. "I'm sorry. I didn't introduce myself. I'm Jingyi."

The woman nodded again before she put her hand to her chest. "Kristine."

"It's nice to meet you, Kristine." Jia held up the rice. "And thank you."

Jia stepped back, and Kristine promptly closed the door.

Jia headed downstairs to her apartment and walked inside.

"Hey, Jingyi," Rick called out. "Can you come here for a minute?"

"Yeah. What is it?" She moved past the counter, where the bug was planted, irritated on principle that she had to censor her speech because of it.

"I thought you might want to take a look at this."

She followed Rick's voice into the office, and he stood as she entered. Without another word, he gestured to his screen.

On it, he had listed all their suspects in the CIA who could have leaked details about her mission.

Next to seven of the names, he had typed in notes that appeared to eliminate the individuals from suspicion. Though some of the reasons fell into the speculation category, such as family members with significant health issues, the one listed beside Dylan Floyd was solid. If this information was correct, Dylan's knowledge of the safe house locations had been limited to those in Malaysia, which meant he couldn't have been responsible for sending Brandt's men after her.

Jia leaned closer and pointed at his name. "Are you sure about this?"

Rick nodded.

Jia focused on the only name that remained without anything beside it: Chesah Abalos. Rather than speak, Jia picked up her cell phone and texted Rick.

Do you know where she is now?

He responded by texting back. *Her phone is still in Malaysia.*

Still texting, Jia typed in her next thought. *Any chance she's passed through any border control?*

Not that I could find.

Jia texted again. *Where's Dylan Floyd? Maybe you need to have another chat with him.*

Rick traced the location of Dylan's phone and stood. "Want to go for a walk with me?"

"That sounds great."

Rick grabbed his mini backpack, stopping at the refrigerator to grab two water bottles and a couple of protein bars. After he put them in his pack, he retrieved both of their MRT passes.

"Where do you want to walk tonight?"

He pulled the door open. "I'm sure we can find someplace we've never been."

"Of that I have no doubt."

CHAPTER 26

Erik didn't like what he'd seen in his report. Not only was Chesah Abalos the only person who he couldn't logically eliminate as the leak within the CIA, but her phone also hadn't moved in two days. If he was right, Chesah was on the move, and she was making sure no one could track her.

They walked out of the elevator and passed by the pool, exiting through the back gate before Jia broke the silence.

"What aren't you telling me?" she asked.

"I'm worried that Chesah hasn't used her phone in the last couple days. And it hasn't moved either."

"In our line of work, going off-grid isn't unheard of."

"I know. That's why I messaged one of my colleagues to dig a little deeper."

"Deeper into what?"

"The beach house Chesah bought four months ago in Florida."

"She bought a house?"

The fact that Jia hadn't heard of the recent purchase raised Erik's suspicions even further. He checked his cell clock, annoyed that the time difference prevented him from calling Kade without waking him. Nearly five o'clock here in Singapore meant it was four in the morning in the eastern US.

"When is she due to rotate back to the States?" Erik asked Jia.

"She got here a year before me, so theoretically, she could transfer back this summer." Jia shrugged. "I assumed with her language skills that she'd want to stay in the field."

Especially if her salary was being enhanced by Brandt and possibly others who would pay her for intel.

"It's hard to believe it's Chesah." Jia walked slowly down the path toward the MRT station. "I didn't think she was the type."

"People who spy on their country rarely seem the type." Although Erik could admit that he still had reservations. Chesah didn't show any red flags, except for the recent real estate purchase, and that behavior wasn't wholly unheard of. If she was looking to move back to the US, a place in a beach community in a state where there wasn't income tax was a smart choice. And it could make a nice rental.

"What about Qian Zhang?" Erik asked. "The only eliminator I had on him was that his grandmother has kidney disease and congestive heart failure. If he isn't close to her, he could be our real mole."

Jia seemed to ponder Erik's question before she asked, "What are the chances he would come into an inheritance when his grandmother passes?"

Erik cringed at the thought of someone wanting a relative to die to increase their own wealth. "None that I know of, but those details aren't public record until after a will or trust is filed after someone's death."

"Did you trace his location?"

"No, but I can have a colleague run it for me really quick." He pulled out his phone and debated which guardian would be both awake and available this time of day. He punched in the number for Troy.

He picked up on the second ring. "Hey," Troy greeted him. "What are you up to? Still playing house in Singapore?"

"Yeah." Erik glanced at Jia, the memory of their kisses pushing to the forefront of his thoughts. Work. He needed to focus on work. Not on Jia's stunning profile or the way humor and determination often lit up her face.

"If you're calling me, you must need a favor and didn't want to wake up Kade," Troy said.

"It's an easy one, I hope." Erik stopped when he reached the bend in the sidewalk that led to the MRT station. "Can you run the location on Qian and do a deep dive into his finances? It's possible R already did one, and it hadn't popped up before I left the apartment," he said, referring to Kristi, the guardian's financial analyst.

"Let me see what we've got." Troy fell silent for a moment, the tapping of keys coming over the line. "Okay, I've got it. It looks like his phone is currently at a restaurant in Bangkok. And no red flags on the finances yet."

"Can you tell if this guy comes from money?" Erik asked. "I specifically want to know if his grandmother has any wealth. Her name is in the database."

"Hold on," Troy said again. More typing. More of Jia staring at him with her gorgeous, dark-brown eyes.

Troy came back on the line. "Oh yeah. Grandma has some money, but it's not like she's totally loaded. Her house is worth a couple million, and it's already been placed in a trust." He paused. "I checked to see if the trust was on file, but it looks like it's still a living trust."

"So no court record yet."

"Nope."

"Thanks for your help."

"No problem. I'll be around if you need anything else."

"Thanks, but in another hour or two, I have to call K. He's supposed to be checking up on something for me."

"I'll call him for you."

The eagerness in Troy's voice was enough to send Erik's suspicions rising. "Why do you want to get involved?"

"I just haven't had any reason to wake him up lately. And you know how fun it is to irritate him."

Erik laughed. He did know. "Okay, go ahead. Tell him to call me when he has anything."

Troy's smile came through the phone. "I will."

Erik ended the call and looked down at Jia, surprised to see her smiling up at him. "What's that smile for?"

"You. You should laugh more often." She put her hand on his arm. "You have a good laugh."

He'd never had anyone say that to him before. But he didn't often have occasion to laugh unless he had some downtime to chat with one of the other guardians.

"So what did your friend say about Qian?"

"It's possible there could be some money coming his way when his grandmother dies, but I'm not sure it would be enough to want to kill for."

"Maybe not, but if he's getting paid for the intel being shared, it could be that he isn't worried about how much longer his grandmother stays alive," she said. "He could even think that he's putting her out of her misery."

* * *

Putting her out of her misery. Her own words had stayed with Jia throughout the MRT ride to Little India. Was she correct that Brandt was motivated by similar thoughts?

Jia stepped out of the crowded train and joined the flow of people heading for the escalators. Rick had fallen behind her, several others now between them, but that didn't surprise her. Right now, they didn't need to act like a married couple. And by not walking together, Rick could pretend he didn't know Jia in case they happened upon Dylan Floyd unexpectedly.

She reached the main level and scanned the signs to determine which exit to take. Rick passed by her and turned to the left. She followed.

When she emerged from the MRT station, the humidity enveloped her. So did the smell of curry. Pedestrians crowded the narrow sidewalk, some people spilling out onto the street as they attempted to walk past the various shops using the sidewalk as an extension of their space.

Rick held his phone and looked down at it as though using his GPS feature for directions. Jia suspected he was using it to determine where to go, but it wasn't a destination he was searching for. It was a person.

They passed by several shops and restaurants, Jia remaining several meters behind Rick as she scanned the faces of those around her. An older woman wearing a traditional sari, the customary red dot on her forehead. A blonde woman and the man beside her who had to be at least a few inches over six feet. Tourists? Then there was the crowd of teenagers all dressed in their school uniforms. Her analysis continued, the others around her ranging from Chinese to Australian, Indian to European, and everything in between.

Rick stopped to browse a display of clothing in a sidewalk shop. He peeked in her direction, no doubt making sure she was still behind him.

The pattern continued, Rick browsing on occasion, Jia closing the distance between them, and then letting herself fall farther behind.

They passed by a Hindu temple, ornate figures carved into the wall surrounding it as well as in the walls and on the roof of the temple itself. The crowd by the entrance expanded into the street, making it difficult for the cars to pass by.

A trickle of sweat dripped down the center of Jia's back, the lack of a breeze making the muggy 85-degree weather feel much warmer. She needed water, but Rick had hers in his pack.

She spotted a man in his twenties a short distance away. A bucket sat at his feet, filled with water bottles and melting ice. She pulled some coins from her pocket and quickened her step so she wouldn't fall too far behind.

She exchanged the coins for the water, barely slowing her pace as she paid. She twisted off the cap and downed a quarter of the cold liquid.

Rick reached the next intersection and stopped. Then he turned and made eye contact as though he now wanted her to join him.

Not sure what had changed, she continued forward until she reached his side.

"Have you seen him?" she asked quietly.

"He should be in that restaurant over there."

Jia debated where they could blend into their surroundings while watching for Dylan and anyone he might be meeting. "We should grab a table at that restaurant over there." She gestured toward an Indian place directly across from Dylan's current location.

Rick nodded. They entered the arched doorway, the scent of curry and Indian spices making her mouth water.

Rick held up two fingers as though he weren't sure which language to speak. She narrowed her eyes. What languages did he speak? She was pretty sure she'd spoken to him in Mandarin before, and he'd understood. But was he conversant in any other Asian languages? Not that such details should matter to her. He was simply her partner on this mission, her partner who could kiss her in a way that made her head feel like it might detach and spin around three times before reattaching to her body.

Using hand signals, Rick pointed at a table that a busboy was currently clearing off, one situated right next to the front window. After a brief wait, they were seated, both of them with menus in their hands.

Rick lowered his menu and leaned forward. "Anything look good to you?" he asked, much like a man on a date with his girlfriend. Or his wife.

CHAPTER 27

Erik skimmed over the menu. He could order half a dozen things on it, but he couldn't risk the possibility of cross-contamination, not right now when a reaction could cripple him and leave Jia vulnerable without adequate backup. And if there was a time she would need backup, it was now.

While surveillance cameras filled the city of Singapore, the one place that had blind spots was here in Little India.

His thoughts went briefly to her last partner. Still no word on where the man might be or if he was even still alive. A hollowness filled Erik, the familiar ache that surfaced any time he faced the possibility of someone passing away so young.

He hated that his own family had been forced to endure that. How he wished he could have told them the truth, that he had died so he could continue to live and so the danger wouldn't draw any closer to them.

The drive-by shooting could have taken his grandparents' lives far too easily, and they deserved to live a full life—even if it didn't include him.

"What are you getting?" Jia asked, breaking him out of his thoughts. She leaned forward and asked in a whisper, "Did you want to order or just get a drink or something?"

"A drink sounds good." He had cash he could drop on the table if they needed to leave prematurely. "Have you decided?"

"I'm debating between the chicken masala and the butter chicken."

"How about you get one, and I'll get the other?" That would help him look natural, and he could take the food home with him, where he could test it for gluten before eating it. Assuming they were here long enough to be served their meal.

A waiter approached the table next to them, carrying two plates. She took a step their way at the same time Dylan emerged from the restaurant across the street.

The waiter reached their table. "Can I take your order?"

Before Jia could answer, Erik said, "We need another minute."

The woman nodded and stepped away just as Jia looked out the window.

"Chesah Abalos." Jia nearly pointed but dropped her hand in time to not draw attention. "She's across the street."

"Dylan just came out too."

Jia shook her head. "Maybe they're both involved."

Dylan turned down the street. Chesah followed from a discreet distance.

"Let's find out." Erik pushed back from the table. "Come on."

Jia stood and exited the restaurant behind him, remaining between him and the wall. It didn't take long for him to realize she needed to stay out of sight of the two people they were following. Dylan might recognize Erik, but Chesah had never seen him.

To reduce the likelihood that they'd be noticed, he took Jia's hand in his so at a glance, they looked like a couple.

Despite the thickness in the air and the bead of sweat on his brow, the mere touch of Jia's hand against his brought with it a connection he'd longed for without his knowing something was missing.

This playing-house thing was messing with his mind. Or maybe the reason he'd thought of Jia so often over the last two years was that his respect for her had blossomed into something more personal.

Ahead of them, Chesah wandered down the sidewalk as though she didn't have a care in the world. Erik could admire her ability while also appreciating that Jia shared it.

Ahead of Chesah, Dylan turned a corner without a backward glance.

"Does he not know he's being followed, or are they going somewhere to meet?" Jia asked quietly.

"If they were going to meet, why would they both be in the same place at the same time and then go somewhere else?" Erik asked.

"She's following him for a reason."

Erik quickened his steps. He could only think of two reasons for Chesah to follow someone from her own office. Either she suspected Dylan of being the mole, or she was here to make sure he wasn't a threat to Brandt.

Jia squeezed Erik's hand. "We need to hurry."

* * *

Jia didn't want to think Chesah would kill Dylan, but the possibility was all too real. They were in the one part of Singapore where cameras were far fewer, the narrow alleyways far more prevalent. And if Chesah had done any surveillance work at the apartment complex, she would most certainly have noticed Dylan with the way he'd been poking around everywhere. And if that was the case, had Chesah also seen Jia?

Jia's pulse quickened. If the CIA learned she'd lied about her whereabouts for the past week, ultimately someone would understand she'd gone off-grid to protect herself and Shaun. But the presence of two other members from her office was suspicious, and not in a good way.

Dylan made another turn, and this time, Chesah quickened her step and closed the distance between them.

"Come on," Rick whispered before he released her hand and broke into a jog.

Jia raced after him. They turned the corner, and this time, they were in a narrow alley rather than on a street, and instead of a crowded sidewalk, only Dylan and Chesah were visible among the stacks of boxes and trash bins lining the back of the buildings on either side.

Chesah's hand went to her waistband, and Jia's heartbeat stuttered. Did Chesah somehow manage to smuggle a gun into Singapore? But it wasn't a gun that was visible when her hand reemerged. The sunlight glinted off the blade of a knife.

"Hey!" Rick shouted.

Chesah whirled toward them. So did Dylan.

His gaze darted to Rick before he spotted Chesah.

"Put down the knife," Jia called out.

Now Dylan's eyes widened. He froze for a split second, and then he ran.

Chesah started to follow, but she didn't even make it four steps before the back door of a business opened, and she ran into it. Chesah fell to the ground, and Jia shouted, "Go after him!" There was no way she could catch Dylan.

"But—" Rick looked down at the knife still in Chesah's hand.

"I've got her."

Rick hesitated a split second more. Then he turned and sprinted after Dylan.

Jia charged forward and stepped on the blade of the knife Chesah held, stomping on her finger in the process.

"Agh!" Chesah cried out in pain before she rolled over and freed herself, sans the knife.

Jia jumped in anticipation, not surprised when Chesah swept out her leg in an effort to knock Jia off her feet.

As Rick disappeared from view, Jia kicked the knife under a stack of boxes and backed out of the danger zone, then lifted both hands, prepared to defend herself.

"What are you doing here?" Jia asked. "Are you the one working for Brandt?"

Chesah merely narrowed her eyes and danced on the balls of her feet. She circled to the right and struck out with her fist.

Jia ducked, the air displacement for the intended punch whooshing by her ear.

Instinct kicked in, and Jia pivoted, throwing her elbow into Chesah's back.

Chesah fell forward, catching the side of her face on the edge of a wooden crate. She turned again, her hands lifted, her body ready to attack despite the trickle of blood on her lip.

"Why are you working for Brandt?"

Chesah's response was another jab, this one landing on Jia's shoulder.

Jia's counterpunch was quick and straight to Chesah's stomach.

The next twenty seconds passed in a blur of fists, elbows, and knees. After multiple blows to her shoulder, back, and cheek, Jia finally managed two subsequent strikes that sent Chesah stumbling backward.

Chesah coughed and leaned over as though trying to catch her breath—the classic posture of someone who pretends to be defeated as a way to draw in an opponent.

Jia stepped away. "Brandt's men tried to kill me. And they have Shaun."

Chesah spat on the ground, a law-breaking offense in Singapore, although Jia doubted Chesah cared about that at the moment.

Jia tried again. "Don't you care about helping get Shaun back? His wife is too young to be a widow."

Chesah wiped at her bleeding lip and straightened. "He should have thought of that before he teamed up with you." Resentment filled Chesah's voice, which didn't make any sense.

"What's your problem with me?"

"Oh, don't stand there like you don't know—Miss First in Your Class, Pick Your Assignment, Do Whatever You Want."

"I have no idea what you're talking about." Nor did it matter. "Is that why you started working for Brandt? Because you were jealous?"

"I'm not working for Brandt." She straightened slightly, and the gleam in her eye gave her intentions away. She charged Jia, but not before Jia grabbed the top of a metal trash bin.

Jia stepped to the side and swung the lid at Chesah's head. A resounding clang followed, and Chesah fell to the ground.

CHAPTER 28

ERIK HATED THE THOUGHT THAT Jia was on her own against someone who was armed, but she'd asked him to trust her, and he hadn't seen a better option.

As it was, she'd been smart to send him after Dylan. The man had enough speed to make chasing him a much larger challenge than Erik had hoped.

Erik struggled to keep the fleeing man in sight as Dylan weaved in and out of the people clogging the sidewalks. If it weren't for the constant flow of cars whizzing by on the main street, he would have given up using the sidewalk completely. As it was, he had no choice.

He glimpsed Dylan's gray T-shirt as the man ducked into an electronics store that was little more than an open counter and shelves of outdated computer equipment.

Erik arrived in time to spot Dylan headed toward the back door of the shabby building.

Though he hated to draw attention to himself, today Erik had little choice. He sprinted to the counter, used his hands to vault himself onto and over it, and then took off running amid the protests of the shopkeeper.

Dylan burst through the back door, but Erik managed to reach it before the door closed completely. He caught the edge of it, yanked the door open, and ran into the back alley that could have been a clone of the one they'd started in—trash cans, boxes, overripe garbage, and Dylan running away.

Erik's lungs and thighs burned as he followed Dylan once more, struggling to close the distance between them.

The sound of moving vehicles rumbled toward Erik, growing louder with each step.

Dylan reached the end of the alley and grabbed the edge of the building to keep his momentum from thrusting him into the passing traffic.

Another couple of meters and Erik would catch up to him.

A car skidded as his target emerged from the alley, the sound and the nearness of the vehicle causing Dylan to jump back, nearly landing on top of Erik.

Erik grabbed Dylan from behind, hooking an arm around the man's neck.

Dylan threw his body back, knocking Erik off-balance, but Erik didn't let go.

"Stop. I'm not trying to hurt you." Erik grabbed both of Dylan's arms, gripping them tightly before he knocked his knees into the back of the other man's legs.

Dylan's knees buckled, and he fell forward, but Erik held his arms firmly to keep him from dropping to the ground.

"Why were you at my apartment complex this morning?"

"I told you. I was checking out a rental."

"I know better." Erik lowered his voice. "And I know you're CIA."

Dylan tensed. "I don't know what you're talking about."

"That's fine." Erik didn't really expect an intelligence operative to share classified information with him, even if it was simply the truth about his employer. "Let's catch up with your colleagues and see if you're more comfortable giving one of them some answers."

"You don't know who you're dealing with."

Erik pulled Dylan forward, keeping one hand on the other man's arm. "Actually, I think I do."

* * *

A hotel. This was certainly not where Jia had expected Rick to want to meet her, particularly with a prisoner in tow, but he'd texted her an address and an electronic room key along with instructions on which back door to use when she arrived.

Chesah had tried to break free twice on their walk from Little India to the hotel, but they'd finally made it, and thankfully, Rick was waiting at their room with the door open when they arrived.

The moment they passed through the door, Rick took Chesah by the arm and forced her into the empty dining room chair beside Dylan.

No longer responsible for protecting herself against Chesah's escape attempts, Jia closed the door behind her and took in her surroundings.

This wasn't a typical hotel room. It was almost half the size of their condo, complete with full living and dining rooms. Two doors opened off the main living space, likely both bedrooms.

In the dining area, Rick used zip ties to secure Chesah's wrists in front of her. He then used a bedsheet to tie her body to the chair. Dylan already sat in the spot beside her, his hands and body also secured so he couldn't try to get away.

"Jia." Dylan lifted his gaze to meet hers. "I should have known you were the one working with Brandt."

Jia didn't respond, instead searching for any tells on his face or in his demeanor that would give him away. She saw none.

Turning her attention to the woman who currently ranked among their top suspects, Jia asked, "Who's paying you for information?"

Chesah clenched her jaw, the simple reaction telling Jia far more than she'd expected.

Rick looked at Jia and tilted his head toward Dylan.

Jia gave a subtle nod. They were in agreement. Chesah was the traitor.

Acting as though she didn't have any care about extracting more information from Chesah, Jia pulled one of the other two chairs away from the dining room table and set it in front of Chesah and Dylan. She sat and turned her body so she was looking at Rick instead of their two prisoners. "I'm not sure why she was jealous of me, but I guess there was something she had an issue about."

Rick crossed his arms over his chest. "That could explain why she leaked the location of the safe house."

Dylan turned his head to look at Chesah. "You did what?"

"We figured you knew," Rick said. "Seeing as the two of you have been working together."

"I'm not working with anyone," Dylan insisted.

"Someone sent you to check out the condo complex," Rick said. "The question is whether you were looking for Jia or you were there to meet with Brandt."

"Who are you?" Dylan asked.

"He's one of us," Jia said. "I requested support from someone outside the local offices after Brandt's men showed up at the safe house."

Dylan seemed to ponder his options.

"If you weren't involved, you should tell us what you know," Jia pressed.

"Why didn't you come back into the office if you were in trouble?" Dylan asked.

"Because I had no idea which of you was working with Brandt." She paused. "Or if he has more than one person from the CIA on his payroll."

"Whoa." Dylan shook his head. "I'm not working for anyone but our common employer." He looked from Jia to Rick and back again. "And I don't know anything about a leak other than the report that came through about you going off on some rogue mission without authorization."

Jia fisted her hands at the mere thought that someone would accuse her of such a thing. Then again, here she and Rick were, accusing two CIA operatives of being spies.

"Why were you at the condo complex?" Jia asked again.

Dylan tensed again before he seemed to relent to the need to share information. "I was tasked to follow Brandt to see if you showed up."

"Who tasked you with that assignment?" Rick asked.

"Andrea."

"She thought I went rogue?"

"Yeah. The mission report we got from Bangkok said you called in telling them that Shaun had gone missing, and then you disappeared," Dylan said. "When your passport flagged in Singapore, we figured you must be working with Brandt."

"How did you find Brandt?"

"After your passport flagged both here and in Batam, the Singapore office set up extra surveillance at the docks and the airports."

"So you were looking for me, but you found Brandt." Jia hadn't expected that.

"We think we know where Brandt is staying now," Rick said, likely trying to build a bridge of trust. "But we don't know who else is involved."

Jia leaned forward in her chair. "Do you know who else sailed in with Brandt?"

"The Singapore office has the photos."

"How did you get brought in?" Jia asked.

"They wanted someone who would recognize you in a crowd." Dylan shrugged. "You aren't always easy to find."

That was true, especially in locations where most of the residents were either Chinese or of Chinese heritage.

Jia turned to Rick. "What do we do now?"

"I'll have a friend verify Dylan's story and check out both of their travel orders," Rick said. "If we're right about Chesah being our mole, my guess is that she didn't travel here on the government's dime."

CHAPTER 29

Erik had no doubt. Chesah wasn't talking, not because she was protecting intelligence but because she was the person who had been leaking it.

It had taken less than an hour to determine that Dylan had indeed traveled to Singapore on official travel orders, and Chesah had not.

Erik paced the hotel bedroom and debated his next move. He would need to involve the local FBI liaison to take Chesah into custody, but he suspected she might be a bit more cooperative if questioned by Jia rather than the FBI.

A knock sounded on the door, and Erik answered it. Jia stood on the other side. Not that it could have been anyone else. The other two were still tied up.

Jia stepped into the room, pulling the door slightly closed so she could still see their two prisoners while giving them some privacy. "Any luck?" she whispered.

He nodded. Respecting the training the two CIA operatives had received, he put his hand on Jia's waist and leaned down to speak in her ear so the other two couldn't read his lips. "No official record of Chesah's travel."

"With the way she's acting, I really think she's the problem." Jia put her hand on his shoulder as though to steady herself and remained close enough to him to make sure their words weren't heard and their lips remained unseen as they spoke.

Erik whispered in her ear. "I think you should question her."

"I've tried. She's not giving me anything."

He breathed in the scent of Jia's shampoo and reveled in their closeness. With some effort, he focused on the reason they were currently in a hotel together. "It's nearly dinnertime. Why don't you order something from room service?"

"You're going to feed them in the hope of getting on their good side?" Jia asked.

"That and you need to eat something." He tilted his head slightly, his cheek brushing against her hair.

"What about you? You need to eat too."

"I'll be fine. And while you get the food, I'll keep digging to see if I can find anything you can use during your interrogation."

She nodded slightly, and her breath feathered over his skin. "I'll need something to hold over her." She lifted her eyes to meet his, and for a moment, she simply stared.

Instinctively, his gaze dropped to her lips, and all too easily, he could imagine kissing her again. But this wasn't the time or the place.

His heart sank. It might never be the right time or place again.

Jia pressed her lips together. "Maybe I should go downstairs to order our food. We don't want the room-service waiter to see these two tied up."

"True." He eased back slightly. "We can call in the order and then one of us can go get it."

"I'll call it in. What do you want?"

"I have a protein bar with me."

"That's not going to fill you up."

That was true, but he couldn't afford to eat anything here. Not when one of the people in the other room might very well be able to break this case open and help them find Shaun.

Erik turned so he was facing away from the doorway. "Remember how I said I have to eat gluten-free? We can't risk me getting sick right now."

"I'm sure they have something you can eat."

"Really, I'll be fine." And he did have two bars with him.

"Okay. I'll call an order in for everyone else." She leaned closer again before she added, "See what you can do to give me an upper hand with Chesah."

"I will." Erik glanced through the crack in the door to where Chesah was currently staring in their direction, a look of pure hatred on her face. "Any idea why she doesn't like you?"

"Until today, I didn't even suspect this, but it seems there may be some jealousy issues going on here. I have no idea why," Jia said. "Maybe if we can tease that answer out of her, we'll know more about how she ended up working for Brandt."

"Maybe you should go down to order," Erik said, considering. "And take your time. I may need a few minutes to lay the foundation for you."

Jia lifted her eyebrows, clearly curious, but she nodded. "Okay. Good luck."

She started to move back, but Erik held her in place. Might as well set the stage now for what he had in mind.

He pushed the door open so he and Jia were in full view of Chesah and Dylan. Then he leaned down and brushed a kiss across her cheek. "Don't be too long."

A little smile played on Jia's lips before she eased out of his arms. "I won't."

* * *

Jia crossed the lobby toward the restaurant and tried not to think about the way her skin still tingled from where Erik had kissed her cheek.

Had he been trying to make Chesah jealous? She supposed it was possible, especially if Chesah had somehow put herself in competition with Jia. Although why anyone would want to do that was beyond her.

Jia came from a simple background, without a lot of opportunities growing up. She'd had to work to pay for her school supplies and clothes from the age of twelve, and ultimately, she'd chosen her university based on the scholarships available to her. And everyone knew she didn't have a life outside of work.

She reached the restaurant and asked the hostess for a menu. After a quick scan, she put in her order for three dinners, opting for finger foods for Chesah and Dylan so she could avoid the need for them to use utensils of any kind. There was no way she was going to give Chesah anything she could use as a weapon.

"It'll be about twenty minutes," the hostess told her.

"Thanks." Jia gestured to an open seating area located in the lobby a short distance away. "I'll wait over there."

She sat with her back against the wall, where she could see the restaurant entrance and still observe anyone passing through the hotel lobby.

Her phone rang, and she pulled it from her pocket. She expected Rick had changed his mind about ordering something, but the contact popped up with a single letter: T.

Jia hit the Talk button. "Hello?"

"Is this Jia?" a man asked, a wisp of a European accent evident in his voice.

"Who is this?"

"I'm Ghost."

"Excuse me?" Jia lowered her voice. "This isn't Ghost."

"I'm another ghost," the man clarified. "Your ghost asked me to give you the details on Chesah. It sounded like he couldn't talk when I called him."

Jia's reservations subsided. Whoever this man was, he clearly knew her situation. And his name, or rather initial, was programmed into the phone Rick had given her. "What do you have?"

"A lot of suspicions," Ghost said. "Chesah has been traveling to Malacca at least once a month, and she's flown to Phuket four times in the past five months."

Jia narrowed her eyes. "We both travel a lot for work. Since both of those locations are vacation spots, it would make sense to meet potential informants there as a way to cultivate relationships."

"That's true, but when I ran her travel patterns against known foreign intelligence operatives, I got a partial hit."

"What?" She straightened in her seat and had to remind herself to keep her voice down. She amended her question and asked, "Who?"

"Wei Guo. He operates out of Hong Kong, but we've identified him as Chinese intelligence. If I'm right, Guo is Chesah's handler, and she's been feeding information to the Chinese government through him."

Then Chesah really was a spy. But how did she go from spying for the Chinese to feeding intel to Brandt? Unless someone in the Chinese government supported his plans.

A couple passed by. Jia did a quick look around at the few other people in the lobby. "You think that organization could be involved?"

"I'm not sure the Chinese have goals that line up with Brandt's, especially not after taking the blame for COVID-19."

"Then how are you connecting the dots?" Jia asked, careful to make sure her words wouldn't give away the true nature of her conversation.

"My guess is that either Wei Guo is involved, or Brandt paid Chesah's handler to coerce her to help with a side job," Ghost said.

"Chesah is too smart to be tricked into doing something like this. It's more likely he was either her middle man brokering a deal to have her feed information or she is working for more than one person," Jia said, still trying to wrap her mind around the fact that her coworker had been working against her. "Any clues on what might have motivated her to get involved in the first place?"

"I have a few thoughts. I'm sending a link to your phone with our initial psych profile. It might help with your interrogation."

"Thanks." Jia started to end the call, but when someone walked out of the restaurant with a takeaway bag, she asked, "Hey, do you by chance know what our mutual friend can eat here at the hotel restaurant?" She gave the name of the hotel in case Ghost didn't already have that information. "I'm picking up food, but he's planning on sticking with protein bars." When Ghost didn't immediately respond, she added, "I'm aware of the dietary issues."

"Do you have an order number already?"

"Yeah." Jia read it to him.

"I'll see if the kitchen is up to standard," Ghost said. "If it is, I'll put in an order for him and have it added to yours."

"You can do that?" Jia asked.

"Yes, it's not a problem." He ended the call, and Jia's phone chimed with an incoming message.

She clicked on the link Ghost had sent her, a detailed report popping onto her screen. She checked the time. Another fifteen minutes until her food would be ready. Might as well start reading now. And maybe something in this report would explain why a woman who had pledged to protect American citizens had been meeting with a Chinese intelligence officer and was also helping a man who planned to kill countless innocent people, both in the US and around the world.

CHAPTER 30

Chesah still wasn't talking, but now Erik had a new weapon: the psych profiles Troy had sent him on her. Troy had included one on Dylan as well, but it hadn't taken long to determine that Dylan's file supported Erik's and Jia's belief that the man was telling the truth.

He skimmed through Chesah's background, immediately seeing the similarities between her skills and Jia's. Both women were black belts in their chosen forms of martial arts, both fluent in multiple languages, both graduates of the CIA's career training program.

Erik turned to his laptop and dug a little deeper. After he retrieved Chesah's training records from the farm, he pulled up Jia's and split the screen so he could see them side by side.

Jia and Chesah had scored in the top quarter of their class in nearly every aspect. And in every category, Jia ranked slightly above Chesah—speed, shooting accuracy, tactical analysis, defensive driving. And the list went on.

Erik looked at the top of the reports, and suddenly, the competition made sense. Jia and Chesah had trained together.

With this new tidbit of information, Erik looked up from his laptop. "So, Chesah, did this competition thing between you and Jia start before you went to the farm? Or was it at the farm when you first realized she's better than you?"

Chesah clenched her jaw.

Erik read a little further. "That must have been tough. I mean, you came from a wealthy family, you went to a better school, and you still couldn't beat Jia in anything."

Fury lit Chesah's eyes. "Shut up!"

"It's true though," Erik said calmly.

"You don't know what you're talking about."

But she was talking now, so maybe they could finally get somewhere.

"I know she scored higher in her CIA training courses than you," Erik said, hoping to needle her into sharing more than she might otherwise say. "She told me so herself."

"Of course she did." Chesah scowled.

"What I don't get is why you care." Erik turned to Dylan. "I mean, did Jia get better assignments than Chesah?"

Dylan glanced down at his hands, which were still bound in front of him. Then he looked at Erik, a glimmer of cooperation reflecting in his eyes. "It's hard to compare the two," he said. "Jia was a lot better about sharing her intel and letting us know which sources she was cultivating."

"But not Chesah?" Erik asked.

"No. It was like she was afraid someone might take credit for her work." Dylan tilted his head toward Chesah. "Then again, since we're sitting here tied up because of her, my guess is she was hiding the fact that she couldn't do the job. Maybe that's how she ended up working for Brandt."

"It wasn't just Brandt she was working for. It was the Chinese government."

"I don't know what you're talking about," Chesah said. "And I don't know who this Brandt guy is other than Jia's stories about him being some bioweapons terrorist." Chesah shook her head, her contempt obvious. "She's probably making up intel again to get more attention."

"She doesn't seem the type who cares about the attention."

"You obviously don't know her very well then."

Erik rubbed his thumb over the back of the ring on his finger before he held up his left hand. "I know her well enough to be married to her."

Chesah's eyes widened. "You married her?"

"Jia's married?" Dylan said in the same instant.

"Yes." Erik lowered his hand and did a quick analysis of the two people in front of him.

A flicker of disappointment crossed Dylan's face. As for Chesah, Erik could only describe her expression as pure shock.

"What?" Erik looked at both of them as though he couldn't understand why they were so surprised.

"When did this happen?" Dylan asked. "I didn't even know she was seeing someone."

Erik couldn't tell if he was asking the question because he really wanted to know or if he was playing along in the ruse to get more information out of Chesah. Probably both.

"We've known each other for a couple years." That was sort of true. "But we haven't been married that long."

Also true. Sort of.

Chesah narrowed her eyes and shook her head. "If you're stupid enough to marry her, you deserve whatever you've got coming to you."

"What exactly do you think I've got coming to me? Jia wasn't the one you were trying to stab in the alleyway. That was our friend here." He gestured to Dylan. "And officially, Jia isn't even in Singapore." Erik paused for a moment, pondering his last statement. "Did you know she was here?"

Chesah pressed her lips together.

He turned to Dylan. "Did you know she was here?"

"I wasn't sure where she was. I only knew that Brandt was here. My assignment was to get eyes on him and see if I could determine if he was meeting with anyone I might know."

"Someone like Jia?" Erik prodded.

Dylan hesitated a moment before nodding. "Jia's passport flagged as coming both here and Indonesia. We weren't sure where she ended up."

The door opened, and Jia walked in holding two bulging paper bags. She kicked the door closed behind her. "Did you miss me?"

"You know I did." Erik kissed her cheek before he took the bags from her and set them on the table. "Apparently, your coworkers didn't know we got married."

Jia put her hand on his chest. "Chesah was already jealous enough of me as it was. Can you imagine how she would have reacted if she knew I married someone like you?"

Before Erik could fumble for a response, Jia opened one of the paper bags and pulled out a Styrofoam container. Even though they were standing across the table from Chesah and Dylan, Jia spoke as though their two prisoners weren't present. "Did she admit to working with Brandt yet?"

"No, but I'm still not sure if she knows she was working for him or if her Chinese handler tricked her into it."

"Guo is a tricky one." Jia nodded. "I could see him pulling her into something without her knowing it was a side job to put money in his pocket."

"I thought of that too." Erik nodded.

"That has to be it," Jia said. "Otherwise, I think she would have been smart enough to leak some intel on Brandt to the CIA. That might have gotten her a promotion, even if the agency were too late to stop him."

"True." Erik put his hand on her back. "Unless she leaked the safe-house intel just so someone would eliminate her competition."

"That's sick." Jia looked up at Chesah, the truth of Erik's assumption evident on Chesah's face.

Erik had no doubt Jia saw the same thing he did. Regardless of who had been pulling Chesah's strings, part of her motivation for falling in line was to see Jia dead.

CHAPTER 31

A PAPER PLATE. SHAUN EYED the latest meal their guards had provided and the flimsy vessel it had been served on. The wooden bowls and plates they'd eaten off of before were basic, but the shift to the paper version made him wonder if their captors were worried he would turn the wooden plates into a weapon. Or maybe they no longer wanted to wash dishes.

Their guard had left their food on the floor just inside the door before closing them in again and flipping the lock.

Shaun leaned down and picked up the meal, carrying it to where Nur sat on the couch. "Looks like someone was in the mood for Indian food tonight." He held out the plate, offering her first choice of the chicken satay and naan.

Nur took a piece of naan. "What will we do if we really get out of here? We're in the middle of nowhere."

"We hide in the jungle and keep going until we find a way to reach my friends." He took a bite of chicken. The meat was tasty enough but far cooler than he would have liked.

"It could take days to find anyone," Nur said.

Judging from the private runway, it was likely that she was right. Although their guards were certainly making sure they remained in custody.

Shaun took another bite and pondered their captors' logic. "Something or someone has to be out there," Shaun finally said. "Otherwise, they wouldn't have so many guards still here watching us."

"Even if someone is out there and we do escape, who is going to believe us?"

"I'm hoping one of my friends is already telling people the truth right now," Shaun said. If Jia was still alive.

* * *

Her own coworker wanted her dead. Jia glanced out the hotel room window. She still couldn't quite wrap her mind around that detail. Was she such a horrible person that she could elicit such hatred?

Across the room, Rick spoke with the FBI liaison who had arrived to take Chesah into custody. He'd tried questioning her further, but once it had become obvious she wasn't going to share any more information, he'd made the call. Dylan rubbed his hand over his wrist, the restraints now gone.

"Thanks for showing up when you did," Dylan said. "But next time, I think I'd rather skip the zip ties."

"Noted," Rick said.

"Let's go," Special Agent Graymore said, escorting both Chesah and Dylan out of the room.

Jia folded her arms over her chest, automatically taking a defensive posture against the events of the day.

As soon as the other three left, Rick closed the door. "Are you okay?"

Her body trembled, likely from a combination of adrenaline and hunger. "It's a little unsettling to think that someone you respected and considered a colleague wanted you dead."

"She obviously has some issues." He closed the distance between them and put his hands on her shoulders, the offer of a hug laid out before her.

Jia opened her arms and stepped into his embrace. She rested her head against his shoulder, comforted by the way he held her. Tears tried to surface, but she blinked them back.

"You can't take responsibility for what others do," Rick said softly. "None of this is your fault."

He was right. Logically, she knew that, but the unsettled emotions still churned inside her.

After a moment, she eased back. "Sorry. I'm not usually the needy sort."

"That wasn't needy." His gaze remained on her for a moment before he gestured to the food on the table that neither of them had touched. "You should eat something before we head back to our apartment."

"Maybe we should stay here tonight." Jia looked out at the bank of windows. "I'm not sure I want to show up at our building this late at night. We're too likely to be noticed by the wrong people."

Rather than respond, Rick pulled out his phone and tapped on the screen. After a moment, he grabbed the bags of food. "Come on. We're switching rooms."

"Do you have to go back down to the desk to do that?"

"No." He led the way into the hall and then to the stairwell. They went up one flight and down the hall to where Rick used his phone to unlock the door of a room that appeared to be right above the one they'd been in a moment ago.

He pushed the door open and waited for her to pass through before following her inside. Sure enough, the suite was identical to the one below them.

Rick set the food down. "Come on. Let's eat."

Jia pulled out the food she'd ordered for herself and carried it to the microwave in the adjoining kitchenette. After she put it in to warm, she asked, "Do you want me to warm yours up too?"

"That's okay. I can just eat my bar."

Jia shook her head. "You should eat this. I'm not sure what it is, but your friend ordered it for you," she said. "Hopefully, he knows what you like."

"My friend ordered it?" Rick opened the second bag.

"Yeah. I'd already put the order in for the rest of us when he called. When I asked if he could help me find something gluten-free for you, he said he would make sure the kitchen would be up to your standards so he could call it in and have it added to my order."

The microwave beeped.

Rick opened his takeout container and nodded his approval. "Thanks for this. It looks good."

"What is it?" Jia asked.

"It looks like rice noodles with pork and veggies." He sniffed it. "It smells good."

He retrieved his gluten sensor from his bag and proceeded to test the food to ensure it didn't have any gluten.

"What's that?"

"It's a device that tests for gluten." He looked up at her. "I don't use it unless I'm alone so people don't know about my dietary issues."

"But I'm here." She smiled at him hopefully. "Does that mean you trust me?"

"I do trust you."

As he heated his food, the sensor finished, and it appeared that it had indicated the dish was safe for him. They both sat at the table to eat.

Jia plucked a shrimp up with her chopsticks. "Do you think Chesah was really working for the Chinese instead of Brandt?"

"Honestly, I think she was working for both, but I have no clue if she contracted out to Brandt or if her handler did," Erik said.

"I think she did," Jia said.

Erik finished chewing a bite. "What makes you think that?"

"Because I acted so quickly on the intel about Brandt, I don't think she would have had time to funnel it to the Chinese and then have Brandt coincidentally figure out that he would need intel to try to catch me." Jia shook her head. "The only thing that makes sense is if Chesah saw the message that I was heading to a safe house, and then she fed the intel to Brandt as a way to get rid of me."

"But how would she have known how to get in touch with Brandt?"

"I had his suspected contact info in my files." Maybe Jia should have been more careful about the size of her circle of need to know at the office. "If Chesah managed to access my intel, she could have simply called him."

"That might give us exactly what we need."

"How so?" Jia asked.

"If we can pull the phone records, that could give us the phone number she was using to call Brandt and tell us if it was a single contact or multiple."

"And if we can prove she was behind the leak, we can bring the agency in on our hunt for Brandt."

Erik furrowed his brow. "Yeah, I guess we can."

CHAPTER 32

ERIK SHOULD HAVE BEEN RELIEVED that Jia would be able to work with her own agency again. But he wasn't. Instead, he found himself wishing their time together would continue.

He never should have kissed her. Okay, so maybe that decision had protected Jia from being seen, but he shouldn't have let his guard slip. He shouldn't have let himself enjoy it so much.

Jia stood and threw away her food container. "You're quiet all of a sudden."

"Just thinking." He took a drink of his water bottle and tossed it into the recycling before clearing off the rest of the table.

When he turned, Jia was standing behind him, only a meter of space between them. "What are you thinking about?"

"About how it won't be long before you won't need me anymore." He should step back so he wouldn't be tempted to fall into the illusion of being a couple. But he didn't.

She narrowed her eyes as though trying to read his thoughts. "You aren't getting rid of me that easily. We still don't have Shaun back, and we have no idea where Brandt plans to distribute his virus."

"Yes, but the CIA has people who can help with that," Erik said. "My job is to help people when they get in over their heads."

"In case you haven't noticed, I'm definitely in over my head." She put her hand on his arm. "And we've already established our cover as a married couple with the residents at Brandt's complex."

"Not just with them." Erik cast an apologetic look at Jia. "I hope it won't be too awkward when Dylan learns that we aren't really married."

"You're assuming I'm going to admit to it." Her hand trailed down his arm until her fingers laced with Erik's.

The familiar butterflies took flight in his stomach, and he had to remind himself that this wasn't real. But what if it could be? Was it possible Jia would ever consider a future with someone like him, someone who was destined to live in the shadows?

She rubbed her thumb over the back of his hand. "Dylan isn't the sort of guy I would ever date. It's easier if I don't have to tell him why I don't want to go out with him."

Then Erik had been right about Dylan being interested in Jia. He squeezed her hand, his eyes fixed on hers. "What kind of guy would you want to go out with?"

Her next word came out breathless. "You."

"Someone like me?"

"Not someone like you. Just you."

Me? Erik's chest lurched, his wonder overshadowing all the challenges he'd faced to get to this point.

Unable to resist, he released her and lifted both hands to frame her face. Her eyes darkened as though challenging him to take the next step, as though daring him to walk into something real.

Unwilling to resist, he leaned down and kissed her. He thought he knew what to expect, but he was wrong. The kiss might have had the same dreamy effect as before, but this wasn't part of a cover story. This was real.

He slid his arms around her waist, drawing her closer until he could feel her heart thudding against his chest. Jia slipped her arms around his neck, her fingers brushing across the skin there and sending a shiver through him.

Joy burst in a bubble that enveloped them both, a vibrant rainbow of colors filling his thoughts. Right now, he didn't have anything else to worry about besides needing to be in Jia's arms.

When he finally pulled back, he leaned his forehead against hers. "Wow."

Her lips lifted into a smile. "You're acting like you've never kissed me before."

"Before it was Rick kissing Jingyi." He straightened so he could see her better. "This was the first time it was really us."

She slid her hands from his neck to his shoulders. "But it isn't really us. Not quite."

"What do you mean?"

"I still don't know your real name." She let out a little sigh. "But I can understand if you can't tell me."

He wanted to. "You know this is going to get complicated with us, right?"

She shook her head. "It only has to be as complicated as we let it." She kept her gaze fixed on his. "I'm intelligence. You're intelligence, even if I can't know exactly who you work for. We both know there are some things that are need to know."

"And if I tell you my name is one of them?"

Disappointment flickered on her face. "Then I guess I'll have to keep calling you Rick."

* * *

Jia stood by the hotel room window and tried to focus on the positives. She and Rick had found the person responsible for leaking the safe-house location. At least, she was pretty sure they had. Her developing feelings for Rick weren't one-sided, a possibility that had left her unsettled. And they'd narrowed down where Brandt was staying.

She only wished Rick would tell her his real name. It shouldn't bother her that he hadn't. Logically, she understood how highly classified his mere existence must be. But she wanted him to trust her, and sharing his real name would prove that he trusted her as much as she trusted him.

But that trust was clearly still limited to the small circle of need to know that she currently didn't occupy in his life.

At the moment, Rick was behind closed doors in his bedroom. He'd disappeared into the private space to take a call several minutes ago, leaving her alone to process everything that had happened today.

Had it really only been earlier today when she and Rick had tracked Dylan to Little India? It felt like days ago.

Jia stifled a yawn and crossed to the couch. She should go into the second bedroom, but she didn't want to lock herself away from Rick right now, especially if he had more information to share.

She lowered onto the couch and stretched out her legs, using the arm as a pillow. Her body relaxed, and her eyes fluttered closed. The thought that she should stay awake until Rick finished his phone call flitted through her mind as she drifted off into that blissful state of semiconsciousness.

The bedroom door opened, and Jia jolted.

Rick emerged, apology on his face. "Sorry. I didn't mean to wake you."

"It's okay. It's just been a long day."

"A very long day." He sat on the chair to her right, his expression serious.

Jia sat up. "Is everything all right?"

"By chance, are you missing a KA-BAR knife like the one we took from Chesah?"

"I have one, but I left it in my apartment when I went to Bangkok. Why?"

"Because the FBI ran the fingerprints on the knife Chesah had in her possession."

"And?"

"And they were yours."

Her fingerprints. Jia stood, her mind racing. "You think Chesah stole my knife."

Rick nodded. "She would know when you weren't home, and someone with CIA training would know how to bypass any security system you have in place."

Understanding crested. "She was going to kill Dylan and make it look like I did it."

Again, Rick nodded. "It was nearly a perfect plan: She sets you up. She gets rid of the only other operative who's been close to Brandt. And you get blamed for creating an elaborate story of being followed to the safe house as a way to throw everyone off your trail."

"And I'd be arrested for espionage and blamed for everything Chesah did." Jia paced to the window, the possibilities and what-ifs flooding through her. Had it not been for Rick, she would have been blamed for everything, and Dylan would be dead. And no one would know how dangerous Brandt really was.

That thought simmered for a moment before she turned back to face Rick. "Dylan checked out the condo complex, but that was in my source notes. The station chief would have had that information, too, so why would Chesah see Dylan as a threat?"

"Unless he knows something else, maybe something we haven't found yet."

Jia's heartbeat quickened at the thought. "If that's true, someone could try to take him out again."

Rick pulled out his cell phone and dialed. The faint ring carried into the room, but the call went unanswered. "Agent Graymore must be driving."

"I'm sure he has a partner with him," Jia said.

"Yeah, but we know Chesah isn't working alone."

Jia grabbed her purse and headed for the door. "Come on. We need to make sure they get to the embassy."

Rick tapped on his cell phone screen. "Our ride will be here in two minutes."

"They have a fifteen-minute head start on us."

Rick rushed into the hall. "I know."

CHAPTER 33

Neither of the FBI agents was answering their phone. Dylan wasn't either.

Erik hurried outside with Jia to where a policeman waited beside his car. Erik hated involving the local authorities, but tonight, he didn't have a choice. If the lack of communication was any indication, the FBI agents and Dylan were all in danger.

Erik flashed his fake credentials and yanked open both passenger doors.

Surprise lit Jia's face, but she slid into the back seat without comment.

Erik closed her door for her and took the front.

Jia leaned forward and asked, "How are we going to find them?"

"We're going to call in some help." Erik dialed Troy's number.

"Tell me about the girl," Troy said in greeting.

Erik didn't question why Troy would think to ask about Jia. "No time. I need you to track down the car Special Agent Graymore is driving. He's not answering his phone."

"On it."

The police officer took his spot behind the wheel. "Where to?"

"I'm trying to locate our people now," Erik said.

After a moment, Troy came back on the line. "They're on River Valley Road, headed west. Based on their speed, it looks like they're caught in traffic."

Erik gave instructions to the officer on their intended destination before he spoke to Troy again. "I need a way to slow them down. Since no one is answering their phones, they might have a signal jammer interfering."

"Didn't you search Chesah before you let them take her?"

"Yes, but that doesn't mean someone didn't attach one to the car when the agents came upstairs to get her."

"Let me see if I can override the street lights," Troy said. "That might give you time to catch up."

"If you can, try to push them off course," Erik said. "I don't want to chance someone trying to rescue our suspect."

"Got it."

"And send me the link to the GPS tracker."

Troy didn't respond, but a few seconds later, Erik's phone chimed, and the link popped up. Erik clicked on it and connected the mapping app into the onboard navigation system.

"We're trying to get to that car," he told the policeman.

The officer nodded.

Erik checked the time calculation for their intercept route. Twelve minutes. Twelve minutes too long.

Troy must have shared Erik's sense of urgency. "We need to call Kade. He's better at hacking systems than the rest of us. If anyone can get your target off course, it's him."

"True. Let me see if I can pull him in on a conference call so you can both help me." Erik tried to dial in Kade, but the call failed. With no time to deal with phone issues, he opted for a different solution. "Put the link on the message board for him." Erik swiveled in his seat so he could see Jia. "I need you to pull up K in the favorites list on your phone. Tell him what's going on and to check the message board for details."

Jia nodded and dialed her cell.

Trusting Jia to do what he asked, Erik turned his attention back to Troy. "Anything?"

"The chief of station handed the Brandt case off to Dylan after Shaun went missing and Jia was listed on leave."

"And? Can you track his movements? Or are there any new notes in there?"

"Looks like a meeting with Jia's source. The notes aren't clear, but it appears that he was looking into connections between Brandt and a medical researcher from Germany."

"A partner, maybe?"

"That would be my guess," Troy said. "Like I said, his notes are pretty cryptic, but it looks more like someone went in and redacted part of it rather than him code talking. If that station really does have a mole, it's possible he reported something that put him on a hit list."

"That's what I'm worried about." And the only way to know what information was missing would be to get to Dylan before Brandt did.

* * *

Jia held her phone to her ear as the ghost known as K on her phone continued to give her directions to help them intercept the FBI's vehicle. She hadn't needed to hear both sides of Rick's conversation to understand the gravity of the situation. Dylan knew something, and whatever it was, Chesah, or someone she worked for, considered it worth killing for.

The man on the other end of her call spoke in clipped tones and short, efficient phrases. "Tell the cop to take the next left."

Jia leaned forward and passed on the message. The police officer changed lanes and did as he was asked.

She wasn't sure how the guardians had solicited the help of the local authorities, but right now, it didn't matter. All she could think about was that Shaun was still missing, and she wasn't about to lose another colleague to Brandt. Dylan might not have a wife like Shaun did, but he certainly deserved to live his future. And if they didn't reach Dylan in time, he might very well lose that opportunity.

Jia checked the navigation screen on the center console. Two minutes until intercept.

Their target slowed to a stop, no doubt because the ghost on the other side of the phone overrode yet another stoplight. Traffic was already snarled in this part of the city, and Jia suspected it would continue to worsen until the guardians stopped messing with the lights.

The police officer came to a crowded intersection and hit his siren once to gain access to the street beyond the dozens of cars blocking them.

Jia studied the map again. Then she spoke into the phone. "Can you switch the light at the next intersection? I think if we can block them there, Rick and I can reach them on foot."

"I can turn it early, but that's still half a kilometer from you."

Jia looked down at the running shoes on her feet. "That's not a problem." She checked their position before she put her hand on Rick's shoulder. "I say we catch them on foot. It'll be faster."

Rick debated a fraction of a second before he spoke to the policeman. "Let us out up here and then see if you can meet up with us at . . ." He trailed off.

"The intersection of Devonshire and Exeter," Jia finished for him.

The man behind the wheel nodded and pulled over when he reached the intersection. With their route already memorized, Jia jumped out of the car and hurried down the perpendicular street. "This way."

CHAPTER 34

Erik's lungs burned as he sprinted beside Jia, both of them weaving through cars and pedestrians. The traffic had turned into a complete nightmare, even worse than normal for seven o'clock on a weeknight. His consolation was that whoever Chesah had working with her would be just as affected by the traffic jams as they were. He just hoped Chesah's allies hadn't already made their move.

He shook that thought away. The car was still moving. If they'd already been intercepted, the likelihood was that the vehicle would be parked somewhere on the side of the road.

Jia took a right, cutting through a side street that wasn't nearly as well-lit as the one they'd turned off of. Shops that had already closed for the night, a bakery—also closed. The pedestrian traffic was nonexistent, but the cars in the street were bumper-to-bumper.

Jia picked up her pace, and Rick timed his steps with hers. He'd seen her aptitude scores, but he hadn't expected that someone who was a good six inches shorter than he would be this quick.

"They should be around the next turn," Jia puffed out.

Erik resisted the urge to pull his weapon. That would draw far too much attention in this city known for its strict laws and zero tolerance for violence. But violence would occur on these streets tonight, and Erik was determined to make sure it didn't spill beyond the people trying to cause it.

They turned the corner, and the SUV from the embassy came into view a half dozen cars in front of them.

"There they are!" Jia gestured with a tilt of her chin.

Erik did a quick check of the area. At first glance, everything seemed normal, except for the heavy traffic. Then he caught sight of two men approaching from the other direction, two men with guns beneath their T-shirts.

Erik put his hand on Jia's arm to slow her pace to a walk. "Got two."

"One of them was at the lab." Jia spoke the words as one of them zeroed in on her and pointed.

"We've been made." Erik reached for his gun in the same moment the two men reached for their weapons.

"Everyone get down!" Jia shouted in English.

Erik repeated the command in Mandarin.

Both of them darted behind the nearest car as bullets hit the vehicle's rear bumper.

A woman inside the car screamed, the noise muffled by the windows. Footsteps pounded against the sidewalks. Someone on the street shouted.

Up ahead, Agent Graymore opened the passenger-side door.

"Stay with the prisoner!" Erik shouted.

The agent either didn't understand him, or he ignored him.

"We can't communicate with them as long as the jammer is in effect," Jia said. "I'll work my way up to the FBI's car. You cover me."

She was offering to take the more dangerous role. Erik didn't like that one bit. "How about you cover me?" Erik suggested.

Jia shook her head. "No. They're more likely to try to make a move if they see me. You'll have a better chance of picking them off."

"I don't like it."

"Me neither." She pointed her weapon at the ground and took a step toward the center of the street. "But it's our best option."

Tactically, her plan made sense. She was smaller, more likely to stay out of sight, and the most likely to draw fire.

No, he really didn't like this. He put his hand on her shoulder. "Be careful."

She nodded. Then she slipped around the far side of the car and disappeared from sight.

* * *

Jia was crazy to do this. Three times, gunfire had sparked around her, and three times, Rick had been forced to lay down cover fire for her.

She was halfway to her target, only three cars remaining between her and the FBI's SUV.

Agent Graymore crouched beside the vehicle, his door open, his weapon drawn.

Jia reached the front of the car currently shielding her from the gunmen's bullets and still had a full three meters in front of her to reach the car.

A siren rang out in the distance, likely from the police officer who had driven them here.

Jia peeked over the hood and spotted one of the two men opposing her. Rather than try to close in on the FBI vehicle, he'd tipped over a thick, wooden table on the side of the street to use for cover. Jia doubted the owner of the café the table belonged to would be happy to find bullet holes in it when he returned to work tomorrow.

The pedestrians on the street had disappeared, and Jia hoped they all remained uninjured. The lack of foot traffic also meant she could hear the movement of the other agents nearby.

The cars on the street had already gone into conservation mode, and the sounds of whimpers and frantic voices were the only noises competing against the occasional gunfire. But as hard as she strained, she couldn't sense where the second gunman had hidden.

Using hand gestures, she signaled the FBI agent to cover her.

He nodded.

She counted to three, lowering her fingers with each number. As soon as she fisted her hand, the agent popped up and fired in the direction of the man behind the table.

Jia sprinted forward.

More gunshots sounded, and this time, Agent Graymore's body jerked as he took a round in the chest.

He dropped to the pavement, and Jia sprinted the rest of the way to reach his side, more bullets sparking through the air.

Jia skidded to a stop beside the fallen agent. She took a quick glance across the street to where the gunman had taken cover, surprised that he hadn't made a move to come closer to the vehicle to try to liberate Chesah. Focusing on Graymore, Jia asked, "How bad is it?"

He winced in pain, and his voice was strained when he spoke. "I took one in the vest."

Judging from the man's expression, Jia suspected he'd broken a rib or two, but that was far better than the alternative. She ducked and searched beneath the car. She quickly spotted the jamming device wedged beneath the vehicle beside the rear passenger tire.

"What is it?" Agent Graymore asked, trying to adjust his body so he could see what had pulled her attention from the current standoff.

"A jamming device." Jia pulled her phone from her pocket and turned on the flashlight. She lay on the ground to get a better look. Then she spotted the glowing red numbers. "Oh no," she whispered.

"What?"

"It's a bomb."

CHAPTER 35

SOMETHING HAD CHANGED, AND ERIK wasn't sure what to think. The gunman behind the table hadn't tried shooting for nearly a minute, and the second gunman had disappeared from sight between the cars in the oncoming traffic. Why hadn't they made their move yet?

Jia's frantic voice carried to him. "Get everyone out!"

Erik glanced in her direction, surprised when she yanked open the back door of the FBI vehicle and pulled Dylan from it.

"Cover me!" the agent driving shouted.

Erik popped up and fired two shots, one at the man behind the table and the other at the ground near where the other shooter had hidden. Neither man attempted to fire back, nor did they leave their hiding places.

The agent in the driver's seat climbed out and reached for the back door. He had it halfway open when the person in the back seat kicked both legs at the door and sent the agent stumbling backward.

Chesah rushed out of the car. Before the agent had a chance to recover, both gunmen emerged from their hiding places and laid down cover fire.

Chesah ran between them until she reached a BMW, the female driver screaming as Chesah ducked out of sight.

Erik sprinted forward as the gunman behind the table abandoned his spot and retreated. Erik fired twice more, one of the bullets causing the man to break his stride.

Jia ran toward Erik. "There's a bomb beneath the car. I don't have the tools to defuse it."

Now everyone's behavior made sense. The gunmen weren't coming closer because they didn't want to be in the blast zone.

Erik tried to open the door of the closest car. When it held firm, clearly locked, he yelled and pointed away from the FBI's vehicle. "Get out and run that way. There's a bomb."

The couple inside the vehicle didn't have to be told twice.

Jia, Dylan, and the two FBI agents had already started warning the passengers closest to the vehicle, Jia and Dylan working together as the agents warned the drivers and passengers in the cars on the other side of the SUV.

Erik warned the next vehicle, his gaze straying to where Chesah had disappeared a moment ago. She and her rescuers were nowhere to be seen. And with Chesah's escape successful, Erik couldn't help but wonder who the bomb was intended to kill and if Chesah would have been one of the casualties if Brandt's men had failed to free her.

* * *

The countdown continued in Jia's head, the three minutes on the timer going far too quickly. Working together, she, Dylan, Rick, and the two agents had cleared more than two dozen vehicles, the perimeter now secure around the SUV that would blow up in the next fifteen seconds.

The policeman who had driven them from the hotel had arrived in time to help with crowd control, sending the civilians to safety while ensuring no one else approached the danger zone.

Rick reached her side and took her hand as they ducked behind a car a block away from where the SUV currently remained in the middle of the street, surrounded by abandoned vehicles. Dylan followed and took cover on the other side of Rick.

"How long?" Rick asked.

"Ten seconds. Maybe less." Jia put her hands over her ears.

Rick and Dylan did the same.

Ten seconds passed. Fifteen. Thirty.

Jia turned to face Rick, the confusion in his expression matching her own.

Keeping his hands in place over his ears, he peeked around the edge of the car. Then he lowered his hands.

Jia caught the scent of a chemical burning. She lowered her hands as well and straightened enough to see the SUV.

Smoke poured out from beneath the vehicle, creating a thick haze that billowed outward.

Jia's jaw dropped, and her embarrassment crested. "A smoke bomb?"

"Let's hope that's all it was," Rick said.

"I can't believe this." Jia replayed the last few minutes. "We panicked all those people for nothing."

"It wasn't for nothing," Rick insisted. "We erred on the side of caution."

"That's a nice way of looking at it." Jia looked past him to Dylan. "Why would Chesah or Brandt want you dead?"

Dylan's eyes widened slightly. "This wasn't intended to be a rescue, was it?"

Rick shook his head. "We don't think so. We think this was their attempt to target you."

An oversized police vehicle arrived, using the sidewalks to pass some of the abandoned cars.

"It looks like the bomb squad is here," Rick said. "The FBI agents can talk to the local police. Let's get you back to the hotel, and we can decide on our next move."

Dylan cocked an eyebrow. "You aren't going to zip-tie my hands again, are you?"

"I think we can bypass that this time," Rick said. "But let's leave here before the police want to haul us downtown to get our statements." He gestured for Dylan and Jia to follow him.

Dylan rubbed his wrists. "Gladly."

* * *

Erik waited for Dylan to sit in the hotel living room before taking the spot beside Jia on the couch.

"What did you find out after I went to Thailand?" Jia asked without preamble.

"I did a lot of research, but if someone wants me dead, my guess is that the information your source gave me was more accurate than I thought."

"What did she tell you?" Jia asked.

"She received a photo in the mail from Singapore. No return address. No letter. Just a photo." Dylan leaned forward and rested his elbows on his thighs. "The postmark was the same day she last spoke to her sister."

"What was the photo of?" Erik asked. "There's no record of it in your report."

Dylan's jaw dropped, and surprise lit his expression. "You read my report?"

"Yeah." Erik tapped a finger restlessly on his leg. "And it looked like someone went through and pulled pieces out of it."

"So what was in the photo?" Jia asked, circling back to Erik's question.

"It was of two men, Brandt and another man," Dylan said. "I ran the other man's image through facial recognition. His name is Kenneth Ackerman."

"Who is he?" Jia asked.

"He's a medical researcher who specializes in infectious diseases."

Erik's blood ran cold. "Exactly the sort of person Brandt would need to develop his virus." Exactly the sort of person whose research could kill Erik and millions of others.

"Who else knew about your scientist?"

"Only whoever read my report. I got the intel on Friday afternoon, so most everyone had gone home for the weekend, but I messaged the chief of station to make sure she knew I'd made progress."

"I wonder how Chesah found out about it," Jia said.

"She was probably monitoring everything she could for Brandt," Erik said.

"I still can't figure out how she ended up working for him." Dylan gripped the arms of the chair he currently occupied. "When you questioned her, it sounded like she was in league with the Chinese."

"I think she is," Erik said, speculating on what might cause someone to deliberately share intel. "My guess is that when she realized Jia's case was tied to Brandt and his deep pockets, she saw an opportunity she couldn't resist."

"Especially since it would help her get rid of me," Jia said, clearly still shaken by that fact.

Erik couldn't deny he was shaken by it as well, especially now that Chesah was on the loose. "Is there any chance Chesah knows that Jia and I are staying in Brandt's building?"

"I doubt it," Dylan said. "I only stumbled across you because I followed Brandt into Singapore and was hoping to stake out the place."

Erik's interest heightened. "Wait. You followed Brandt into the country?"

Jia leaned forward. "From where?"

"Malacca. Why?"

"Because we still haven't found Shaun," Jia said. "We're hoping wherever Brandt came from is where Shaun is now."

Dylan looked at Erik. "You can access my CIA reports from here?"

"I can, but my laptop is back at the apartment."

"Then maybe we should spend the night there. That way I can show you everything I have from when Brandt was in Malaysia."

Erik checked his watch. "It's already almost midnight, and our apartment is bugged, which makes it hard to talk there. I'll have one of my colleagues start looking at the photos and pull copies in case anyone tries to redact any more of your reports."

He turned to Jia. "You're exhausted, and the hotel is closer than our apartment. We can go back there, and I can get Dylan a room next to our suite. That way, we can all get a good night's sleep. Then tomorrow, we'll tackle finding Shaun and Chesah."

"And stopping Brandt," Jia said.

Erik nodded. "That too."

CHAPTER 36

JIA HADN'T THOUGHT THROUGH WHAT it would be like to return to the apartment with Dylan in tow. Even with the listening devices in place, the space had become sort of an oasis from the world without her even realizing it.

Now she sat in the living room with Rick and Dylan, all the curtains closed and the images from Dylan's reports displayed on the television screen on the wall. The listening device in the living room had been carefully moved into the master bedroom closet, and Rick had set up his spare laptop to play a movie to provide background noise to mask their conversation in the living room.

"Most of these photos are from the port," Rick said. "How did you track him there?"

"His yacht was spotted when it docked, and the passport for Brandt's boat captain was scanned when he came ashore," Dylan said.

"You were watching for the boat captain?" Jia asked. "That was good thinking."

"I thought you'd approve."

Rick cast a curious glance at her.

"I trained Dylan when he first arrived in the country," Jia explained before focusing again on the photos on the screen.

Rick clicked to the next one—a mansion she'd seen before when she'd been surveilling a drug trafficker almost a year ago. Jia stood. "Why did you take this photo?"

"A bunch of cargo was brought there before the yacht continued to Batam," Dylan said. "Based on the size of the crates, it looked like furniture."

Rick pushed to his feet. "If Shaun is still alive, they could have put him in a crate to transport him. No one would think twice if something that size was being taken to a house that big."

She prayed Shaun was still alive. "Did you see Brandt?"

"No, but if you look here, you can see a small airfield." Dylan pointed at the edge of the screen. "That's new since the last time this place was photographed."

"So it's possible Brandt could have come by plane or by boat," Rick said.

Or more likely, by using a combination of both to bypass passport controls in certain locations. "The government took over the mansion almost a year ago after they busted the drug dealer operating out of there. Who owns it now?" Jia asked.

"I'm not sure," Dylan said.

"I'll check." Rick grabbed his laptop and sat back on the couch. "It's a company out of Bulgaria."

"And who owns the company?" Jia asked. With all of Brandt's holdings, it was entirely possible he had companies operating out of multiple countries, not just the United States and Singapore.

"It's one shell after another." Rick kept hitting keys.

Jia paced across the room, her mind whirling. "Dylan, you said you didn't ever see Brandt at the mansion?"

"No, but the cars going in and out of there had tinted windows. I couldn't tell who was in the back seats."

"The mansion is outside the city limits, and it has a private dock. Once they cleared the initial check by the coastal patrol, anyone who came in by boat would be free to come and go as long as they weren't pulled over by the police."

"Same thing with a plane," Dylan said. "With the private airstrip, people could come and go without being seen or their passports scanned."

Rick looked up from his laptop. "I've got it. The person running the parent company is Kenneth Ackerman."

"He's the one in the photo with Brandt." She gestured to the screen again. "This could be where they're holding Shaun."

Rick turned back to Dylan. "You said the yacht continued on to Batam. Is it possible Shaun could have been taken there?"

"I don't think so, not unless he was kept on the yacht," Dylan said. "The yacht didn't dock until the day it sailed back to Singapore."

"So it's possible the yacht was there to pick someone up rather than drop someone off?" Jia asked.

Rick gestured to Dylan. "I need everything you know about that mansion."

"The floor plan should be included in the government seizure documents," Dylan said. "Do you think we can get the military to send someone in after Shaun?"

Rick nodded. "I think I can convince them."

"How?" Dylan asked.

"Sometimes it pays to know the right people." He stood up again. "I need to make a call. Get me whatever you can on that mansion and everything that's happened there since Shaun went missing."

"Will do," Dylan said.

Rick disappeared into the office, and Jia watched him go.

"You okay?" Dylan asked.

"Yeah." Except for the fact that she was developing feelings for a man who was a complete mystery.

* * *

Erik closed the office door to ensure that the listening devices wouldn't pick up his conversation. He was so ready to have those gone.

He dialed the number for the liaison officer who connected the guardians and the president. A quick calculation told him it was already ten at night in Washington, DC, but this couldn't wait. And with the evidence they'd found, it was unlikely anyone within the military would act without the president's authority anyway. Might as well jump straight to the top. As a guardian, he had that privilege.

The phone rang four times before Vanessa's voice came over the line. "Have you found Shaun Fleming?"

Typical Vanessa. More often than not, she guessed at the reason for his call before he could get a word out. "I think so. He's possibly in Malaysia." Erik proceeded to give her the details and the information he and his current partners had uncovered so far.

When he finished, Vanessa said, "The president will likely need more intel before he gives the go order, but the Saint Squad is still in the area."

"How long until they can be mission ready?" Erik asked.

"As soon as we have enough intel to send them in with an achievable mission plan, they'll be ready. Best guess, twelve hours or so."

"I'll put everything we've got into the guardian database," Erik said. "The sooner we can get Shaun out of there, the better."

"Agreed." Vanessa paused. "Do you have any indication of whether he's still alive?"

"No, but we haven't had any indication that he's not either."

"I'll inform the president and let you know as soon as I have any updates."

"Thanks, Vanessa." Erik hung up and returned to the living room.

"Any luck?" Jia asked.

"Things are in motion," Erik said. He wasn't about to announce that a squad of SEALs would soon be prepping for a rescue mission. At least, not yet.

He grabbed his laptop and uploaded the photos and latest information to the guardian database. Once he finished that, he turned to Jia. "Remember when you were saying that you wanted a dog?"

"Yeah, why?"

"I have an idea, and I think a dog could help us get what we need."

"A dog?" Dylan looked from Erik to Jia. "How can a dog help?"

"If we can find the right one, it will be the perfect distraction."

CHAPTER 37

Jia would have preferred to research what was required to buy a dog in Singapore, but instead, she'd ended up on a secure conference call with her chief of station.

Rick had chosen to sit in front of her, behind the laptop she was currently using, no doubt to stay out of view. Dylan had taken the spot on the couch beside Jia.

"The agent who was shot last night is in stable condition, but we haven't found Chesah yet," Andrea said.

They already had the update on the injured agent, thanks to Rick's contacts, but Jia had hoped for good news about Chesah.

"How is it possible that she managed to disappear?" Dylan asked. "There are CCT cameras everywhere in this city."

"The local authorities traced her and the men with her as far as Little India. From there, they dropped out of sight."

Jia blew out a frustrated breath. "Little India is becoming our nemesis."

"Unfortunately, the camera coverage is lacking there," Andrea said. "Most likely, they had a car stashed somewhere nearby or had someone drive them out of there."

"It would have had to be some sort of delivery van or the cameras would have picked them up through the windows," Jia said.

"The Singapore chief of station had the same thought. He's already working with the locals to lock down borders to help them search."

"With how effectively Chesah's rescuers played us to get her back, I'm not holding my breath on them being found."

"Me neither," Andrea said. "I'm also not thrilled with the two of you remaining in Singapore when we know she wants both of you dead. I want you back in Malaysia as soon as possible."

Jia should have anticipated being recalled to Kuala Lumpur, but the thought of going out in the city, of leaving this mission unfinished, was more than she could do. She lifted her gaze to meet Rick's before she pulled her attention back to the screen. "I can't leave."

"You can, and you will," Andrea insisted. "The FBI is arranging to have someone escort you to the border."

"The FBI is shorthanded," Jia countered. "And I'll be far more effective working from here." Before Andrea could argue, Jia asked, "What's the latest on Brandt? Is there an arrest warrant issued for him yet?"

"No, which is another reason I want you back here," Andrea said. "The local authorities don't believe our evidence is strong enough to bring Brandt in for questioning."

"Then we have to stay," Jia said.

"I agree," Dylan put in. "No one is going to get this kind of access to him."

"And if Chesah shows up?" Andrea asked. "The Singapore field office is doing what they can to track her down, but they don't have the resources or the access to stake out your building."

"We know." Jia glanced at Dylan, appreciative that he was on her side. "But with Dylan and me here, we can keep Brandt under surveillance, and we can back each other up if Chesah does show up."

"And she doesn't know that Jia was staying here in the first place," Dylan added. "That was all done off book."

"And we need to keep it off book in case Chesah still has any backdoor access."

"We all agree on that point." On the screen, Andrea tapped her finger against her chin. "I don't like it, but you win. I'll approve you both staying in Singapore, but I want regular updates."

"Understood," Jia said. "There's just one more thing."

"What's that?" Andrea asked.

"I think it would be a good idea to put in a report that Dylan was injured last night and is now in one of the local hospitals," Jia said. "It might help draw out Chesah and her friends."

"I'll see what I can do," Andrea said. "But you guys be careful."

"We will." Jia clicked on the mouse pad and ended the call.

Rick stepped forward and shut the laptop before speaking. "Now that we have your status with your employer settled, I say we dig into the background on Kenneth Ackerman and work on our plan to gain access to the apartment upstairs to plant some listening devices of our own."

"Can I just say how crazy it is that we're plotting a break-in when the person who we're trying to spy on is spying on us?" Jia asked.

"I know, but we're working around it," Rick said.

Dylan stood. "You two have already made yourselves known here, so I say you work on the break-in plan. I'll research Ackerman."

Jia nodded. "Great idea."

* * *

A sense of urgency tugged at Shaun, and he fought against it. Impatience could get him killed. It could get Nur killed. But he also knew they couldn't wait much longer. If he had his dates right, the first event where the virus was scheduled to be released would take place the day after tomorrow.

It had already been a day and a half since Nur had admitted to having the bobby pins, but their meals since then had come on paper plates or in flimsy plastic bowls that wouldn't harm anyone or anything regardless of the force put behind throwing them. Maybe their guards somehow learned Shaun and Nur planned to escape.

Shaun pulled the bobby pins from his pocket, the protective tips now removed and both of them pulled open so he could use them in tandem to pick the lock to their room. He'd already practiced on the bathroom door to make sure he could do it. Now they just had to decide when and figure out how to disable the men standing watch in the hall.

Nur had taken to sitting beside the door, listening to their guards, searching for any moment of vulnerability.

She stood now and walked quietly across the room. Leaning close, she whispered, "Every night around this time, one of the guards leaves for a few minutes. I think he may be going to get his dinner."

Shaun's heartbeat quickened. "Is there only one there now?"

"Yes, but if it's like yesterday, it won't last long enough for you to unlock the door and us to get past. But if we wait until tomorrow—"

"We can be ready." He glanced at the lock on the bathroom door. "And I have an idea of how we can get past him."

* * *

Even though Dylan was already working on the background information on Kenneth Ackerman, Erik opted to do a little digging of his own, specifically on the connection between Brandt and Ackerman.

He'd already done his research on how to adopt a dog, a prospect that had far more requirements than he'd anticipated, which had resulted in his calling Kade for assistance. He still couldn't believe he was considering a pet, but this situation required some out-of-the-box thinking. And seeing Jia's interaction with Elanora's dog had brought this solution to the forefront of his plans.

Erik pushed one of his earbuds more firmly into place while the clicking of Kade's keyboard echoed over the line. Continuing his own search, Erik conducted a comparison of the educational backgrounds for Brandt and Ackerman.

Through Erik's earbuds, Kade grumbled as he worked on the other side of the world. "I can't believe I had to stay up late to get you a dog. I live out in the middle of nowhere, surrounded by woods, and even I don't have a dog."

"Ace does," Erik countered.

"Yes, but Ace's wife is always home. And they live on an island."

Literally.

"Once your son gets older, you may have to reconsider your stance on no pets," Erik said.

"Maybe." A softness came into Kade's voice that only surfaced when he spoke of his wife and son. "What are you going to do once you get to Brandt? The dog is going to need a home somewhere."

Erik leaned against his desk and took in his office. He stayed in Taipei as often as not because he preferred his apartment there, but oddly, this apartment in Singapore already felt more like home, even with the limited privacy due to the listening devices.

He missed having a dog, and he couldn't deny the excitement inside him at the thought of owning one again, even if only for a little while. "I'm sure there's some embassy family who would love a new puppy."

The irritation in Kade's voice was back. "Are you going to make me look for the dog's new home too?"

Normally, Erik would be more than happy to delegate such a task, but not today. "Let's not worry about that quite yet."

"Just remember that when it is time to worry about it, it's going to be your problem to solve."

"I think I can manage." With Jia's help.

Erik's lips turned up in an involuntary smile, and a warmth swelled in his chest. He rather liked the thought of Jia being close, of her being part of his future in whatever way she would let him.

He finished his check of the educational backgrounds for Brandt and Ackerman. And while they hadn't gone to school together, their fields of study were eerily similar. Brandt had graduated in biology, followed by a masters in hospital administration and a PhD in genetics. Ackerman had graduated in biochemistry before continuing his study in pharmacology, followed by a PhD in biology.

Brandt had gone to school in the US, Ackerman in Germany and the UK. So where had the two men crossed paths? And how had they come to work together in such a nefarious way?

Kade interrupted his thoughts. "Okay, I uploaded all the paperwork you'll need into the pet store's system. As soon as they pull up your name, they'll see that you've already undergone all the home and medical checks needed to adopt."

"Kade, you're the best."

"I know that, but all it's getting me is a lack of sleep."

"Will you feel any better if I send you some Turkish delights?"

"You're not in Turkey."

"No, but Cas will fly through there on her way back home." Erik leaned back in his office chair. "She can pick them up and ship them for me."

"Delegating again, huh?"

Erik laughed. "Yeah, I guess I am."

"Tell Cas I like the ones with chocolate."

"I will." Erik grinned. "And thanks for your help."

"I'd say anytime, but then you'd think I meant it," Kade said. "I'm going to sleep."

"Good night," Erik said, despite the sunlight shining through the window.

"Night." Kade ended the call, and Erik pulled out his earbuds, setting them in their case to recharge.

After sending a quick text to Cas to ask for Kade's payment, Erik opened his office door. For the benefit of whoever was on the other side of the listening devices, he called out, "Hey, hon, we're all set. We can leave for the store whenever you're ready."

CHAPTER 38

She was getting a dog. Jia knew this was only temporary, but that didn't make her feel any less like a little girl about to pick out her own Christmas present.

"I can't believe you pulled this off," she said to Rick. After getting off the call with her chief of station, she'd done some more research on getting a dog in Singapore, and she'd pretty much immediately discounted the possibility. Now, here she was, driving to a pet store with her pretend husband by her side.

Rick signaled and made a left turn before responding. "You should know by now I can do anything."

"Right." Sarcasm dripped from the single word, but in truth, she was starting to think he really could do anything. Broaching a different subject, she said, "It's weird having Dylan staying with us."

"Yeah. We should probably pick up some clothes and basics for him while we're out," Rick said. "It's too risky for him to go back to his hotel."

"How are we going to explain why we're sleeping in separate rooms? He still thinks we're married."

"Easy. Just say I snore, and we sleep better in our own rooms sometimes," Rick said. "Unless you want to tell him the truth."

"The snoring excuse works," Jia said. She'd rather not deal with giving Dylan any hope of a future romantic relationship with her. "How long do you think it'll take for Chesah and her friends to show up at the hospital to silence Dylan?"

"I don't know, but it was smart of you to set a trap." He pulled to a stop at a red light and glanced at Jia.

This wasn't the first time he'd called her smart, but the simple compliment still warmed her. "It's a long shot, but it's worth a try."

"If Brandt has any way to track him there, my guess is he'll send someone in after Dylan." Rick pulled into a parking spot and turned off the car. He shifted in his seat to face her. "Are you ready?"

Jia was ready, but there was something she had to do first. She put her hand on his and leaned forward until her lips touched his.

He lifted his free hand to the back of her neck, drawing out the kiss and sending a kaleidoscope of butterflies fluttering inside her.

When the kiss ended, she fixed her gaze on him. Opting for complete honesty, she said, "I know there hasn't been an 'us' for very long, but I already miss having time with just you and me."

His expression softened, and he took her hand in his. Sincerity filled his voice when he spoke. "I know our living situation is only temporary, but I don't want this to end."

Now the butterflies took flight. Jia leaned in for another kiss. "Me neither."

For several seconds, Rick just stared at her. Then he smiled. "Come on. Let's go pick out our puppy."

* * *

Erik hadn't been prepared to fall in love in less than thirty seconds, but that was exactly what happened. His new love, a chocolate-colored mini labradoodle, had stolen his heart the moment the pet store worker had brought him into the room. And Erik wasn't the only one who had fallen hard.

Despite the dog crate in the trunk of the car, the puppy sat in Jia's lap, alternating between trying to look out the window and lick her face.

Jia shifted him in her lap to limit the puppy's kisses. "He's the cutest thing I've ever seen." She ran her hand down the puppy's back, calming him until he settled into her lap.

Erik made the turn toward Marks and Spencer, where he planned to make a quick stop to gather some clothes for Dylan. "What are we going to name him?"

"I don't know." Jia looked out the windshield before she pointed at the store they were approaching. "What about Mark? Or Spencer? This store seems to be where we always end up when we need something fast."

Erik pondered for a moment. "Mark has too many hard consonants for a dog name. I say we go with Spencer."

"Okay. Spencer it is." The puppy leaped up and licked Jia's face. She laughed. "I think he likes it."

"Good." Although how long he would keep the name or they would be able to keep him, Erik didn't know. Nor did he want to think about it. Erik pulled into the parking garage and found a spot. "Do you want to shop, or do you want me to?"

"You go. You're faster than I am, and you'll have a better idea of what Dylan needs."

"Okay. I'll be back in fifteen minutes." Erik handed her the car key. "Be right back."

"We'll be here."

Erik ran his hand over the puppy's head before he leaned in to kiss Jia. "I'll be quick." He climbed out of the car and made it all the way across the parking lot to the elevator before he glanced back and caught movement by a pillar only a half dozen cars from his.

Someone else in the parking garage shouldn't have been cause for alarm, but Erik remained in place, waiting to identify whoever had passed into his view.

The fact that whoever he'd seen remained behind the pillar heightened Erik's sense of alarm. He watched and listened and waited. Nothing happened.

His plans to shop for Dylan took a back seat to ensuring Jia's safety. He pulled out his phone and texted her. *Can you see the person behind the pillar? Six cars over to your right.*

No.

Erik texted back. *Then we may have a problem.*

* * *

Jia wanted to think Rick was being paranoid, but experience told her he likely wasn't. If he was worried, she had a reason to be too.

Was it really too much to ask for the two of them to experience a normal hour or two together?

She fought against the surge of adrenaline. It wouldn't do to have unsteady hands right now, not if she might need to use her weapon, but she couldn't ignore the tremor that worked through her body.

She set Spencer on the driver's seat and dug through the shopping bag on the floor behind her until she found the leash.

"Okay, little one, you need to stay here." Her hand trembled slightly as she looped the leash through the door handle in the back seat and then clipped it to the puppy's collar.

Spencer wagged his tail and tried to jump up on her.

"Stay down." She set him on the back seat, and Spencer immediately tried to climb back to the front to be with her. Jia held up her hand to block the puppy's path. "Stay."

Her phone chimed with another incoming text. *I'm circling behind him. Give me one minute. Then get out of the car. I'll see if I can flush him out.*

Jia hit the Like button and retrieved her weapon from her purse. Then, not wanting to leave the car running, she rolled down the windows partway and turned off the engine.

She counted the minute Rick had asked for in her head. She drew a deep breath with the last four seconds, then pushed open the car door, her pistol at her side.

Almost instantly, she heard Rick's voice. "Hey! What are you doing there?"

Jia had hoped Chesah would suddenly appear before her, but instead, it was a man around her age—short, dark hair, loose-fitting clothes, empty hands.

He stared at her for a brief moment. Then with barely a hesitation, he sprinted toward her. Or was he running away from Rick?

Jia lifted her weapon. "Stop right there!"

But he was almost to her, and she couldn't shoot an unarmed man. Could she?

"Jingyi!" Rick shouted as though trying to warn her of the danger right in front of her.

Unable to pull the trigger, Jia lowered her weapon and jumped to the side.

The man thrust his arm out, no doubt intending to knock her over so he could continue running past her, but Jia ducked, and the man missed her entirely. He stumbled forward from the lack of contact, and Jia jabbed her elbow into his side.

He whirled around, a brief flash of indecision in his expression. Then he lifted both hands, clearly ready to fight.

"Who are you working for?" Jia asked.

Rick sprinted toward them, and out of the corner of her eye, Jia could see his pistol in his hand aimed at her would-be attacker.

"Put your hands up," Rick demanded.

The man's only response was to pivot behind Jia and throw a punch at her head.

She evaded again, her hip bumping into the car as she moved.

Spencer yipped, and the scratching of his little paws against the glass sounded behind her.

"The police are already on their way," Rick said, his voice even. "Give it up."

He was trying to use words to defuse the situation, but he couldn't shoot. Not only did he not have a clear shot, but Jia suspected that he, too, would be restricted by his training and ethics when it came to shooting an unarmed man.

The man struck out again, and this time when Jia ducked, his hand connected with the car.

He cried out in pain.

Balancing on the balls of her feet, Jia lifted her own hands and went on the offensive. With the man off-balance, Jia kicked her foot into his stomach and sent him crashing to the concrete floor.

Rick rushed forward, and Jia lifted her weapon to cover him. Rick produced a zip tie from his holster and secured the man's hands.

The man tried to fight against him, but Rick simply knocked the man back down and forced him onto his stomach.

With his knee pressing down on the man's back, Rick tossed Jia a second zip tie. "Secure his feet."

Jia leaned down and knelt on the back of the man's legs to make sure he didn't kick her while she complied.

"Did you really already call the police?" Jia asked.

"Yeah. They should be here any—"

Blue lights flashed as a police car approached.

A police officer climbed out and joined them. After a brief conversation and a flash of Rick's ID that identified him as FBI, the policeman took custody of their prisoner and secured him in the back of his car.

As soon as they gave their reports, the police officer returned to his car and left them in the garage, the puppy still yipping behind them.

Jia opened the back door and scooped Spencer into her arms. "It's okay."

Rick put his hand on her back. "Are you all right?"

"Yeah." Other than the throbbing in her hip. No doubt she'd have a nasty bruise, but that was a minor inconvenience compared to the injuries she could have suffered. "I can't be sure, but that guy may have been there when Chesah escaped."

"Maybe, but it was too dark to really tell." Rick rubbed his hand up and down her back. "You'd think that if Chesah is involved, she'd have told Brandt to send more than one man against you."

"You're right." Jia furrowed her brow. "Maybe this man was simply following us because Brandt wanted to know about his new neighbors."

"He's going to learn a lot about his new neighbors," Rick said. "But I'm not sure if he's going to enjoy the experience."

Jia snuggled the dog in her arms. "No, I doubt he will."

CHAPTER 39

Erik checked the car twice before he found the tracking device hidden next to the battery. He confirmed that it didn't also contain a listening device before he closed the hood and stepped away from the car.

Jia whispered. "Was there a tracker?"

He nodded.

"Now what?"

"Let's go home." He gestured to the car door. "If we come back, it will look like Brandt's man simply didn't find us."

"Brandt is going to suspect something when his man doesn't report in."

Erik opened her door. "Maybe, but the best thing we can do is act like we have no idea what happened."

"No, I think we face it head-on." Jia remained standing. "When we get back, we need to tell Dylan that someone came running at me, and we were lucky that a cop was nearby."

"So we give Brandt the reason his man can't check in." Erik nodded. "Might as well try it your way. I'd like another day to go over our plan to breach Brandt's apartment before we make our move."

"I agree. We need to make sure Spencer here will play his part." Jia slid into the car.

As soon as Erik took his spot behind the wheel, Jia pulled out her phone and tapped her screen. When she finished, she turned her cell toward Erik so he could read the message she'd just sent to Dylan instructing him to move one of the listening devices back into the living room.

Erik nodded his approval, hesitant to say anything in the car for fear that there might be a listening device he'd missed. He turned on the engine and pulled out of the parking garage and onto the street.

Reminding himself that it would sound odd for them to remain silent on the way home, he said, "I still can't believe that happened to you."

"I know. Me neither," Jia said. "At least the police were nearby. Otherwise, I don't know what I would have done."

"I guess Spencer here isn't ready to be a guard dog yet." Erik turned onto Orchard Road. When they arrived at their apartment, he drove slowly to make sure there weren't any other surprises lurking behind the various pillars and vehicles. He parked in their designated spot. "We should probably take him out for a quick walk in case he needs to go to the bathroom."

"I'll do that if you can take the kennel and the rest of the stuff to the apartment," Jia said.

"After what just happened, I'd rather stay together." Erik gathered the bags out of the trunk and left the kennel. He nodded at it. "I can come back for that."

Jia put the puppy on the ground, and Spencer immediately tried to scamper away from her.

They walked to the elevator, and Erik said, "Looks like leash training is in his future."

Jia pressed the Up button. "I'm sure there's a lot of training in his future."

They took the elevator up one flight and walked the dog out to the front of the complex, to a grassy area where Spencer could relieve himself. After he was done, they continued upstairs to their apartment.

Dylan stood from his spot on the couch. "Hey, how did it go?"

Jia grinned. "Dean, meet Spencer," she said, using Dylan's usual alias.

"Oh, he's a cutie." Dylan bent down and held out his hand. Spencer wagged his tail and licked Dylan's hand. Dylan looked up. "So what took you guys so long anyway? I thought you'd be back at least an hour ago."

Playing along with the ruse that he didn't already know the situation, Erik said, "Jingyi had a bit of a scare at the mall when we stopped to pick something up."

"What kind of scare?"

Jia proceeded to give an abbreviated version of what had happened, making sure it sounded like the police officer was the hero who saved her from a possible attack.

"Man, I'm so glad you're all right," Dylan said once she finished.

"Me too," Erik said.

"If it's okay with you two, I'm going to lie down for a bit," Jia said.

"Let me know if you need anything," Erik said. "I have some work to do, so I'll be in my office."

"Do you mind if I work in there too?" Dylan asked. "I have some emails I need to check."

"Yeah, no problem." Erik led the way down the hall and walked into his office.

Jia went into her bedroom before circling back to the office, entering right behind Dylan. She turned on some music on her laptop to provide background noise. Then she walked to the far side of the room and leaned against the front of her desk. "What did you find out?" she asked quietly.

"Ackerman's been working in the pharmaceutical industry for the past ten years, which makes sense if he's involved with trying to engineer something that would be drug-resistant."

"But why would he be involved with this?" Erik asked. "Why is he trying to kill people?"

"I think this might have something to do with it." Dylan held up his phone. "I found an article he wrote about the challenges of caring for the elderly, even predicting that there would be a shortage of medical supplies within the next thirty years if something isn't done to correct the problem."

"And he thinks that releasing a virus that could kill millions is the way to fix the problem?" Jia asked, her eyes wide.

"In everything I've found that he's written, he shows a radical tilt," Dylan said. "He honestly seems to believe that the medical industry can't keep up because it's artificially prolonged life for people who should have been allowed to die."

"That's twisted." Jia shook her head. "First, we have Brandt, who seems to think anyone with a genetic health issue should be eliminated, and now this. These men are both mad."

"Agreed," Erik said. But at least they were relatively sure that they had the right suspects. They just had to find and stop them before they endangered lives, including his own.

Erik's phone rang, and he checked the screen before he answered the call from Vanessa. Apparently, Kade wasn't the only person burning the midnight oil in Virginia. "Hey, what's up?"

"Just wanted to let you know the approvals came through," Vanessa said. "The Saint Squad will go in tomorrow night to extract Shaun Fleming."

Hope filled Erik. "Thanks for the update. And let me know as soon as you get word."

"You know I will." Vanessa's yawn carried over the phone. "We'll talk tomorrow."

She ended the call, and Erik lowered his phone as well as his voice. "They're going in after your partner tomorrow."

Jia's eyes brightened, and relief shone in the sheen of tears that surfaced. She juggled the puppy in her arms and leaned forward to kiss Erik's cheek. "Thank you."

Erik had to take a moment to find his words. "We should hear something late tomorrow night or first thing the next morning."

"I just hope we hear good news," Jia said.

Erik nodded, and his gaze swept over Dylan before he focused on Jia again. "We all do."

CHAPTER 40

Jia cuddled Spencer on the couch and stifled a yawn. The puppy had gotten up once during the night, and then he'd awoken again at five thirty this morning. Not exactly what she'd planned when she'd gone to bed last night.

She still couldn't believe Rick had cut through the complications to allow them to adopt a dog so quickly. Granted, they'd adopted the dog under their aliases, but still. The little bit of research she'd been able to do on pet-adoption procedures had made it seem nearly as complicated as when she'd joined the CIA and the government had learned that her maternal grandmother was still a Chinese citizen.

And then getting the rescue mission approved. How Rick had managed that was still a mystery. In her experience, such things usually took twice as long as they should, and often the political red tape prevented action from being taken.

She was starting to think his ghost status was a cover to hide his supernatural powers. Either that, or he had friends everywhere. With the speed he was able to access resources, she suspected it was the latter. Rather surprising for a man who wouldn't even share his real name.

A little sigh escaped her at that thought.

Rick and Dylan emerged from the office. It was time.

Their plan was simple: She would go upstairs and use Spencer to create a distraction while Rick planted as many listening devices as he could along the window of Brandt's apartment. Or if Rick couldn't find the opportunity, she would try. She hoped Spencer's energy would give one of them the chance they needed.

It really was crazy. Brandt's people had planted bugs in their place, and now Erik and Jia were using Brandt's own methods against him.

Rick stared at her for a moment before he gestured toward the door. "Does he need to go out?"

His question was undoubtedly for the people listening. What he was really asking was whether she was ready.

Jia drew a deep breath and let it out in a rush. Time to get this over with. She stood, lifting the puppy with her. "Yeah, I should probably take him out. It's been a while."

"I'm going to head upstairs to take this back to Elanora." Rick passed two listening devices to her and pocketed two more.

"I can come with you," Jia said as though they hadn't already planned out this conversation. She slipped the listening devices into the pocket of her shorts before she clipped Spencer's leash to his collar. "We haven't introduced the puppy to any of our neighbors yet."

"Sounds good. Then we can go for a walk afterward."

Jia and Rick headed for the back door, leaving Dylan behind. As soon as they reached the service elevator, Rick put his hand on her back and leaned closer. "Are you ready for this?"

"I can't believe we're really using a puppy as a distraction technique," Jia said, even though this had largely been her idea. "It's crazy."

"It is," Rick said. "And if you hadn't wanted a dog so badly, I probably would have tried to figure something else out, but this might just be crazy enough to work."

The doors slid open, a woman standing inside with an armful of groceries.

"Your puppy is so cute!" She shifted the bag in her right hand to her left as Jia and Rick walked into the elevator. "Can I pet him?"

"Sure." Jia stepped closer to give the woman easier access. "I'm Jingyi, and this is my husband, Rick. We're your new neighbors."

"I heard someone new had moved in," the woman said. "I'm Puan. I work for the Wilsons in 1006."

"Good to meet you," Jia said.

"It's good meeting you too." The elevator stopped on her floor. "If you ever need someone to dog sit, let me know. My boss's kids love dogs."

"Thanks so much," Rick said. "We'll keep that in mind."

Puan left the elevator, and the doors closed, leaving Jia and Rick alone. They continued upward to the sixteenth floor.

Even though Jia doubted anyone was listening, she said, "The puppy's getting antsy. I'm going to head downstairs. Meet me down there when you're ready."

"Okay. See you in a minute." Rick stepped out, and Jia hit the button to hold the door open for a moment longer to give Rick time to head downstairs before she reached Brandt's floor.

Spencer wiggled in her arms, and Jia let go of the button. As soon as the doors slid closed, she set the puppy down and prayed this crazy plan would work.

* * *

Erik slowed his steps on the stairs as he neared the landing. The open stairwell brought him to within a few meters of the spot where Brandt's bodyguard had been positioned the last time Erik had been on this floor. With the elevator on the other side of the guard, he and Jia would have him flanked. But they weren't going to battle today. Today was all about planting the listening devices that would hopefully give them the information they needed to stop Brandt and whatever he was planning.

The elevator dinged, and Erik continued to the fourteenth-floor landing in the stairwell. He stepped out and lifted his hand in a nonthreatening wave. "Hey, how's it going?" he asked.

The guard narrowed his eyes as though trying to determine whether Erik was a threat.

The elevator doors slid open.

Spencer yipped and then ran out of the elevator.

Jia cried out. "Oh no!"

As they'd hoped, the guard focused on the puppy now scrambling at his feet. Unfortunately, instead of moving forward to help catch the puppy, the guard took a step back. Judging from the sudden apprehension on the man's face, he was afraid of dogs. Great.

"Sorry," Jia said, not yet attempting to grab Spencer's leash. "He's friendly."

The guard took another step back, his body now blocking the window where they needed to plant the listening device.

Apparently realizing that the guard was continuing to go in the wrong direction, Jia scooped up the puppy and held him up. "Do you want to pet him?"

"No. We don't want any dogs up here."

Resigned, Erik stepped forward. If the dog couldn't draw the guard away from the window, Erik would have to try a different tactic. Adopting his best jealous tone, he asked, "So is this where you keep running off to every time you leave our apartment? Are you coming to see this guy or whoever he works for?"

Jia turned toward him, an innocent expression on her face. "Honey, I didn't see you there."

"Right." Though squaring off against the guard hadn't been part of the plan, Erik should have known that anything involving using an animal was likely to get interesting. Erik took an aggressive step forward. "Are you the one my wife's been flirting with?"

"I don't know what you're talking about." The guard took another step back, now a full four meters away from Jia, but Erik couldn't tell if he was trying to stay away from him or the dog.

"Honey, you're overreacting." Jia put her hand on his arm, her body now between Erik and the window.

"I got you this dog to keep you company, not give you an excuse to go check out all the neighbors."

Jia shifted the puppy in her arms so her free hand was now the one closest to the window. She spoke to the guard and slipped her hand into her pocket. "I'm so sorry about all this. My husband can get a bit jealous."

"Just back off," the guard said.

Erik pushed forward again until he was nearly nose-to-nose with the guard. "Don't talk to my wife that way."

The guard straightened his shoulders and lifted his chin, his gaze now even with Erik's. "Look, you and your wife get out of here, or I'm going to help you back onto that elevator."

"Honey, let's go," Jia said, her hand on his arm once more.

Spencer wiggled in Jia's arms, trying to free himself.

"And get that dog away from me," the guard demanded.

"Fine." Erik took one step back and then another, his stare remaining on the guard until he was certain Jia was safely behind him.

Jia spoke again. "Come on, Rick. Let's take the stairs."

Erik joined her at the stairwell, not breaking his focus on the guard until he turned to join his current family on their descent to their apartment.

CHAPTER 41

Jia paced the living room. She'd connected a pair of wireless headphones to the laptop currently recording the audio from the listening device she'd planted on Brandt's apartment window, and now she listened, hoping for some clue as to where the virus would be released and when. The listening device that Brandt's man had left in her living room had once again been relocated to the master bedroom closet.

Brandt's man had managed to plant three bugs, but they'd managed only one. Not ideal, but with the limited access she'd had to the window and with Spencer wiggling in her arms, she'd been lucky to get one down at all.

The puppy was currently curled up on Rick's lap, Rick's laptop balanced on the arm of the couch so he could see the screen without disturbing Spencer. The mere sight of them together warmed her heart. She enjoyed seeing the domestic side of her pretend husband.

She glanced at the kitchen, where Dylan stood washing dishes. Rick had cooked dinner. Dylan was cleaning up. And all because she'd been willing to make tacos for lunch. She was liking this arrangement.

Dylan turned off the water and set a pan on a dish towel to dry. He walked out of the kitchen, and Jia slid one of the earphones aside.

"I'm going to take a nap," Dylan said. "Wake me when you need me to take over."

Jia nodded. "Okay."

"Anything?" Rick asked.

"A woman said she'd finished the laundry." Jia shrugged. "Not exactly exciting stuff."

"You know, wearing a path on the floor isn't going to make them give you information faster."

"I know."

Rick ran his hand over the puppy's head. "Can you take him for a minute?"

"Sure." Jia sat beside him, and Rick shifted Spencer into her arms.

The puppy barely stirred, simply snuggling into her as she nestled him on her lap.

With nothing currently coming over her headset, Jia kept one side off her ear and asked, "What are you working on?"

"Trying to get the update on when the SEALs are expected to be back in communication range after they go in after Shaun."

The mere thought of Shaun in captivity for so many days made her sick to her stomach. "Do you think there's a chance he's really still alive?"

"Don't go there." Rick reached over and put his hand on her shoulder. "We'll know soon enough if he's where we think he is. Asking those questions isn't going to help us get the answers we want."

"I know, but it's hard not to feel guilty. I'm the one who left him behind."

"And if it weren't for you, we wouldn't know about the threat. And had you not left, you probably wouldn't be alive right now." He leaned toward her and brushed his lips over hers. The kiss sent a familiar thrill rippling over her skin. He eased back, his gaze on hers. "I can't imagine my life right now without you in it."

Though she hadn't planned to have the relationship talk now, not with everything else going on, Jia couldn't keep her question from spilling out. "What's going to happen after all this is over? I mean with us. I live in Kuala Lumpur. You live—I don't even know where you usually live."

"I can live anywhere with a major airport and access to a port." He trailed a finger along her neck before settling his hand on her shoulder again. "Kuala Lumpur qualifies on both counts."

"You're saying you would move to Malaysia so we could be together?"

"Would you mind if I lived nearby?" Rick asked. "We'd have to keep our relationship quiet. With my situation, I'll always have to live in the shadows."

"Will that ever change?" Jia asked.

"No." His gaze met hers, his expression serious. "When I told you I was in the wrong place at the wrong time, I wasn't exaggerating." He set his laptop aside. "If I hadn't joined the guardians, the people who wanted me dead would have killed me."

"Who were they?"

"It doesn't matter." His expression clouded. "They killed two people when they tried to kill me. I couldn't risk more people getting caught in the crossfire."

"They're the ones who shot you?"

Rick nodded. "Yes. I chose this life rather than giving them the chance to try again."

Jia put her hand on his knee. "Rick, I'm sorry."

"Me too, but you should know what you're getting into with me." His gaze intensified. "I really care about you, but my life will never be like everyone else's."

Jia tried to imagine it, sharing even the near future with someone who she had to pretend didn't exist. Her coworkers wouldn't know she had a boyfriend; neither would her family. That also meant she wouldn't have to suffer through her parents' inevitable scrutiny of every part of her relationship. And with Rick knowing who she really worked for, she wouldn't have to lie about where she was when she traveled or make up excuses when a mission needed to take priority.

A flicker of disappointment flashed in Rick's eyes. "I'll understand if you can't live this way."

Live in the shadows or not see Rick again? That choice was easier than she'd expected. "In case you haven't noticed, my life isn't exactly a home in the suburbs."

Hope bloomed on his face. "So you're not breaking up with me?"

"No." She leaned in for another kiss. "I'm not."

CHAPTER 42

Their plan was risky, but Shaun couldn't wait any longer. Unless something had changed, and as long as he'd counted the days correctly, the planned attack was happening tomorrow. He had no idea how long it would take for him and Nur to find civilization, assuming they could get past the guards in the first place.

From her spot beside the door, Nur waved to get his attention and whispered, "The second guard is leaving."

Shaun's heartbeat quickened. "You ready?"

Though fear shone in her eyes, she nodded. She took her position behind the door, and Shaun quickly used the bobby pins to unlock it. The moment it clicked, he yanked the door open and rushed into the hall.

The single guard stood directly beside the door, and his eyes widened when he realized that the door was open. He fumbled for his weapon at the same time Shaun grabbed for it. The two grappled for the rifle, each of them gripping it with both hands.

Shaun pulled on it and backed up, drawing the guard with him as he reentered his makeshift prison. The moment the guard was beside the door, Shaun called out, "Now!"

Nur shoved the door forward. It thudded into the guard and sent him stumbling.

Shaun lost his grip on the rifle, the guard still clinging to it. Shaun rushed back to the guard and grabbed him from behind, hooking one arm around the man's throat and using his free hand to grab the man's arm. Then Shaun rammed his knee into the back of the guard's leg, causing the man's knee to buckle.

The guard grunted, but he quickly regained his footing. He shoved his elbow back into Shaun's ribs, pain shooting through Shaun and causing his eyes to tear. The guard then stomped his heel on Shaun's foot.

Shaun fought to keep from crying out. This was their one and only chance to get out of here—their one chance to stop the virus.

With a new determination, Shaun tightened his hold on the man's throat, cutting off his air supply.

The guard tried to fight against him. When he couldn't get free, he dropped his weapon and used both hands to pry Shaun's grip loose.

"Get the gun!" Shaun called to Nur.

She hurried forward and leaned down to grab the fallen weapon. Her fingers brushed against the barrel, but the guard kicked it away from her, catching her hand with his foot.

Nur gasped and backed out of range, moving in the same direction the weapon had skidded across the floor.

The guard elbowed Shaun again, and this time, he managed to break free of Shaun's grasp.

His rifle no longer in reach, the guard reached for the pistol holstered at his side.

Shaun backed up a step. He might be able to take cover in the hall, but what about Nur? He couldn't abandon her. They'd kill her for sure.

A blur of movement flashed in the edge of his vision as the guard drew his weapon. The guard must have sensed it, too, because he turned just as Nur swung the rifle at him.

He tried to duck, but the edge of the stock clipped his forehead and sent him stumbling to the floor.

Shaun quickly leaned over and relieved the guard of his sidearm. Then he stood and motioned to Nur. "Come on. Let's get out of here before the other guard gets back."

With the rifle in hand, she nodded and raced to the door.

Shaun peeked into the hall, relieved that none of the other guards had appeared despite the fight that had just occurred. He gestured with his free hand for Nur to enter the hall.

Across the room, the guard struggled to sit up and shook his head.

"Come on," Shaun whispered.

The moment Nur entered the well-lit hallway, Shaun flipped the lock on the door to trap the guard inside. Then he looked both directions and listened.

No audible footsteps. No sign of anyone.

Taking the lead, Shaun gripped his pistol and started toward the main entryway. He reached the end of the hall and peeked out. Through the windows beside the front door, he could see two men, one on either side of the door.

Two known barriers in one direction, unknown threats in the other. Shaun chose the unknown. There had to be a back door somewhere or a window on the front side of the house that he could use to climb out. Suspecting that a back door would also have guards, he crept across the entryway, past the stairwell, and into the hall opposite him. He glanced back to make sure Nur was still with him. She was, the rifle held awkwardly in her hands and her eyes wide.

They hurried down the next hall, this one spanning a dozen meters before they reached a formal living room, which was blessedly empty. Unfortunately, even though the window faced the front of the house, it had security bars lining the outside of it and was in full view of the guards by the main entrance.

Shaun started past the living room, but footsteps sounded on the tile floor.

Nur darted into the living room, no doubt to stay out of sight. Shaun followed.

Only a few seconds passed before shouts echoed from their former living quarters. Someone had discovered they were gone, and once again, they were trapped.

CHAPTER 43

Shaun peeked into the hallway. The three guards had rushed to their old room as though their arrival might prove they hadn't escaped after all. Not that making it to the other side of the house constituted a real escape.

"Maybe if we hide here, they'll leave and look outside." Nur gestured toward the sofa behind him.

Shaun considered if such a simple ruse were possible, and he shook his head. "They're going to look everywhere. We have to leave here and get into the trees. It's the only way."

"They'll shoot us."

"We have guns." Shaun swallowed. "We'll shoot back." His heart pounding and his palms sweating, he gathered his courage. "We'll go through the front door."

"But the guards—"

He might have to kill the guards in order to gain his freedom.

"Do you know how to use a rifle?" he asked.

She shook her head.

"Trade me. The pistol will be easier for you to handle." Shaun held out his hand and took the rifle from her. Then he passed her the pistol and gave her a quick rundown on how to fire it.

"We'll go through the front door. You shoot the man on the left. I'll take the one on the right."

"I don't know if I can."

"It may be the only way."

Nur swallowed hard. Then she nodded.

Shaun peeked into the hall again, one of the guards now visible in the distance.

The guard pointed and shouted.

Following the training he'd undergone dozens of times, Shaun stepped clear of the living room, lifted his weapon, and fired.

He didn't hit his target, but the guard jumped into the nearest room to take cover.

"Let's go." Shaun rushed toward the front door just as it burst open.

A guard filled the doorframe, and Shaun fired again. This time, he didn't miss.

The guard dropped his weapon and grabbed his chest before his knees buckled, and he fell to the ground.

Behind Shaun, Nur fired, but Shaun wasn't quite sure who she was shooting at.

The second guard by the front entrance took cover, the barrel of his weapon now pointing in their direction.

"Get down!" Shaun shouted.

He and Nur dove for the floor as bullets flew through the air and thudded into the wall. Shaun tried to adjust his grip on his weapon to return fire.

His heart lodged in his throat when he spotted three men rushing toward the door. He lifted his weapon to take aim. A shot fired before he could squeeze the trigger, but it wasn't Shaun who was injured. Rather, the guard collapsed in the doorway.

The men approaching fanned out, no longer in his sights. Then one appeared at the fallen guard's side. He kicked the guard's weapon out of reach before he called out. "Shaun Fleming?" Shaun was so stunned to hear his name that he didn't answer at first. "Shaun," the man said again. "US Navy SEALs. We're here to take you home."

Relief whooshed through Shaun, and he pushed to his feet. By the time he was vertical, two men dressed in combat gear were in the entryway, one positioned by the far side of the hallway, the other standing over Nur.

Shaun reached down and helped Nur stand. "She needs to come too. She's our source."

The man towering over him nodded. "This way."

Shaun ushered Nur through the front door behind the SEAL, with the second man taking up position behind them. They were all the way to the trees before reality crashed over Shaun. He'd escaped. And maybe, just maybe, he could share what he'd learned to stop Brandt and his partner from releasing the virus.

CHAPTER 44

JIA HAD FORCED HERSELF TO sleep, promising that when she woke up, she'd receive the good news that Shaun was safe. Now, here it was, four hours after the mission had started, and still no word.

The predawn light already shimmered on the horizon, spilling through the living room windows.

Hungry and tired, she put a piece of bread into the toaster and prayed new details would come forward soon.

The laptop she'd set on the counter remained open to the message board Rick had given her access to, but so far, nothing had popped up on Shaun or the SEALs.

In the living room, Rick adjusted the headset on his ears. He'd taken over for Dylan an hour ago, insisting Dylan get some sleep.

Jia could admit that while she missed the alone time she was accustomed to having with Rick, having Dylan here to help share responsibilities had been a huge help, especially with the puppy needing to go out every three to four hours.

Jia buttered her toast and took a bite. Suspecting that eating her breakfast too close to the puppy wouldn't go over well, she left her toast on a plate on the counter and walked into the living room.

Rick lifted his gaze to her and pushed one side of the earphones off his ear. "Still nothing going on upstairs."

"Do you want me to fix you something to eat?" Jia asked. "I can make you some eggs."

"That's okay. I'll fix something in a minute."

"If nothing's going on upstairs anyway, why don't you let me listen while I eat?" Jia held out her hand. "That way you can fix yourself some breakfast now."

"Thanks." He handed over the headphones.

Jia slipped them on, leaving one ear free so she could still hear Rick.

He crossed into the kitchen, and Jia took a seat on one of the stools at the serving bar. Rick opened the cabinet below the sink and pulled out a cleaning wipe, then rubbed down the counter that was already spotless, except for a few breadcrumbs.

Jia lifted an eyebrow. "Do you always wash the counters before you start cooking?"

He looked up as though surprised by the question. "Yeah. I can get a little overzealous on making sure I don't accidentally get exposed to gluten. Sorry."

"Don't apologize. I like having a clean kitchen." She took another bite of toast.

Rick pulled out a frying pan and proceeded to make an omelet. The aroma of sautéed mushrooms and eggs filled the kitchen, replacing the lingering scent of toasted bread.

Even though Jia finished her breakfast before Rick, she remained at the counter, the silence from upstairs still filling the headset.

Rick settled into the seat beside her and took a bite of his food.

"That smells amazing," Jia said.

"Do you want to try it?" He grabbed another fork and scooped a bite onto it for her.

Unable to resist, she leaned forward and accepted the offering.

The perfect blend of cheese and egg delighted her taste buds. "Oh, that's good."

"Do you want more?" he asked. "I'll share."

"No, it's okay." She turned her attention back to the screen. "I can't believe we haven't heard anything yet."

"Depending on how far they had to walk to get to their ride, it could still be a while," Rick said. "The SEALs tend to be overly cautious when scheduling their extraction times."

"You sound like you work with them a lot."

He nodded. "I do."

* * *

The helicopter shook, and Shaun gripped the edge of his seat. Nur sat on one side of him in the back of the helicopter, one of the navy SEALs seated on the other. Though Shaun had learned that the house where he and Nur had been held was only a couple hundred kilometers from his current residence, the fact that the SEALs had come in without authorization from the local government forced them to remain hidden on their trek through the surrounding area.

As a result, it had taken them nearly three hours to hike through the jungle to where their ride had waited for them. Undoubtedly, it would have gone much faster had it not been for Nur. Shaun hadn't realized how weak she was until after they'd escaped, but her lack of activity over the past couple of weeks had caught up to her.

The helicopter shook again, and Shaun tightened his hold until his knuckles went white.

Something was wrong. He wasn't sure what, but beyond the unexpected turbulence, the tension of the six navy SEALs had heightened, which was saying something after seeing how efficiently these men had cut through the walls of the security Brandt had erected at the house.

Shaun tapped on the shoulder of the man sitting next to him, a dark-haired man named Craig. "What's wrong?"

Craig tapped the headset covering his ears. Then his voice came through over the headset Shaun was currently wearing. "There's a problem with the helicopter. We're going to have to put down."

A problem with the helicopter? Shaun's body stiffened, and his grip on the seat tightened. A prayer circled through his mind. Surely they hadn't escaped captivity only to die in a helicopter crash. He wanted to live.

"We'll be fine," Craig assured him.

The words should have soothed, but the helicopter shook again and lowered in altitude.

Then words Shaun had hoped to never hear came over his headset when Craig said, "Brace for impact!"

CHAPTER 45

Erik paced the living room and willed new information to pop up on the navy's communication feed. Music played in the office to mask any noise he and Jia might make in case anyone was monitoring the bugs that had been planted, all of which were currently in the back of the apartment.

Tired of wearing headphones, he'd turned on the speakers on his laptop so he could hear the feed from the listening device as he watched and waited for news.

The SEALs should have checked in hours ago. He knew it, and so did Jia.

For the past two hours, Jia had alternated between pacing with him, staring at the computer screen, and sitting silently on the couch with the puppy in her lap. At the moment, she was back to staring at the laptop.

And somehow, Dylan remained asleep, blissfully unaware that he and Jia were both unable to function because of the worry that had increased with each passing minute. Not that Dylan or Jia understood his own personal connection to this particular operation.

He wasn't as well acquainted with the Saint Squad as some of the other guardians were, but all of them were well aware of their connection to numerous prominent figures in the US, first and foremost being the president.

But more than anything, these men had worked with the guardians over and over to protect others, and they were known for their incredible good luck that often made it seem like God Himself was watching over them. Erik prayed their luck hadn't run out today.

Jia stood and stepped into his path, her eyes damp. Instinctively, he opened his arms and pulled her into an embrace. She hugged him tight, digging her fingers into the back of his shirt as her body trembled.

Erik wanted to assure her that everything would be okay, but he couldn't get the words out past the lump in his throat. Instead, he just held on, receiving comfort as well as giving it.

After several moments, Jia pulled back. "I don't know if I can stand this much longer."

"Me neither," he whispered, his voice hoarse.

The click of shoes against tile carried over the laptop speakers.

Jia eased out of Erik's arms, and she turned toward the laptop. She sat back on the couch, and Erik settled beside her. They'd been listening for twenty-four hours, and so far, they didn't have anything incriminating. Nor did they have details about the when and where of Brandt's plans.

A crackle of static came over the laptop's audio, followed by Brandt's voice. "Make sure they have the timing right. We can't afford any more mistakes."

Erik tensed. If Brandt was talking about timing, that likely meant the attack was happening soon. And they still didn't know where.

"No more excuses," Brandt said, his voice increasing in volume. "Everything is riding on this."

He paused, obviously on the phone.

"Then get someone else," Brandt said. "I want this resolved within the hour. Call me back when you figure it out."

The conversation stopped, only some muffled movements filtering through now. Then the sound of retreating footsteps, followed by silence once more.

Jia shifted to face him. "The way he's talking, it sounds like the attack is about to happen."

"I know." A burning sensation spread through Erik's chest. "I don't think we can wait any longer to intervene."

"What do you have in mind?" Jia asked. "If we work together, we should be able to get past the guard at Brandt's front door."

"Yeah, but that guy wasn't the same guard who was outside the first time I walked by Brandt's place. Brandt's obviously got more than one."

"We still don't have authorization from the locals to bring him in for questioning." Jia blew out a frustrated sigh before she gestured toward the back of the apartment. "And we can't prove Brandt is behind bugging our place."

Erik pondered that particular detail. "In all likelihood, it's him though."

"It has to be. No one else would have reason to spy on us."

Erik slowly nodded. "So maybe it's time to use their listening devices against them."

* * *

Jia would have preferred to execute Rick's plan with backup, but the fear of creating an international incident left her and Dylan relying on Rick's insistence that he could operate under a different authority. She hoped she wasn't being set up to land in a Singaporean prison.

"You sure about this?" Dylan asked, his brow creased with worry.

"Trust me." Rick gestured to the laptop. "As soon as Brandt sees us as a threat, he'll either send someone after us, or he'll put a second guard by his door. Either way, that will give us the advantage."

Though Jia didn't love going against an unknown number of guards, she couldn't deny the sense of urgency that had been pulsing through her. People were going to die if someone didn't stop Brandt, and right now, they were the only ones willing to try. If nothing else, facing off against Brandt would distract her from her concern about Shaun and the lack of communication from the SEALs.

"How do you want to play this?" she asked.

"We'll start with this." Rick handed her and Dylan a communication earpiece, much like the ones the Secret Service used.

Dylan took his and held it out. "I've never used one of these before. Is it an open channel?"

"Hit this button to mute and unmute yourself." Rick slid his own earpiece into place. "Dylan, can you plant a couple of cameras in the service elevator and by the stairs on the next floor up? I'll disable the main elevator to make sure Brandt can't use it to leave."

"What are you planning for us to do if we see Brandt in the elevator?" Dylan asked. "Is one of us going to need to run out and hit the Down button to make it stop?"

"Actually, I'm going to rig it to stop on the seventh and eighth floors every time it goes down."

Dylan narrowed his eyes. "You can do that?"

"Yes." He retrieved three cameras from a case on the counter and handed them to Dylan.

"I'll be right back." Dylan headed for the back door.

"What about me?" Jia asked.

"Keep listening, but use the headphones." Rick waved toward the hall. "And can you also move the bug from the living room back into place?"

"Yeah, I'll take care of it." She set aside her comm earpiece, slipping the headphones on instead.

Rick grabbed the puppy's leash off the counter, and Spencer immediately wagged his tail and hurried to Rick's side. "I'm going to take him out while I prep the lobby elevator. Once we get back, we'll want to crate him to keep him safe."

Jia shook her head. "No, if you're planning to bring trouble here, it's better not to have Spencer here at all."

"We don't have a lot of options."

"We could ask the helper on the tenth floor who said she'd be willing to dog sit, or better yet, we can ask Elanora to take him for the day."

"I haven't vetted the helper, so my vote is for Elanora," Rick said. "After I take him out, I'll go up to see if Elanora will watch him."

Relieved that her newest little family member would be safe, Jia ran her hand over the puppy's head. "Thank you."

Rick leaned in and pressed his lips to hers for a lingering kiss. "I'll be right back."

Jia nodded and resisted the urge to lift her fingers to her tingling lips. So much had changed over the past two weeks, and she hoped her life could continue with this brilliance long after Brandt was behind bars. And she prayed they wouldn't be mourning her friend as they moved past this mission.

Jia did a quick check of the message board to confirm that there hadn't been any new communication since she'd looked a few minutes ago.

Trying not to think about where Shaun might be right now, she headed for the bedroom and retrieved the listening device she'd moved to the closet.

She walked into the living room at the same time Dylan entered through the front door. Jia held up the bug so he would know they were being monitored.

Dylan nodded his understanding, and Jia carefully placed it beneath the counter where it had originally been planted.

Rick arrived a moment later, his hands empty. "Our friend was thrilled with my visit."

Jia noted that he didn't mention the puppy had been left behind at Elanora's place. "How's Spencer doing?"

"He's just fine." Rick handed a spare pistol and a Taser to Dylan. Then he passed a Taser to Jia along with a communication earpiece. He drew his pistol from the holster at his belt. Ready or not, they were doing this.

CHAPTER 46

Erik was going into a hostile situation with a partner by his side. And not just any partner. Jia was the woman who mattered to him more than anyone. He didn't doubt she could handle herself, but that didn't stop the tension building inside him. He leaned close and whispered in her ear, "Ready?"

She nodded.

Erik turned to Dylan, who gave him a thumbs-up.

Erik adjusted his laptop so he could see the surveillance footage from the cameras outside his apartment, in the service elevator, and by the stairwell above them.

Feeling like a man about to willingly step on a hornet's nest, he spoke for the benefit of whoever might be monitoring them through the listening devices. "I don't think we can wait any longer for proof. We know Brandt is planning to release the virus."

"How sure are you about Brandt?" Dylan asked.

"Sure enough that I plan to request an arrest warrant," Erik said. "This stakeout has gone on long enough. Brandt is here, and now that we know the details, it's time to move."

"How do you want to handle this?" Jia asked.

"Let's have you override the lobby elevator and see if you can get up to his floor that way." Erik thought of how the one guard had been so afraid of Spencer. "Take the puppy with you. He'll be a good distraction."

Jia narrowed her eyes, and Erik shook his head to signal that he wasn't changing their game plan.

"What about me?" Dylan asked.

"We'll go up the service elevator," Erik said. "That way we're protected until we're ready to strike."

"Good idea." Dylan walked to the front door, opened it, and closed it.

Jia followed his example and did the same with the door leading to the lobby elevator.

Erik carried the listening device into his room, careful not to make any noise as he walked. As soon as he secured it in the bedroom closet, he hurried back into the kitchen and checked his computer screen. No movement on any of the camera feeds. "You hear anything?" he asked.

Jia nodded. She hit the button on the laptop to switch the audio from her headset to the laptop's speakers so they could all hear it.

"I don't care who they are," Brandt said. "I want them all dead."

"And then what?" another man asked. "This timing couldn't be worse."

"Leave them in their apartment. By the time anyone realizes there's a problem, it will be too late for them to stop me, and we'll all be long gone."

* * *

Jia stared at the computer screen as the elevator doors slid open on the thirteenth floor. "Got something."

Two figures stood inside, one of whom was the guard she'd seen outside Brandt's apartment yesterday.

Rick pocketed a flash grenade and a syringe filled with a sedative. After he put his communication device in his ear, he leaned close. "You and Dylan take the men in the elevator. I'm heading upstairs."

"Be careful."

Rick gave her shoulder a squeeze. "You too."

"We'll come back you up as soon as we take care of the guards," Jia said. "But don't take any chances up there."

"I'm afraid today we may have to take chances."

And get the local authorities involved. Those words remained unspoken, but they both knew what was in their future. They needed the locals to help them stop whatever attack might be pending and stop Brandt once and for all. Yet with that support came the possibility of them being taken into custody. And even though they didn't have time for a detainment, they couldn't take down Brandt's operation alone.

Determined to take the first steps of detaining the madman, Jia and Dylan rushed out the front door, Rick passing them as he sprinted for the stairs.

Jia took the spot just beyond the elevator, while Dylan pressed himself against the wall on the side closest to their apartment.

The elevator motor hummed, and the sound of Rick's footsteps on the stairs followed.

The elevator chimed, and the doors slowly slid open.

Jia lifted her Taser, and Dylan mirrored her movement. Jia gestured to Dylan and held up one finger to indicate he should take the first person who exited.

He nodded and gulped in a deep breath of air.

A man Jia hadn't seen before stepped out, and Dylan fired, the leads on the Taser hitting the man directly in the chest. The man cried out, his body shaking as he absorbed the electric current.

Jia glimpsed another man in the elevator, this one the guard who'd been afraid of the puppy. She lifted the Taser, but the first man's body blocked her from being able to take a shot.

As the first guard fell forward, the second guard lifted his hand, a pistol gripped in it.

"Gun!" Jia shouted as she darted to her left.

Dylan dove for the ground.

The second guard rushed out of the elevator and shifted his aim in Jia's direction. With no guarantee that he wouldn't fire, even if she used the Taser on him, Jia acted on instinct. She dropped the Taser and grabbed the man's right arm, forcing the weapon upward.

A gunshot echoed, and tiny bits of concrete from the walkway above them scattered in the air.

The scuffle of footsteps sounded, likely from Dylan trying to position himself to help her, but Jia's main focus was on trying to hold her own against a man whose strength exceeded hers.

The elevator doors started to close behind the guard, and Jia planted her foot right behind his leg, shoving at him to knock him off-balance.

His body tipped, his back slamming against the elevator doors, forcing them to reopen. Jia thrust her hand against his right wrist, knocking his weapon free. It clattered into the elevator car, and he turned to get it.

Jia shoved him from behind, and he stumbled into the elevator, his head bumping into the padded side of the elevator wall.

He grunted and whirled toward her, the pistol now at his feet.

Not giving him the chance to retrieve it, Jia struck out, but instead of her fist connecting with his midsection, as she'd intended, the guard grabbed her fist and yanked her into the elevator.

He shoved her back against the bank of buttons. She pushed back, but his grip remained firm. To gain some much-needed space between them, she lifted her hand to his jaw and applied as much strength as she could to force him to turn his head in the hopes of breaking free. The car began to move.

Jia shot her knee up, aiming for his crotch, but she missed, though her action had the desired result. He released her and jumped backward.

Jia lifted both fists, prepared to defend herself. Her weapon remained holstered at her waist, but she didn't dare try to retrieve it in these close quarters.

The guard's fists came up, too, and he didn't hesitate to take the first punch.

Jia ducked and danced to the side. The guard's momentum pulled him a step forward, and Jia jabbed her elbow into his back.

The guard took another forward step and pressed his hand against the elevator wall.

Jia didn't give him time to regroup before she punched him in the stomach.

The guard's breath heaved out, but he shoved her away, and Jia rammed into the wall opposite him.

Before she could regain her balance, he grabbed both of her arms and lifted her off the ground, her feet now dangling several centimeters above the floor.

"Do you even know what your boss is planning?" Jia asked, her eyes even with his. "He's trying to kill millions of people."

No response. Either the man didn't care, or he was beyond listening.

The elevator continued its downward descent, now coming to a stop.

Jia kicked her leg out, her foot connecting with his kneecap.

The guard's eyes watered, and he dropped her to the ground. He started to lean down to reach for the gun, but Jia stepped on the weapon as the elevator doors slid open.

The guard grabbed at her ankle, pulling her off her feet and sending her crashing down beside him.

On the other side of the elevator doors, a dog barked and rushed into the elevator car, a woman holding the end of its leash.

The guard scrambled back, the weapon still lying on the floor.

Jia grabbed the gun and hit the Door Open button. She peeked out at the woman. "Hey, can you do me a favor and go get the guard? We need the police."

The woman's eyes lowered to the gun in Jia's hand, and she swallowed hard.

Jia reached out her free hand. "And one more thing: Let the dog stay here. He's keeping this guy where he needs to be."

The woman gave a hurried nod. "I'll be right back."

CHAPTER 47

Erik had run halfway back down the stairs to check on Jia and Dylan, but Jia spoke into his earpiece. "Guard secure. Dylan, bring the other one downstairs."

Her breathing came more quickly than usual, likely due to whatever confrontation she'd just endured. Thank goodness Jia could take care of herself. Now it was his turn to do his part to stop the spread of the virus. If he didn't, he would lose his life and the chance to build the future he had started to dream about with Jia. And even though he already had a death certificate, he had no interest in losing the ability to breathe anytime soon, especially now that he had Jia in his life.

He climbed back up the stairs until he reached the fourteenth floor and peeked around the wall that separated the stairwell from the main walkway leading to Brandt's apartment.

A man stood in front of Brandt's door, dressed in cargo shorts and a loose-fitting T-shirt, his gun visible at his belt.

Erik had hoped Brandt's security staff was limited to the two guards in the elevator, but it appeared Jia and Dylan weren't the only two who would have a face-off today.

Erik fingered the syringe in his hand. Suspecting a direct approach would likely get him shot, Erik pulled the flash grenade from his pocket. So much for staying invisible.

He muted his comm unit. Then he pulled the pin, glanced around the corner again, and sent the grenade through the air. It bounced a couple of meters from the guard's feet, but Erik didn't wait to see the other man's reaction. Instead, he took cover behind the wall and put his hands over his ears.

The walkway vibrated beneath his feet, and the boom of the grenade mixed with the guard's cry.

Erik rushed from his hiding place, noting the broken window beside where the guard stood bent over, his hands over his ears.

The guard didn't even acknowledge Erik's presence when Erik sprinted to his side and thrust the needle from the syringe into the man's thigh.

The man fell back against the door, his body sliding down until his backside hit the floor.

Erik nudged him aside and tried the doorknob. Locked.

He pulled a skeleton key from his pocket, inserted it into the lock, and turned. Then he pushed the door open slowly.

He peered inside. No sign of life.

He passed through the laundry room and into the living area. To his surprise, Brandt sat in a recliner, his feet up. A man stood at his side, the pistol in his hand aimed at Erik.

Erik jumped back into the laundry room, using the wall between it and the kitchen to protect himself. "Give it up, Brandt. We know about the virus."

"So you're the person who thinks he can stop me." The distinctive sound of the recliner's foot rest lowering clicked. "It's too late. There's nothing you can do."

"You're wrong about that." Erik prayed it wasn't too late to stop Brandt's plans.

"I don't think so."

The calm, arrogant tone sent a chill through Erik. "Give up, and we can have a nice chat with the police downtown. Otherwise, you aren't likely to live to see whether I'm right or not."

"Who are you?"

"I'm the person who helps when everyone thinks all hope is lost."

"We have all the hope in the world today. We're paving a new road for mankind." Brandt's voice was a little louder, a little closer.

Erik bent down and looked around the corner again. Brandt stood in his direct line of sight, and the guard now stood beside the broken window. Erik spotted the gun in Brandt's hand and jumped back as both Brandt and his guard fired in tandem.

"You may have gotten past my other guard," Brandt said, his voice still eerily calm, "but you aren't getting out of here alive."

* * *

Jia heard the gunshots when she stepped out of the service elevator on the fourteenth floor. She'd left Dylan with the dog and the captured guards downstairs.

Now it was time to give Rick some much-needed backup. She took a quick moment to evaluate the scene in front of her. A guard lay on the walkway outside Brandt's door, and the window beside it was mostly gone, jagged glass edging the frame.

She started toward Brandt's apartment, but when she caught sight of the broad-shouldered man standing inside the apartment next to the shattered window, she took cover in the little alcove between the elevator and the stairwell.

"Was that gunfire?" Dylan asked through her earpiece.

"I think so." Worry gnawed at her. She hadn't heard any sound from Rick since before the gunfire started. "Rick, status."

Another shot fired, and Jia's heartbeat quickened. She was fourteen floors up, the main-lobby elevator was still shut down, and Rick was nowhere in sight.

"Give it up," Rick shouted.

Relief pulsed through her. He was okay.

"I'm working my way up to you," Dylan said.

Though Dylan could be exposed when he arrived, Jia ignored him for now and instead spoke to Rick through her comm unit. "Rick, I'm right outside Brandt's apartment."

This time when Rick's voice sounded, it came through her headset. "I'm outnumbered."

That wasn't what she wanted to hear. Concerned for both Rick and the danger Dylan would find when he arrived, she said, "Dylan, make sure you take cover when you get here. I don't want you to take on fire."

"Got it," Dylan said.

Rick spoke now. "Do you have a shot at Brandt or his guard?"

"One of them is partially exposed through the window."

"Take the shot," Rick said.

Jia lifted her weapon and aimed at the man's arm to avoid hitting him in his bulletproof vest, assuming he was wearing one. Then she drew a breath, held it, and squeezed the trigger.

The man jerked and disappeared from view.

A second shot fired as Jia sprinted across the walkway to the spot between the door and the window. She ducked so she was below the windowsill, keeping her head out of sight.

As though he had anticipated her movement, Rick spoke. "Are you in position to fire through the window again?"

Jia clicked once into her comm unit to signal the affirmative.

"On the count of two," Rick said, his voice low. "One, two."

Jia straightened to a stand and aimed through the window. The man she'd shot was on the floor, his pistol still in hand. Brandt stood just off to the side, his gun aimed across the room.

Jia took a shot and immediately called out, "Drop your weapons!"

The guard didn't listen. He turned his weapon toward Jia and fired.

She jumped back, taking cover behind the wall.

"Give it up," Brandt said. "You can't win this."

More gunfire pierced the air.

"Rick? Are you okay?"

"Yeah." The impatience in Rick's single word carried far more meaning than telling Jia he was uninjured. He was ready to have this stalemate broken.

"Dylan, where are you?" Jia asked. They needed someone else to help them break this standoff.

"Almost there." A few seconds later, he appeared at the top of the stairs.

With the guard and Brandt close enough to hear her words through the open window, Jia used hand motions to signal Dylan to take her place.

Keeping his head down, he made his way to her side. "Now what?"

"You cover us from here. I'm going to help Rick." Staying clear of the window, she crept past the front door and continued around the corner to the back door. As soon as she reached it, she spoke into her comm set. "Rick, I'm coming in behind you."

He clicked once to acknowledge her words without speaking.

Slowly, she opened the door and slipped inside. Rick held his position beside the door leading from the wet kitchen into the main kitchen, his weapon at his side. He tilted his head, signaling for her to take the spot on the opposite side of the door to where he stood.

"What now?" she whispered.

Rick hesitated, and Jia did her own tactical analysis. The two men in the living room didn't know she was here with him. And with her smaller size, it made sense for him to cover her, for her to rush into the main kitchen and use the counters for cover. But he clearly didn't like putting her in danger.

Taking the initiative, she said, "Cover me. On the count of three."

The muscle in his jaw twitched, but he nodded. He lifted his free hand and signaled to himself and to the right. Then he pointed to her and to the left. Message received. He would take the person on the right side of the room. She would take the left. But first, she had to move into position, where she would have the right angle to shoot.

She held up her weapon, indicating she was ready. Then Rick held up three fingers, counting them down. When he fisted his hand, he swung his gun hand through the doorway and opened fire with two shots.

Jia ran into the kitchen and ducked behind the counter. Both Brandt and the guard had taken cover behind the sofa, and it was time for Jia and Rick to use their advantage. She spoke low into her mic. "Dylan, flush them out."

A shot fired from the window. Movement sounded.

"Get him!" Brandt ordered his guard.

"Now!" Rick called out.

Jia popped up, now able to fire at the guard, who was still trying to use the sofa as a barrier. She fired a shot, this time the bullet hitting the guard's leg.

Rick stepped into the room, and Brandt fired.

Jia's heart stopped, afraid he'd manage to shoot Rick, but Rick had already dropped to the floor. He squeezed off a shot of his own, and Brandt stumbled back a step.

Despite being off-balance, Brandt struggled with Rick, fighting to maintain control of his weapon.

The guard lifted his gun. Jia fired a warning shot. "Drop your weapon, or the next one won't miss."

This time, the guard complied, releasing his gun and dropping it to the floor beside him. Brandt didn't. He swung his gun toward Jia.

Before Brandt could shoot, Rick charged him and tackled him to the floor.

Both men's weapons fell to the tile. Rick punched Brandt in the jaw, and Jia quickly collected the fallen weapons. As the two men on the ground wrestled, she handed the guns through the window to Dylan, grabbing the guard's pistol as she went.

Brandt tried to free himself from Rick, but Jia closed the distance between them and stepped on his hand, pointing her gun at his head. "It's over. You can stop, or I can kill you."

The older man looked up into the barrel of Jia's weapon, and fear flashed on his face. He stilled, and Rick took the opportunity to secure Brandt's hands with a zip tie he produced from the pocket beside his holster.

Dylan kept his pistol aimed at the guard. "You both okay?"

"Yeah." Breathless, Rick stood. "I'm going to clear the rest of the apartment." He jutted his chin toward the guard. "How bad is he?"

"He'll live."

Jia handed her pistol to Rick to make sure he would be armed while he searched the rest of the apartment. She then crossed to Dylan and took Rick's weapon from him. Rick disappeared from view.

Jia considered the likelihood that the cops would want to take them in for questioning. "Dylan, I hate to do this to you, but we're going to need you to deal with the police. We can't take the chance that all three of us will end up at the police station all day."

"I'll call the paramedics now. Just let me know what I can tell the police so I don't sound like an idiot."

Rick emerged from the back of the apartment and holstered his weapon.

"I'll text you," Jia said, "as soon as Rick tells me what story we're going to share."

CHAPTER 48

Erik did a quick search of Brandt's apartment, but he didn't find a single clue as to the date or venue for the event where the man planned to spread the virus. And as much as he'd hoped capturing Brandt would stop his plans, Erik also found no sign of the virus. Which meant Brandt's partner could very well still move forward.

Erik entered the living room, where Brandt lay on the floor, Dylan at his side.

Dylan held up Brandt's cell phone. "He reset it to factory settings."

Jia emerged from one of the other bedrooms. "I didn't find anything."

"You two had better get out of here," Dylan said. "I'll make sure Brandt's laptop is checked and see if the lab can pull anything off his phone."

Erik nodded. "Keep us in the loop."

Jia started out the door to the walkway, but Erik motioned her to the lobby elevator. "This way. I can override the main elevator. It'll be easier to avoid the police."

Jia followed him through the door, closing it behind them.

After a few quick commands through the app on his phone, Erik overrode the elevator and pushed the Down button to make it come.

"You know Brandt is going to claim you broke in and assaulted him, right?"

"Yep. Technically, I did." Erik hit the Down button again, hoping it would speed up the elevator's arrival. "That's why I don't want to get caught up here."

They could hear more people in the apartment, and Erik willed the elevator to come faster.

After a few seconds, it reached the floor they were on.

The elevator doors slid open, and Erik and Jia hurried inside.

As soon as the doors closed, Jia trembled.

Erik took her hand. "You okay?"

"Today hasn't exactly gone the way I'd hoped." She sighed. "First Shaun, and now we catch Brandt, but we still have no idea where Ackerman or Chesah are. They could still try to release the virus."

"I know." They reached their floor and entered their apartment. "Let me grab my laptop and see if we can get an update."

Erik stepped up to the kitchen counter and logged in. A new message popped up, a request for a secure comm link with the USS *Lawrence*. "Hey, I've got something."

Not wanting to deal with the bugs still in the living room, he grabbed his laptop and took it into his office. He set it down on his desk, and Jia pulled her chair next to him.

As soon as they were both seated, Erik pressed the button to open the comm channel.

The image popped up of a ship boardroom, two men in the center. Relief swept through Erik. Jia's partner, Shaun, was front and center. At his side was Brent Miller, the commander of the Saint Squad and the son-in-law of the president of the United States.

* * *

Jia could barely believe her eyes. She sat beside Rick in the office, their chairs pushed close together as Shaun's image flickered on and off the laptop screen before the feed stabilized. A navy SEAL stood beside Shaun, but Jia couldn't think about anything beyond the fact that her coworker had survived.

She lifted her hand to her mouth, unable to speak.

Beside her, Rick took over. "Status?"

"I'm okay," Shaun said, his focus clearly on Jia. "And so is Nur. Brandt was holding her too."

Rick straightened. "Can you positively identify Brandt as one of your captors?"

"Yes. He was on the plane with me when they transported me to the villa where we were being held." Shaun lifted his hand as though waving that issue away. "The more important thing is that he's planning to release the virus at an event sometime tonight."

"Where?" Jia asked. "How?"

"An event in Singapore. I think it might be at some sort of concert."

"Here?" Jia asked. "What else do you know?"

"They plan to hide vials of the virus inside some of the stage equipment and then release it in different cities," Shaun said. "It sounded like it's an airborne virus. After Singapore, the next cities are Tokyo and Seoul, then Berlin, Paris, Rome, and London. They plan to hit the US in New York."

"All huge-population centers," Rick said.

The SEAL beside Shaun furrowed his brow. "Did you say Singapore, Tokyo, Seoul, Berlin, and Paris?"

Shaun nodded.

"In that order?"

"Yes," Shaun said. "Why? Do you know what the event is that they're using?"

"Maybe." The SEAL stepped back, and he spoke to an ensign standing nearby.

Rick was already on his laptop, pulling up possible events in Singapore. "Oh no."

In the same moment, the SEAL came back to Shaun's side. "It's got to be Kendra's concert."

Rick nodded. "I agree."

"Kendra?" Jia looked at the screen on Rick's laptop. "Kendra Blake?" The woman was not only one of the most popular singers in the world, but she was also the daughter-in-law of the president of the United States.

"I'll put the request in to get to Singapore," the SEAL said.

"Brent, you need to stay where you are," Rick said.

Jia furrowed her brow. The SEAL hadn't introduced himself, yet Rick was on a first-name basis with him? They must work together a lot.

"You know I need to be there," Brent insisted. "Kendra has her baby with her."

"I'm not sure all your family will agree," Rick countered. "Besides, once Kendra finds out her concert is a target, she'll cancel, and she and the baby will get out of here."

"Call Vanessa," Brent said. "She can get the orders cut faster than if I go through regular channels."

"I'll let her know what's going on."

Another officer stepped into view long enough to pass a note to the SEAL. "Commander, this just came in."

Brent read the message, and a muscle in his jaw tensed. "We just got orders. A hostage situation on a cruise ship, and we're the closest unit. Looks like pirates."

"Pirates?" Jia asked.

"It happens more often than most people realize," Rick said.

"Yes, but of all the vessels in the South China Sea, they took hostages on one filled with American tourists." She shook her head. "Does this feel a bit too coincidental to anyone else?"

"It's definitely too coincidental," Brent said, clearly not happy with the turn of events.

"Brandt must be behind this. He's trying to stretch our resources."

"Whether that's the case or not, we have our orders," Brent said. "Take care of Kendra for me."

Rick nodded. "I will. And be safe."

"You too," Brent said.

CHAPTER 49

Erik tightened his grip on his cell phone. He'd already tried Kendra's private phone number a half dozen times as well as her concert manager's and the main number for the stadium. No one was answering, and time was running out. The concert would begin in less than two hours, and he had little doubt that those attending were already lining up to get in.

He checked the detailed information on Kendra in the guardian database once more. He'd met Kendra only a handful of times when helping run extra security during her last tour in Asia, but he'd been impressed with her kindness and concern for those around her.

Jia hurried down the hall toward him. "I updated the CIA station chief. He's going to reach out to the local authorities."

"Good, because I can't get anyone on the phone."

"Have you tried calling the venue directly?"

"Yes, but no one picked up. I'll try again."

Jia plucked the car keys off the counter. "You call. I'll drive."

Erik's heart seized. "You want to go over there?"

"It's the only way we can be sure to stop this," Jia said. "We know who we're looking for. The locals are going off photos."

"We're going off photos for Kenneth Ackerman." And if they were too late, they'd both be exposed to the virus.

Jia opened the door leading to the lobby elevator. "I know Chesah, and you've seen her in person. We have the advantage."

"And she knows us." Erik tried to push aside the panic welling up inside him. He'd faced countless men and women with guns and knives. He'd even disarmed a few explosives during his time as a guardian. But facing a fatal illness terrified him.

He forced himself to follow Jia, his brain trying to process any option that would keep them away from the stadium and still prevent the spread of the virus.

On their way to the garage, Erik dialed the stadium again. Still no answer. Same with Kendra and her manager. Erik dialed Kendra yet again. Two rings and then nothing.

"I don't get why no one is answering. Kendra keeps her phone on until right before she goes on stage."

Jia narrowed her eyes. "How do you know that?"

"Experience." Erik gave as much truth as he was able. "I helped with her security team two years ago when she came to Asia."

"I didn't realize ghosts helped civilians too."

"We don't usually," Erik said. "That was an unusual circumstance. Her father-in-law was running for president at the time."

"Right. She's married to President Whitmore's son." She furrowed her brow. "Then Kendra's baby is President Whitmore's grandchild."

"Yeah."

"We can't let her become the wrong kind of headline." Jia jogged to their car.

Erik opened the hood and removed the tracking device Brandt's man had planted and tucked it behind the nearest pillar.

As soon as they were both inside, Jia started the engine. "I'm surprised she's touring with an infant."

Erik clicked his seat belt into place, and his mind raced. "That might actually help us." He dialed again, only this time, he called Vanessa, his liaison with the White House.

Jia pulled out of the garage as Vanessa answered on the second ring. "Hello?"

A little surprised that Vanessa sounded alert even though it wasn't yet six in the morning in DC, Erik said, "I need a favor. I have to get in touch with Kendra Blake before her concert. We need her to cancel."

In true Vanessa fashion, she addressed his request before asking questions. "I'll text you her number."

"I've got it, but she isn't answering. Is her husband with her? Or do you have the number for her security team or her nanny?"

"Charlie is still in the US, but I can send you the security team's phone numbers. I'll try the nanny and her band members."

"Thanks."

"If I get through before you do, what do I tell them?" she asked.

In Erik's relief to have the extra help, he'd forgotten to share details. "Tell them to cancel the concert and get as far from the stadium as possible."

Jia made a quick turn, and Erik pressed his hand against the dashboard to keep his body steady.

"What's the threat?" Vanessa asked.

"The virus. We think her concert is where they're going to release it."

"Oh no." Vanessa's words came out in a whisper. "I'll let you know if I get through."

"Same goes here." Erik hung up.

A moment after he ended the call, his phone buzzed with incoming text messages. He clicked on one and tapped on the phone number for the first shared contact.

"Who are you calling now?" Jia asked.

"Kendra Blake's security team."

* * *

Jia checked the GPS calculations on the center console. What should have been a fifteen-minute drive had already taken twenty, and they still had another two kilometers to go.

"No one is answering," Rick said. "Brandt's people must have set up some sort of signal blocker."

"They thought of everything," Jia muttered. But Brandt's preparedness only heightened her determination.

Taillights of the vehicles in front of them competed with the fading sunlight in the distance. "This traffic must be because of the concert." She gestured to the pedestrians walking under the covered sidewalk beside her, several of whom wore Kendra Blake T-shirts.

Jia's phone rang.

Rick picked it up from the cupholder, where she'd left it. "I'll put it on speaker."

She nodded. As soon as he hit the Talk button, she said, "This is Jia."

"Jia, it's Kyle Mack." The CIA's chief of station for Singapore.

"What's the status with the locals?"

"They're sending extra units in to look for Ackerman and Chesah, but as of now, they're unwilling to cancel the concert."

"You've got to be kidding me." Jia shook her head.

Rick held the phone a little higher. "Do they know there's a signal jammer in use at the stadium?"

"Who is this?" Kyle asked.

"That doesn't matter," Jia said. "Let them know about the jammer, and do whatever you can to limit the number of people at that stadium."

"I'll keep trying."

Rick hung up the phone and gestured to the front of the car. "See if you can use the car to block off both lanes. We can pretend it stalled and walk from here."

"You want me to make this traffic worse?" The words were barely out of her mouth before she caught up to his idea. "Of course you do. We'll be able to delay people getting there."

"And keep them out of the danger zone," Rick finished for her.

"Okay, but get ready for some very angry drivers."

"Just hit the hazard lights as soon as you get into position. I'll pretend to call for help, and then we take off down the sidewalk and lose ourselves in the crowd."

"Let's hope this works." Jia signaled to change lanes, waiting for two cars to pass her on the right before she was able to angle the car as though changing lanes. Then she cut the engine and threw the car into park.

"Pull the handle so I can put the hood up."

Jia pulled it, and by the time she reclaimed her phone and pocketed her keys, Rick already had the hood up and his phone to his ear.

Someone behind them honked their horn. Jia ignored it and crossed to the sidewalk. A dozen teenagers approached, and Jia took another step away from the street so the teenagers would have to pass between her and the car.

Rick joined her, pointing at their vehicle. "It's stuck there for now."

He lowered his arm and eased closer to her as the teenagers reached them. Then he and Jia walked forward, using the teenagers as a screen.

"We don't have time to walk the whole way," Jia said.

"I know. As soon as we reach the next intersection, we'll run."

Run more than half a kilometer right into potential exposure to the virus. She swallowed hard and nodded. "Any idea how we're going to get inside?"

Rick sent a text message. "I'm working on it."

CHAPTER 50

A BEAD OF SWEAT TRICKLED down Erik's spine as he ran beside Jia. Only a few hundred meters separated them from the stadium, and any second, he suspected his cell would stop working. He willed the backstage passes to come through before he lost his signal.

In front of them, a mass of people filled the space between them and the various entrances.

Erik slowed to a jog and checked his phone again. It still showed it was in a service area.

Jia matched his stride, but urgency filled her voice. "They're already letting people in." She checked her watch. "I didn't realize it was so late. There's only an hour until the concert is supposed to start."

Erik looked at his phone again. "Come on, Vanessa."

He slowed to a walk and dialed Vanessa's number, relieved when it rang.

"I just got them," Vanessa said by way of greeting. "I'm texting them now."

"Thanks. We're almost there, but we'll probably lose comm soon." Erik kept moving forward. "Any word on the locals?"

"They still aren't convinced that Brandt is a threat. They're believing his guard's story, that Brandt and his guards were injured during a home invasion."

"We need the police to stop the flow of people coming in," Erik said.

"I know, but at this point, we can't be sure the cops won't make it worse," Vanessa said. "If Ackerman sees people trying to evacuate, he could very well release the toxin prematurely."

"You're assuming he hasn't already released it." Erik's heart plummeted at that thought.

His phone chimed with the incoming text message, and he pulled up the images of the backstage passes. "Got the passes. Thanks, Vanessa."

"Good luck."

He needed luck. Erik ended the call and picked up his pace, Jia right beside him. They headed for the nearest entrance and used their passes to cut to the front of the line. After a brief back-and-forth with the gate agent about their weapons and a lot of ignoring the people who weren't happy that they'd cut, Erik passed into the stadium. He took a breath of what he hoped was untainted air. There was no turning back now.

* * *

Excitement buzzed through the stadium, and Jia scanned for any sign of Chesah or Ackerman. "Do you think our suspects will even be here?"

"I don't know. I'd think they'd steer clear of here when the virus releases."

That wasn't good. If they didn't know who they were looking for, how were they supposed to figure out where and how to stop the virus from being released? Jia paused when she spotted the little glass box on the wall with the fire-alarm trigger encased inside. "Maybe we should take the easy route and pull the fire alarm."

"If they have a signal blocker up, it's possible they're close by. We don't want to take the chance that we'll spook them."

Which could cause Brandt's people to release the virus prematurely. Even though thousands of people were still trying to get inside, Jia suspected there were at least thirty thousand already in the stadium.

Rick glanced in both directions and pointed. "This way."

Jia had no idea how Rick knew where to go, but she hurried beside him, weaving in and out of the hordes of people coming into the stadium, their phones and concert tickets in hand.

Jia and Rick circled past a dozen openings that led into the seating area, finally coming to a door where a man in a security vest stood.

Rick pulled out his phone, retrieved the backstage passes, and showed them to the guard.

"Who are you going back to see?" the guard asked.

"Kendra Blake."

"I'll have to call her to make sure you're cleared." He retrieved his phone from his pocket.

"Phone service is messed up," Rick said. "That's why we need to get back to see her."

It took the guard a few seconds to try, lower his phone, and try his call again.

"Look, we don't have time for this," Jia said. "We have the passes. Let us back there."

"But—"

"This is a matter of life and death. So my friend and I are going to go backstage, and if anyone asks, we're happy to verify with Kendra in person that we're allowed to be here." Rick kept his gaze on the guard. "Sound fair?"

The guard hesitated, and Jia took his inaction as a signal to move past him. Rick followed.

Beyond the security guard, men and women hurried by, crew members preparing the stage, checking the instruments, and setting up the various special effects.

Rick reached Jia's side and grabbed her hand. "This way."

They sidestepped a man holding a guitar and approached a door where two men stood, both of them wearing dark suits, both of them armed.

"We need to speak with Kendra," Rick said.

"She isn't expecting anyone," the blond guard said.

"I know, but her phone isn't working. Neither are yours." Rick pulled out his phone and retrieved something on his screen. "These are my orders from the president."

The guard inspected Rick's phone screen. Then he showed it to the dark-haired guard. Or rather, the dark-haired Secret Service agent.

The dark-haired man handed Rick's phone back to him and knocked on the door.

Kendra answered the door herself, an infant in her arms.

For a moment, Jia could hardly believe she was standing in front of such a well-known celebrity. Jia's tongue tied itself in knots, and her body trembled.

Kendra spotted Rick, and her eyes widened.

"Sorry to interrupt, but we need to talk to you," Rick said.

Kendra stepped back. "Come in."

Rick waved Jia inside, and she had to remind herself how to walk. She entered the dressing room, noting the portable crib in the corner and the woman sitting beside it, a paperback novel in her hands.

Rick turned to the Secret Service agents. "I don't know how many agents you've got with you, but you need to prepare to get her out of here." He lifted his phone again. "And if you see either of these people, let me know."

Both men nodded.

Rick continued into the dressing room and closed the door behind him.

"What's wrong?" Kendra asked.

"First, have you seen either of these people?" Rick showed Kendra the images of Kenneth Ackerman and Chesah Abalos on his phone.

Slowly, she nodded. "I'm pretty sure they're both local hires working on the tech team."

"What does the tech team do?" Jia asked, finally finding her voice.

"They're in charge of all the special effects." Kendra waved in the general direction of the stage. "It's everything from the video feeding to the mega screen to the smoke machines to the lasers."

The pieces of the puzzle fell into place: An airborne virus. Stage equipment. "The smoke machines," Jia said.

"That must be it." Erik nodded. "Where are the machines, and when are they first supposed to be used?"

"They're at the front of the stage. Three of them—two on the sides, and one in the center," Kendra said. "There are also two in the upper bleachers to get an all-around effect."

"And does someone set them off by remote?" Jia asked. "Or are they on a timer?"

"The tech team has a remote that sets them all off at the same time during my first song," Kendra said. "Why? What's all this about?"

"Jia and I have been tracking down a group who are intent on starting a global pandemic by spreading a deadly virus," Rick said. "All indications are that they plan to release it here at your concert."

"Here?" Kendra cuddled her baby tighter.

The woman in the corner stood. "What?"

Kendra ignored her. "I need to get my baby out of here."

"I want all of you out of here," Rick said.

"What about the people coming in for the concert?" Kendra asked. "Will they be exposed?"

"We're hoping to stop it," Jia said. In an effort to put Kendra at ease, she added, "And just so you know, the virus is designed to be deadly to people with autoimmune and other serious diseases. The majority of people here would be fine, but we need to make sure it can't spread."

"Autoimmune diseases?" Kendra turned her attention back to Rick. "Including celiac?"

"Yes," Jia said, confused about why Kendra had singled out that particular disease. Quickly, her confusion turned to horror. Rick ate gluten-free. Was it because he had celiac?

Kendra's face paled, and she turned to Rick. "Then you shouldn't be here."

"Get whatever you need," Rick said, ignoring her comment.

Moments replayed in Jia's mind: Rick's comment that he ate gluten-free, the way he almost always cooked for himself, his use of a gluten sensor, how he always cleaned the counters and any other kitchen items before he used them. He didn't just eat gluten-free. He had celiac, and the virus would likely kill him.

"Your Secret Service agents can take you back to your hotel." Rick opened the door to reveal not two agents but four—three men and a woman. "We'll let everyone know that the concert will have to be rescheduled."

Kendra gathered her bag and instructed her nanny to do the same. Then they passed through the door, and the agents surrounded Kendra and her baby, the nanny falling in with the group.

"We need to get the stadium manager to close off the entrances and help us search for the virus."

Jia grabbed Rick's arm, more concerned right now for the man in front of her. Hoping she was wrong, she asked, "You have celiac?"

Rick's expression clouded. "Yes."

"Then you need to get out of here with Kendra."

Rick shook his head. "I'm not the only person here who's at risk, and I'm not leaving you to deal with this alone."

Panic welled up inside her. "But—"

"Come on. We need to find Chesah, and we need to find the virus."

Jia wanted to argue, but she doubted it would do any good. For now, she needed to stop the virus from being released, or she could very well lose the man who had captured such a huge piece of her heart.

CHAPTER 51

Shaun hadn't been trained for this, yet here he was on board a helicopter heading straight into the danger zone. Although it was hard to consider Singapore a danger zone, with the tall buildings illuminated against the setting sun. But hidden danger lurked down below, and thousands of innocent people were drawn to the center of that danger like moths to a flame.

Shaun had hoped the SEALs who'd rescued him would be able to get their orders changed, but the American hostages off the coast of Malaysia had taken priority. Yet Commander Miller had somehow managed to get Shaun authorization for a ride to Singapore.

The pilot's voice came over Shaun's headset. "The closest I can get you is on top of a hotel two blocks from the stadium."

"Roger that." Shaun was pretty sure that was what he was supposed to say in acknowledgment.

The helicopter circled once and then lowered until it jolted slightly in the landing.

Shaun unclipped his harness.

"Good luck," the pilot said.

"Thanks." Shaun pulled off his headset and left it on his seat before climbing out of the helicopter. The whoosh of air from the propellers pressed against him, and he lowered his head as he hurried toward the door that appeared to lead into the hotel.

The helicopter lifted off, and Shaun entered the plush hallway of the hotel. He simply had to locate the stadium and find a way inside.

* * *

Eric could feel Jia's stare, but he couldn't think about her concern for him right now. They had a job to do, and he preferred not to think about the consequences of what would happen if they failed.

"Rick—"

"I think we need to split up," Erik said, focusing on the immediate tasks at hand. "You go find the stadium manager. I'll look for Chesah and Ackerman."

"No. You find the stadium manager," Jia insisted. "And I'll look for possible distribution devices."

She was trying to protect him. He didn't particularly care for this role reversal, but he nodded. It didn't matter who took which task as long as they succeeded. And the truth was he had more fake credentials at his disposal when dealing with people in power.

"Be careful," Erik said.

"You too." She moved toward the stage, and Erik debated where to look first for the stadium manager.

A woman's raised voice caught his attention. "What do you mean she left?"

Erik turned toward the sound and spotted a woman in her early forties, a man in his twenties standing in front of her.

"I'm sorry, Ming," the man said. "I tried to stop them, but her security pushed right past me."

"Where did she go? Is she coming back?"

Erik crossed to the man's side. "If you're talking about Kendra, I can give you the details." Before the woman could respond, he asked, "Are you the manager?"

"Yes. Who are you? And what do you know about Kendra?"

Too many people were passing by them for Erik to speak openly. He gestured to Kendra's dressing room door. "We can speak in there."

The man beside him started to move away, but Erik put his hand on his shoulder. "You too."

As soon as the three of them entered Kendra's dressing room, Erik closed the door and turned to face them. "We have a serious threat here at the concert," Erik said. "We've already evacuated Kendra, but we need you to close down all the entrances to keep anyone else from coming in."

Skepticism flickered over the manager's face, followed by frustration. "What's the threat?" the manager asked. "And how credible is it?"

"Very, and I can't go into details, but we need to do this as quietly as possible."

The man at Erik's side took a step back. "I'll pull the fire alarm."

"No." Erik grabbed his arm. "If you do that, the people behind this will know we're looking for them." Erik waved toward the entrance. "For now, just close off the doors. Say you need to let people get to their seats before letting the next wave in."

The manager turned to the man. "Start calling the gate attendants and have them shut everything down."

"Your phones won't work. There's a dampening field around here somewhere."

The manager clearly didn't believe him because she pulled out her phone and tried to make a call. After a moment, she lowered her cell. She huffed out a breath and spoke to her employee. "You start at entrance one and work your way toward the center. I'll start at the other end."

"And when you finish, it might be best to stay outside," Erik said.

The young man gulped and nodded.

"What are you going to do?" the manager asked.

"I'm going to see if I can neutralize the threat." He opened the door. Then, leaving the manager and her employee behind, he headed toward the danger.

* * *

Jia sidestepped yet another set worker as she moved toward the stage. Rumors were already buzzing about Kendra and her sudden exit, but apparently, word hadn't reached the setup crew, who were still prepping the stage.

Jia moved past the portable stairs that made up part of the set and peered into the open space filled with instruments and people. Two men set up an artificial wall on one side of her, and a woman set an electric guitar on a stand before adjusting the settings on the amplifier beside it.

Jia spotted the three black boxes placed equal distances apart on the stage, two of which had someone standing beside them. To her left, a man had the cover off one and seemed to be adjusting the settings. Opposite him was none other than Chesah. And right behind her, hundreds of fans were filing into the seats in front of the stage.

Though her gun was holstered at her waist, Jia couldn't use it here, not with so many people so close to Chesah. Jia needed a different plan, one that would ensure no one would be able to release the virus.

Though she had to assume the man fiddling with the smoke machine was working with Chesah, she couldn't be sure. He was also a possible operative who Rick wouldn't be able to identify. With that in mind, Jia circled behind the ring of pillars flanking either side of the stage until she reached the man.

She leaned down in time to see him snap the cover of the smoke machine closed. "Need any help?"

The man looked up, his eyes wide and guilt written all over his face.

Hoping to get him away from the fans and out of sight, Jia said, "One of the guys over there said they need some help adjusting some of the lasers."

"Sorry, I'm supposed to stay with the smoke machine."

"Is that what Brandt told you? Or maybe Ackerman or Chesah?"

The man didn't try to fight. He tried to run.

Jia grabbed his arm, and the man fisted his free hand and swung.

Jia dodged the punch and countered with a jab to the man's stomach.

An echo of gasps carried to her, no doubt from the fans who were seated nearby.

The man coughed and tried to straighten. Jia started to grab a zip tie from her holster to secure the man's hands when someone knocked into her from behind.

Jia stumbled forward and whirled. Chesah stood behind her, her hands lifted in front of her as she prepared to fight.

"You might as well give up," Jia said as she caught a glimpse of Chesah's partner scampering away. Keeping her focus on Chesah, she added, "Brandt is already in custody."

Chesah's only response was to throw a left jab at Jia's midsection.

Jia used her arm to block the punch, and she balanced on the balls of her feet. It appeared the showdown between her and Chesah was about to repeat.

CHAPTER 52

ERIK SPOTTED THE MAN RUNNING off the stage. It didn't take a genius to figure out that he was trying to escape.

Erik changed his direction to cut the man off, deliberately walking so he wouldn't appear to be a threat. Then, just as the man tried to pass him, Erik stuck out his foot and tripped him. The collision sent pain shooting through Erik's leg and caused the man to stumble to the floor.

The man tried to stand, but Erik pushed him back down, thrusting his knee into the man's back. A scuffle ensued, the man bucking his body to get Erik off him.

Despite the man's struggles, Erik reached into his holster and retrieved a zip tie. He secured the prisoner's hands and yanked him to his feet.

"Security!" Erik waved at one of the men wearing a security vest nearby. The prisoner tried to jerk free, but Erik dug his fingers into his arm and held tight.

"What's the problem?" the security officer approached.

"Hold on to him. We need to turn him over to the police for questioning."

"What did he do?" the security officer asked.

"No time to explain. Just don't let him go." Erik handed the man over to security and headed to the stage to help Jia.

He'd taken just a handful of steps before something thudded against his back. Pain radiated across his shoulder blades, and Erik took two more steps before he managed to regain his balance. He turned as someone swung a microphone stand at him again.

Erik brought his hand up to block it, grabbing onto it before it could hit him again.

A man stared back at him, his blue eyes sharp, his face angular—the same face mirrored in the image on Erik's cell phone.

"Mr. Ackerman." Erik winced as he said the words, his back throbbing, both hands now gripping the microphone stand.

"I don't know who you are, but you are most definitely in the wrong place." Ackerman put more pressure on the microphone stand, pressing it upward toward Erik's throat.

"No." Erik's arms trembled. "Your presence proves I'm in the right place." Erik sensed movement to his left, but he suspected it was from Jia still squaring off against Chesah.

The simple truth that they'd found their suspects and had the ability to stop the virus from being released gave Erik a burst of strength. He twisted his body to the side and released his hold on the microphone stand.

The sudden change in pressure sent Ackerman stumbling forward. Erik shoved him, creating distance between them. Then he drew his pistol and aimed.

In the same moment, Ackerman held up a remote. "You shoot, and I press the button."

And if he pressed the button, Erik would likely die. He tried to shove that thought aside. "The signal jammer is still on," Erik said, praying his words were still true. "Your remote won't work."

"You sure about that?"

Erik wasn't sure. And he couldn't exactly check his phone right now to confirm his assumption. "Put it down," Erik said, forcing steel into his voice. "It's over."

"Oh, it's not over." Ackerman straightened. He backed up a step and then another.

Erik's finger twitched, but he couldn't bring himself to squeeze the trigger. He couldn't take the chance that the virus would release and spread.

Ackerman darted behind one of the pillars on the stage. Then he turned and ran.

Erik glanced behind him to where Jia now stood with her arm wrapped around Chesah's throat.

"Go!" Jia shouted.

Erik nodded. Then he turned and sprinted after the man still holding the deadly remote.

* * *

Shaun couldn't believe it. He'd finally made it to the stadium, and the doors were already sealed off. He pulled out the cell phone Commander Miller had provided for him and dialed Jia's number. Nothing happened.

Shaun pushed his way through the crowd, several people trying to prevent him from passing.

He ignored the groans of protest and the elbows thrown his way as he approached one of the ticket takers standing in front of a growing line of impatient fans. "Hey, I need to talk to your manager."

"She's busy."

"It's a matter of life and death."

The man shrugged. "Sorry. Can't help you."

Shaun fisted his right hand, but the presence of a broad-shouldered man standing behind the ticket taker suggested violence wasn't an option.

He stepped back and headed for the next door. There had to be a way in.

* * *

Jia's shin throbbed, and her lip was bleeding, but after multiple blows, she finally had Chesah under control.

A security guard emerged onto the stage. "What's going on?"

"This woman is part of a terrorist plot." Jia nodded toward the zip tie that had fallen on the stage when the fight had first begun. "Get that and bind her hands."

The guard complied.

"And get help. She's already escaped once."

Jia spotted a crew member off to the side of the stage. "You!" She jutted her chin in his direction. "Unplug the smoke machines."

"They're battery operated."

"Then disconnect the batteries," Jia said. "But be careful not to spill any of the liquid inside. It's poisonous." She didn't need to mention that this particular poison could kill far more people than just those present in the stadium.

The stagehand froze.

"Now!" Jia ordered.

Her sharp tone shook the man into action, and he approached the smoke machine on the left side of the stage.

The guard took Chesah's arm, and Jia moved to the smoke machine nearest her. It took her a moment to figure out how to disconnect the battery cable, but she managed to unhook it. When she straightened, the stagehand was disabling the one in the center of the stage.

"Where are the other ones?"

"On the upper level." The stagehand pointed in the direction Erik had gone.

Jia swallowed hard. If Ackerman hit the remote, Erik would be right in the middle of the dispersion path.

"Come on." Jia gestured toward the stagehand. "I need you to show me."

CHAPTER 53

Erik weaved through the crowd, his entire focus on catching the man who could at any minute hit the remote and turn on the smoke machines to expose thousands of people to the virus. Ackerman had already made it out of the backstage area and now raced down an aisle where thousands of people struggled to make their way to their seats. Clearly, the fans had no idea that Kendra had already left the building and that the concert wouldn't be happening tonight.

Ackerman dodged a man holding a huge poster declaring his love for Kendra Blake, and Erik lost sight of his target. The man holding the poster continued toward Erik, blocking his view.

Erik shoved past the poster and scanned for Ackerman, unable to spot his blue shirt among the crowd.

A woman cried out and fell onto a seat.

A flash of blue caught Erik's eye, and he homed in on the retreating back of Ackerman.

Erik sprinted forward again. "Security! Clear the way!" he shouted, first in English and then in Mandarin. His command did little to open his path, most of the fans simply staring at him as he pushed his way past them.

Ackerman reached the opening to the terrace area and the concession stands.

Erik's heartbeat quickened. No doubt, as soon as Ackerman reached the exit, he would hit the button and start the chain reaction that Erik and Jia had worked so hard to prevent. But unless a miracle happened, they were out of time, and the poison would soon be in the air.

* * *

Jia gasped as she raced up the steps. They weren't going to make it.

She'd caught sight of Ackerman and Rick when a woman below had cried out a short distance below them, but now Ackerman was out of sight, and Rick was still trying to make it to the exit.

"How much farther?" Jia panted.

"One's up there." The stagehand pointed to a spot another fifteen rows up. "The other one is over there." Now he pointed at the smoke machine visible fifteen rows up and six sections over.

"You do that one," Jia said, sending him to the one farthest away. "And hurry. I need to help my friend."

Although the word *friend* barely scratched the surface of what Rick was to her.

A phone rang and then another. For a second, Jia didn't compute what the sound meant, but then she remembered. Whatever had been blocking their phone signals earlier had been turned off, which meant there was nothing preventing Ackerman from setting off the smoke machines using a remote.

The stagehand turned toward the other smoke machine, but Jia already knew he wouldn't get there in time.

She looked up at the one above her, and her heart seized. If her suspicions were correct, she wouldn't make it either. She could only hope that Rick made it out of the stadium before it was too late.

* * *

Shaun heard Ackerman before he saw him. In his hurry to get inside, he never anticipated the possibility that one of the people he was looking for would appear only fifteen meters away outside.

Shaun froze for a split second, the memory of his last confrontation with Brandt and his men paralyzing him. Then he spotted a remote in the man's hand.

The fear fell away, Shaun's need to protect rising with a vengeance. "Hey!" Shaun yelled. "Kenneth Ackerman!"

Shaun sidestepped a couple with their arms wrapped around each other, dodged a woman in a wheelchair, and dove at Ackerman. Both of them fell hard onto the concrete walk, and the remote dropped to the ground beside them.

Ackerman elbowed Shaun in the side of his head. Pain exploded and left stars dancing in front of his eyes, but Shaun held firm. Ackerman stretched out his arm, his fingertips brushing against the remote.

"No!" Shaun tightened his grip around his opponent's shoulders, but he couldn't prevent Ackerman from regaining control of the remote.

"Everyone back up!" a man shouted. Then suddenly, a foot stomped on Ackerman's wrist, and Ackerman cried out in pain.

The new arrival leaned down and snatched the remote. He then opened the back of it and pulled out the batteries, letting them drop to the ground.

Shaun caught a glimpse of the gun in the man's hand as he tossed a zip tie to Shaun. "Do me a favor and tie him up." The man then spoke to the crowd. "And someone call the police."

CHAPTER 54

It was over. Chesah, Ackerman, and the stagehand had all been arrested. And finally, Erik and Jia were back home in their condo.

Erik yawned as he led the way into the living room, fatigue setting in.

Jia carried Spencer in her arms, the puppy cradled against her. Even though it was already after nine, she'd insisted on picking him up from Elanora's apartment. The puppy had yipped and jumped in excitement when they'd arrived, and Erik already knew he wasn't going to be able to give the little guy up. He doubted Jia would be willing to either, which meant one of them would need to look into some dog-sitting services soon.

Was he really thinking about coparenting a dog with Jia? How had this happened? He closed the door behind Jia and locked it.

Jia set the puppy down. "I can't believe we stopped them."

Neither could Erik, nor could he stop the faint tremor that worked through his body. For so many years, he'd worked in near isolation. He had saved countless lives, yet today, he'd been forced to rely on others. And had it not been for Jia's efforts—He didn't want to think what would have happened had she not been so diligent.

Erik removed his holster and set his weapon on the counter. A note lay beside the sink.

> *Brandt and his injured guard made it through surgery. They've both been moved to the prison ward of the hospital, and the police have taken the listening devices as evidence.*
>
> *I'm staying at my hotel tonight so I can pick up the rest of my things before heading back home.*
>
> *Dylan*

Erik lifted the note and passed it to Jia. "Looks like it's just the two of us again." He looked down at Spencer. "Or the three of us again."

"Not for long." Jia set her weapon beside his. "I'm sure Andrea will want me back in Kuala Lumpur within the next day or two."

Erik turned to face her. He could move to Malaysia to be closer to her, make Kuala Lumpur his home station, but it would never be like this again. Unless—

The thought of marriage flitted through his mind, stunning him speechless.

Not sure he was ready to face such thoughts, not after only two weeks together, he circled the kitchen counter and opened the fridge. "Are you hungry? I can make us a late dinner."

Jia waited until he turned back to face her before she answered. "Why didn't you tell me?" she asked. "Why didn't you let me know you had celiac disease?"

Of all the things they could talk about after the day they'd experienced, his celiac hadn't been anywhere near the top of his list. He struggled to find the right words. "In my line of work, I can't afford to show weakness."

"It's not a weakness. It's a situation, and I'm not just some random person you helped," Jia said. "At least, I didn't think I was."

"Of course you're not." Erik crossed to her and took her hands in his. "And I did tell you that I'm gluten-free. It wasn't so much that I was hiding my celiac from you. It was more that I didn't want to think about what could happen if Brandt followed through with his plans."

"You were scared." She stated the fact so simply, yet a hint of disbelief shone in her eyes. "I've personally seen you go into a hostile country to help me. You went against Brandt today despite three-to-one odds. And who knows how many other dangerous situations you've faced to help others." She lifted her eyes, her gaze meeting his. "What made the virus so much scarier than those situations?"

"I don't know. Maybe it was because I watched my aunt battle cancer for years. And I was there when my grandpa died of sepsis after only two days." Erik laced his fingers through Jia's. "I didn't know what I'd go through, and I've never had so much to lose before."

Her expression softened, and she glanced out the window. "I'm going to miss this."

Erik looked out at the twinkling lights of Singapore before focusing on Jia once more. "Me too." He leaned down and pressed his lips to hers.

The familiar thrill rippled through him, but beyond the simmer of attraction, a new sensation tangled inside him. This woman had fought with him . . . had fought for him. She had been his partner in every sense of the word.

His heart opened, and love took flight. In two short weeks, she had become his everything.

He pulled back, even more startled by that revelation than by the thought of spending the rest of his life with her. With his heart nearly bursting, he pressed his forehead against hers. "Erik," he whispered. "My real name is Erik."

She leaned back, and her eyes locked on his. To his surprise, tears glistened there. "Thank you," she whispered back. "I didn't want to fall in love with someone without knowing his name."

Her casual mention of love kicked his pulse into overdrive. "You love me?"

Her lips twitched into a hesitant smile. "I do."

Joy enveloped him. "That's good." He caressed her cheek. "Because I love you too."

"So does that mean you're really going to move to Kuala Lumpur?" Jia asked, hope humming through her voice. "Or maybe I can transfer here to Singapore." She gestured to Spencer. "Spencer likes it here."

Erik's smile widened. "He does like it here."

"You know we're not giving up the dog, right?"

"I know." Erik leaned in and claimed her lips again. "And for the record, wherever you are, that's where I'll be."

ACKNOWLEDGMENTS

My continual gratitude goes to my editor, Samantha Millburn, who helped usher this project from concept through to the finished product. Thank you as well to the rest of the team at Covenant, who have done so much to support my career.

Thank you to Lara Abramson for your editing and proofreading help. As always, thanks to my fabulous critique partners, Ashley Gebert, Eliza Sanders, Daniel Quilter, Dave Elliott, Ann Feinstein, Brian Godden, Millie Hast, Alan Spira, and Steve Stratton.

My appreciation also goes to the CIA's Publication Classification Review Board for your continued assistance in clearing my manuscripts before publication. And I also want to thank my family for sharing me with my fictional world and my readers who have allowed those fictional worlds to come to life.

ABOUT THE AUTHOR

Traci Hunter Abramson, a former Central Intelligence Agency officer, was born in Arizona, where she lived until moving to Venezuela for a study-abroad program. After graduating from Brigham Young University, she worked for the CIA for six years until she resigned to raise her family.

Traci is a popular writing instructor and keynote speaker. She has written more than forty-five best-selling novels, several of which have won awards. Traci was also honored with an Outstanding Achievement Award for her contribution to the writing community in 2025. She is a 2022 and 2023 Silver Falchion Award Mystery/Suspense finalist and a 2024 and 2025 Silver Falchion Judges' Top Pick, 2022 Rone Award finalist, and ten-time Whitney Award winner, including Best Novel of the Year in both 2017 and 2019. She received the 2021 Swoony Award for Best Mystery/Suspense Romance.

She loves hearing from her readers. You can contact her through the following channels:

Website: www.traciabramson.com
Facebook page: facebook.com/tracihabramson
Facebook group: Traci's Friends
Bookbub: bookbub.com/authors/traci-hunter-abramson
X: @traciabramson
Instagram: instagram.com/traciabramson